GRAB
BAG

12

A Gay Erotica Anthology

FOR LITERARY HEAT

BarbarainSpy
Toronto, Australia

Grab Bag 12

by

habu

Table of Contents

Introduction

Twelfth in the series of eclectic gay male short story collections by habu, the fifteen stories of *Grab Bag 12* offer a variety of gay male stories in terms of theme, sexual interest and fetish, setting, and time period. Laid out in the order in which they were written rather than grouped by theme, these are stories composed during the fall of 2016.

Four of the stories have historical settings, ranging from Virginia, when the Shenandoah Valley was frontier ("A Different Path"), to the British occupation of Egypt in the 1800s ("The Agent's Third Secretary"), up to the twentieth century, in the Baltimore of the 1970s ("Ed, Frank, and Mark") and New York and the Netherlands in the 1980s ("Under the Skin"). Of the eleven contemporary stories, one is set in an unnamed Asian country ("Prince's Choice") and one moves from Arizona to Cyprus ("Making of a Porn Star"). An unusually high number of habu stories for an anthology like this are set in the United States, moving east from California ("Quattro Amici"), Arizona ("Making of a Porn Star"), Wyoming ("Political Biography"), and Colorado ("Hunted") toward the Atlantic seaboard states ("The Capitol Limited," "Oversexed," "TGIF Lexington," "Gorilla," "Avril's Ploy," "Political Biography," "Tantric Teng," and "Ed, Frank, and Mark"). Typically with habu, several of the stories are located in Virginia and the Carolinas (or New York City), but purely coincidentally, two of the stories in this anthology are set in Baltimore ("Tantric Teng" and "Ed, Frank, and Mark").

Thematically, as is always the case with habu's broad range of experiences, the stories in this anthology are "all over the place" in theme, from lust, greed, extreme need, and rough, BDSM sex to physical danger, espionage, paranormal events, mystery, racial discrimination, humor, porn stars, and tantric sex. The stories were all written in the heat of a U.S. presidential election year, so naturally there are stories here about shady and grasping politicians ("The Capitol Limited" and "Political Biography").

The constants in habu's hodge-podge of story writing are to provide variety, surprise, and scintillating gay male arousal. We trust that this twelfth anthology in the series will do just that for its readers.

In the anthology's lead story, "A Different Path," a widower frontier lawyer finds reason to remain on America's eighteenth-century frontier in western Virginia in young men willing to warm his bed. "Hunted" moves out to Colorado and forward two centuries in time, finding a young man looking for action in Durango, Colorado, and receiving more than he alone can handle. In "Oversexed" a satyriasis male model tries to reconnect with someone who will give him constant attention. Going political and BDSM rough, in "The Capitol Limited" a young congressional staffer is pursued and spiked on an overnight train from D.C. to Chicago. The fifth story, "The Agent's Third Secretary," moves back in time to the 1800s and to Egypt, where a young English diplomat makes the most of his body for espionage.

The second third of the stories starts with a rare (for habu) paranormal mystery. In "Quattro Amici," a story written for Halloween, hallucinations help a young man returning to a family winery unravel a long-ago mystery. Returning to something both rough and kinky, "TGIF Lexington" offers up a real estate representative giving special services to a client with kinky demands who is shopping for a horse farm in Virginia but still in shock from a war in eastern Europe. Back to the political again and grasping politicians, in "Political Biography" a biographer finds more then he should on his subject, a man angling for the highest of political offices. "Gorilla" is a playful story of a young man who is attracted to hirsute, dominant sex partners with a sense of humor and the bizarre. Picking up on politics in distant places and espionage, "Prince's Choice" is a Sam Winterberry sex unit spy story in which a young spy is assigned as a spoiled prince's sex toy to keep the prince occupied and out of trouble. Sam Winterberry is a recurring character in habu's CIA "Candy Store" unit spy stories.

The last third of the anthology returns to Virginia, in the United States, with a Thanksgiving sex party story, "Avril's Ploy," in which a college professor plots to keep his wandering live-in boyfriend on Thanksgiving by manipulating the lives of other guests at his party. Habu takes both a playful and sensual swipe at tantric sex techniques in "Tantric Teng." In this story a young man is taken through tantric massage and surrogate sex acts to overcome a barrier to sexual satisfaction with his boss. "Making of a Porn Star," entering the world of gay sex pornographic movies, describes the transformation of an Arizona archaeology graduate student into a Cyprus-based gay male porn star.

The conclusion of the anthology leans toward the romantic in two stories. "Ed, Frank, and Mark" is a Goldilocks story of a young male prostitute seeking the perfect top, and "Under the Skin" is a thought-provoking story of love between the races and of discrimination, told about a black man who loved a white man in South Africa under Apartheid. "That's Jan Martans," he said. "We found each other in Cape Town. His family found out about us. They sent Jan to Amsterdam. They sent me to prison."

Whatever you are seeking in gay male sexuality reading interest, you should be able to find considerable help in arousing your pleasure in habu's eclectic *Grab Bag 12*.

A Different Path

The quiet and loneliness was driving John Sandles to distraction and he couldn't bear being in the house for any longer. Not that he was in an actual house. He'd been working on the room extension of his house on Sligo Creek nearly where the creek fed into the North River at the foot of the Appalachians to the west. The nearest town to him was Mount Solon, Virginia, a good five miles to the southeast. He didn't really need the extra room now, which was framed and sheathed in rock up to his chest, the rock being Susan's choice. The house itself was a two-room log cabin, the rooms being commodious enough—the bedroom with the loft overhead that he'd put stairs up to early in the winter, and the "everything else" room. The extension was to be his office. The loft was for the child and the children afterward until they could build on to the house. He didn't need the loft now, and it remained unfurnished.

Both Susan and the baby had died in a difficult childbirth late in the winter. John could have gone back East, over the Blue Ridge, back to some semblance of civilization then—back to Williamsburg. It had been Susan's dream to go west, for him to establish his law practice in the Shenandoah Valley. He supposed that it was because that had been Susan's dream that he couldn't leave now—and that he had to finish the room for his law practice. Susan and the baby were buried out there, in the copse of chestnut trees near the creek's edge.

That was probably the real reason he couldn't leave. He was bound to their graves.

That and what he had left in Williamsburg where he had studied for the law at William and Mary. He had been indiscreet there. He had thought that what happened in the fears and frustrations of battle would be buried there, but that had not quite happened. Perhaps Mount Solon was far enough away for his indiscretions not to catch up with him. Susan had thought it would be. Susan had never given up on him.

He couldn't stay here longer today in the silence of the cabin, though, and he was tired of lifting rock into place in the frame for his office. It didn't help that Susan had declared this, the golden days of autumn, as her favorite time of the year in the valley. The trees were changing their color, there was a nip in the air, and the creek had lowered enough that he could hear the babbling of the water over the rocks. Further up the creek, at Thad's Mill, before the creek split, giving lesser flow to the Sligo, the water was still high enough to work the wheel.

Thinking on that gave John the excuse he was looking for to pull himself away from the cabin and from the graves he could see from the cabin in the stand of trees. There had been so much for Susan to forgive and she had loved it here, saying it was a new path for them. It was penance for him to stay.

But not for the rest of today. No, he had flour to pick up at Thad's Mill. He had an excuse to pull away from here, if only for a few hours. He went to the shed and saddled up the horse. It was a good three miles to the mill. And the mill was located on the main road out of Mount Solon north and south, along the Appalachians on the western edge of the valley. He had heard talk that there would be a national census taken for the first time in the next year—1790—and census takers were being hired. As a lawyer, one of only a few in the Mount Solon area, he should be able to land that job. He could use the money as he established his law practice. The mill was the social center of the area this side of Mount Solon. He should be able to learn more about the census plans there.

When he rode up to the mill, it too was quiet, which was unusual. In the stand of trees over by the road, there was more activity, as there often was. Two Conestoga wagons, their oxen out of the traces and watering in the creek, were pulled up beside the road, and five men, two women, a few children—who John couldn't count because they were running all around the wagons—were gathered around a fire, cooking a meal. Just more settlers headed up for the Northwest Territory through the Cumberland Gap, where new settlement was under way farther west than John and Susan had come to settle.

As John came off his horse, one of the men—a young, strapping tow-headed man a good eight years younger than John's own twenty-six, he reckoned on first glance—stood up from the fire and strode to the edge of the road, giving John a close inspection. John tried not to notice, but his demons stirred. The young man was fair of face, as yet with nothing on his chin to shave. His hair was curly and fit his head as a halo, and his body was well formed. Although John was dark-headed and taller and more solidly built than this young man, he couldn't help but think back to when he was that young and vulnerable—and about to enter battle and about to suddenly mature in so many ways. John turned and quickly moved into the dimness of the main mill room, calling out "Thadeus," as he entered the chamber.

A voice—one higher in pitch than Thadeus Wainwright's—answered him from the wheel room, telling him the owner of the voice would be there shortly—that he was grinding the last of a job.

Thad, John thought, Thadeus's young son, given the abbreviated name to distinguish the father from the son—as Thadeus's father, the originator of the mill, had been known as Thad, to maintain the same distinction with a name that had gone down the generations from one oldest son to the next oldest son.

John felt the clutch of being in a trap. He wouldn't have come if he had thought that Thadeus wouldn't be here. He wouldn't have come if he had known that the miller's son, of the same age and aspect as the golden young man over at the Conestoga wagons other than being a redheaded version, would be the only one here.

When Thad came out from the wheel room, he seemed a bit flustered, and it perhaps was just John's imagination that the young man was hitching up his belt. He smiled when he saw John, though, and blushed a bit, a redheaded young man not being able to control the flushing of his face as one of another aspect could.

"Hello, Mr. Sandles," he said in a low, soft voice. "Have you come for your sack of flour?"

"Yes, please, if you have ground what I brought in last week yet," John answered.

"We have it, yes. It's just over here." Young Thad backed away to a shelf area off to the side where several sacks of flour were being stored. He kept glancing back at John, though, and John felt he was flushing as well, although his darker coloring wouldn't show it.

"Is your father around?" he asked, hoping that the older Wainwright was just around the corner somewhere. "I thought to ask him what he knew about the organization of this census to be taken next year."

"No, sir," Thad answered, returning to John's side with a sack of flour. John wondered if it was his imagination that Thad maintained contact between their hands for longer than was required to pass the sack, but he didn't really want to think about that. He shouldn't have come, he now realized. He now realized that what had made him so jittery at the cabin wasn't being lonely for his departed wife—it was more the frustration of another sort of loneliness that he had been saddled with through a spring and a summer. He should have known that was the problem as soon as his eyes had met with the blond settler across the road when he'd ridden up to the mill. But at least the young man who had risen to come look at him would be gone the next day. Chances were good that Thad would be here whenever John came to the mill. Perhaps, he thought, he should take note where the other mills were in the area where he could take his business, such as it was. He was a lawyer, not a farmer, so he only raised the grain he personally needed.

"My father is in Mount Solon today. They are meeting to come up with a delegate to send to Richmond in the coming elections. I would have thought you would be there too."

"Was that today?" John asked. "I must have lost track of the days." There was no lie in that. Living alone as he did, John had considerable trouble keeping track of the days. He hadn't been in church on a Sunday since Susan and the baby had died. He hadn't forgiven God for that yet. But perhaps he should start going again if only to have some index of how the days fell.

"Well, I guess I will ride on over to Mount Solon then," John said. "I have to talk to Mr. Haycock about the drawing up of his will anyway. I'll ask about the census there."

"Does that mean you plan on staying in the area?—I mean if you are interested in the census being taken next year." The young man's voice had a hopefulness in it that he couldn't hide. "I'd heard you were thinking of going back east."

"No, I plan to stay on here," John answered.

"I'm glad to hear that," Thad said, his eyes and slight smile again giving away more than he probably intended.

John touched his finger to his hat as a farewell salute and turned and left the mill—being afraid that, if he stayed, he'd give away more than he intended to as well. As he was getting on his horse and trying not to look at the blond young man still standing across the road and looking at him, John was surprised to see Seth Cooper, a farmer who lived nearby almost slink out of the door of the mill and do a double take when he saw that John, who had fumbled a bit at getting the flour sack hooked on his saddle, was still in the mill yard.

John tipped his hat to Seth, who, with a guilty look tipped his back, and disappeared around the side of the mill. There were only the two rooms in the millhouse. Seth obviously had been in the wheel room with Thad when John had ridden up. John wondered why Seth hadn't revealed himself before John left. But, then again, maybe he didn't wonder at all. The thought didn't relieve John's own sense of frustration, though.

* * * *

"You have the roof on but not yet shingled."

John looked up at the sound of the voice. He had been boiling clothes in a cauldron behind his house, taking a break from carrying rock up from the stream bed to continue building up the wall enclosing his office. He was stripped to the waist. It was an Indian Summer day—too warm to do hard work all bundled up, but the air too crisp to remain bare-chested for long without physical exertion. John had built a working-man's musculature. Starting a law office in Williamsburg would not have made the physical demands that clearing his own land and physically building his house and law office in the shadow of the Appalachians had. He had a laborer's physique now—well-defined chest muscles, tapering down to a flat-bellied waist, tanned and with curly black chest hair swirling around his pectorals and descending in a line where it fanned out on his belly—and lower. His breeches were tight and sat low on his hips.

"Aye, I had help framing the roof," John answered the blond-headed young man standing between him and the in-progress addition project. "But I've had to put in the rock walls all myself, and I trust it will be the same with the shingles. Haven't I seen you before—at Thad's Mill? Weren't you with a couple of wagons bound for the Cumberland gap?"

"Yes, that was me, Mr. Sandles, but I was not part of those families, and I had a mind to stop here apiece before going out to the new territories."

"You know my name."

"Yes, I asked at the mill. I was told you were a man of learning. My name is Matthew."

"Well, greetings, Mr. Matthew," John said, giving the young man a closer look, and feeling the old yearnings gripping him. He was so much like Cal—especially the way the sun caught his unruly golden locks and in his thin build. "Is that what brought you out here to my holdings—because I am a man of learning, as you say?"

"Yes, sir, it is. I don't want to go into the new territories without skills that will see me right. I thought to learn sums before I went. Thad, at the mill, tells me you are a man of the law—that you are college educated."

"Yes, I studied law at the College of William and Mary under George Wythe." John looked at the young man, thinking the name of the great scribe of the Revolution would be recognizable, but there wasn't such a reaction. "George Wythe, who taught law to the likes of our wartime governor Jefferson." Still no notable reaction. He sighed. "My name is John to you as you wish to be Matthew to me. Where do you hail from, Matthew?"

"The eastern slopes of the Blue Ridge. And I know of Thomas Jefferson well," Matthew said, almost indignantly. "He hails from close to the hollow where I was raised. Did he learn his sums from this Wythe man?"

"I imagine he learned his sums well before then," John answered gently. "It is a good and useful thing to acquire such learning, though."

"You've raised the rock on your addition, I see, to the level where it would be better to have help to go from there to the roof, and I have nailed shingles to roofs before."

"Have you now?" John asked, realizing why it was the young man was here—what had brought him here to tempt John in his frustration. His mind raced on the possibility of hiring this young man on—but with what money? If John could have afforded the help in building this law office, he would have hired someone locally.

"I can help you finish off your room," Matthew said. "If you will teach me sums in the evening, I will work with you on this addition during the day. Just for a place to sleep— maybe in the shed over there—and a bit to eat."

John realized the temptation of the offer, but it was true that he had reached a point where help would be valuable. He couldn't spend all of this time on the construction and have it finished before winter set in. His law practice was building, and that was crucial.

"The shed is no place for you to have to sleep. The nights are turning cold. You're welcome to sleep in the house and we will work on your sums there as well."

That evening, in the candlelight, the two men with their heads close together over the sums, John was surprised to find Matthew quick on the understanding. The lawyer also was disturbed, though, to find that putting their head this close together in the dim light of the candle had made him go hard.

Seeing a scar on the back of John's hand prompted Matthew to ask, "Were you in the war? Is that a war wound?"

"Aye, I reckon that came from a .25 Long Rifle ball fired by a Redcoat at Yorktown," John answered. "But it was just a graze. A man pulled me down just at the right moment, or it would have been worse." Cal, he thought, looking at Matthew and remembering. "But, yes, I was in the war. My beginning was the war's ending, though—at Yorktown—the fall of '81. Eight years ago. It seems a lifetime. It was after that that I went to the college to learn the law."

"You joined that late?"

"Aye. I couldn't join before then. I was just eighteen. Same as you probably are now."

"I'm nineteen—or will be in November," Matthew answered—again that slight tone of indignation. "I wish I'd been old enough to have been in the Revolution." This said with some force.

"I think you are lucky not to have been," John said, with a sad sigh. "It was a time that took some of the best of us and scarred and scared the 'you know what' out of the rest of us. It did strange things to men—put them on a path they would not have gone on otherwise that was dangerous and fearsome." He was looking into the more-pretty-than-handsome face of the young Matthew, wanting so much to run his fingers into that unruly mop of golden hair—but knowing that would be going down the wrong path. Again. Indeed, the fright of war brought out a great deal in a man that otherwise could be hidden forever.

* * * *

They had been hacking at the abatis, the bracken stretched along the pit in front of the British Number 10 redoubt at Yorktown, almost on the banks of the York River when Cal, slashing at the branches with his bayonet next to John, gave a cry and pulled John down. All of the young, dark and sultry, newly minted colonial soldier dipped below the bracken

17

except his hand. He felt the sting as the bullet grazed his hand, and he called out in pain.

"Where yer hit?" cried out the blond Cal—younger than John by two months but a more seasoned soldier than he by two years as he had lied about his age at his enlistment. He would do anything to get out of the oppressive apprenticeship at the stables outside Philadelphia. John, the son of a Williamsburg doctor, had been held back from the war by his doting parents until they no longer had a say in the matter.

"Nowhere. It's just a graze," John answered through chattering teeth. It was cold in the middle of October 1781, but it was the fear of his first battle—an infantry assault on the Number 10 British redoubt being led by Alexander Hamilton—that had him scared and moving as if under water.

That slight hesitating from getting through the abatis spared them the carnage of being in the first wave over the wall of the redoubt, and the fight was over soon after that, the victory Hamilton's. The first there were told to hold the redoubt and the rest told to fall back into one of the two parallel trenches the revolutionaries had constructed during the one-month siege. John and Cal found themselves alone in a curve of the farthest trench from the redoubt, huddled together, pumped with adrenaline, but on the edge of the shock of the battle they both had just experienced.

"I thought I'd lost you," Cal whispered to John, taking the young man's mouth with his to stifle what the terror in John's eyes might bring forth from his mouth. John responded with a moan. Cal, always the aggressor, albeit the receiver, rolled over on top of John and moved his hands among the folds of their clothing to unbutton here and there and to free them to affirm life and satisfy the arousal of have survived battle by moving into the act that had been pressed upon Cal in the past by the stable owner he had been apprenticed to and had more lovingly then been taught to a frightened and overwhelmed new recruit, John.

Positioning his buttocks over John's crotch and continuing to cover the handsome dark man's face with kisses of assurance, Cal took the first few inches of John inside him. Calmed, thrilled to be alive, and in deep need, John clutched Cal's hips and aided in the rising and lowering of the blond beauty on his cock.

All along John had rationalized that it was just a reality of the demon nature of warfare and would be fleeting. He was betrothed—indeed had been promised for years—to the daughter of another Williamsburg physician, Susan. It was only because there were only men in the army and

18

the conditions were frightful and put men on the edge that John had been coaxed down the path with Cal. After the war, it would all . . . but it hadn't all changed. After Yorktown John returned to Williamsburg to begin his studies with George Wythe at the college. But Cal had come to Williamsburg as well, and worked in a saddlery. It hadn't all changed at all. It had just become furtive until people started to talk. Then, the two married, Susan said she wanted them to move west to start life anew— going down a different path.

But Cal had been so sweet, his channel so satisfying, his kisses even better than Susan's. John could try to salvage what he could by heading west, but he couldn't forget Cal—lying under him once the war was past them, John finding confidence and greater mastery, Cal on all fours under him, with John mounted on his hips, penetrating the blond beauty deep, and pounding, pounding, pounding.

John woke up in a sweat, despite the chill in the air. The fire was burning low in the grate. The covers were off him in the bed, and his hand was under the hem of his nightshirt, gripping his engorged cock and squeezing and stroking it, as he done for himself so many nights since Susan had died. The evidence of what he was doing was covered by the material of his long nightshirt, but he was on his back, legs spread and bent, and the movement of the material at his crotch left little doubt that he had been masturbating himself in his sleep—in his dream of being with Cal.

He looked over toward the fire, spying Matthew stretched out on the pallet between him and the grate, covered with a blanket, but turned toward John, watching him. Matthew's hand was under the blanket and from the rustle of that there was little doubt that Matthew was masturbating himself and he lay there, eyes open, watching John on the bed.

With a groan, John turned over onto his side, facing the wall, facing away from Matthew and the glow of the fire in the grate, picking up the golden highlights in Matthew's mop of hair, giving his head a halo.

John finished himself as quietly as he could. When he turned back facing the fireplace, now under his blanket, Matthew was asleep—or was pretending to be.

* * * *

The nights were getting colder, increasing chill stealing into the cabin as soon as dark had fallen. The rock wall of the law office was completed now, and Matthew was working on shingling the roof. The teaching sessions were going well too. Matthew was a fast learner. The increasing cold of the evenings was bringing the two men closer to each other, touching each other, perhaps not always by chance, as they put their heads together over the paper on which John was teaching Matthew his sums.

John woke up in the middle of one of his "Cal" dreams to find the cabin colder inside than ever before. It was darker too, the fire in the fireplace nearly out, hissing because of the rain coming down the chimney.

Matthew was under his blanket, on the pallet, but his body was shuddering and John almost could hear the chattering of his teeth. As dim as light was, beyond the occasional flash of lightning visible in beyond the glazed-glass windows, John could see the condensation in his own breath, so he knew that Matthew must be suffering.

"Come into the bed, Matthew. Or stoke up the fire at least."

"I'll be fine, sire," Matthew answering in a small voice. "I didn't bring in enough wood this afternoon to keep the fire burning up. It's my fault."

John's heart lurched for the young man—and not just his heart. And Matthew had called him "sire." A term of submission Cal had used after the war, when they settled down to a routine of John's body dominating Cal's. "It's madness, Matthew. I am cold too. We must combine our body heat. We'll both be comfortable enough then."

The young blond sighed and responded to the commanding tone in John's voice. He climbed into bed and turned his back to John. This was not an uncommon practice at the time, and travelers on the road were known to share what beds there were with other men at rooms in the inns, calling themselves lucky to have a roof over their heads and a mattress under them at all.

John, going to sleep with his back to Matthew, drifted off into a wet dream with Cal, coming at least partially awake to find that he now was turned toward Matthew's back and was embracing him, spooning the younger, smaller man's body in to his. Both of their nightshirts had ridden up on their bodies, and John's hard cock was between Matthew's thighs. Being so deep into his dream of fucking Cal that he didn't want to lose it, John fought the urge to come completely awake, apologize, and turn his body. The urge won, encouraged by the mewing sounds and low moans coming from Matthew and the way that Matthew's thighs were squeezing John's cock and chaffing against it in slow waves of movement. Matthew turned his face to John's and they went into a prolonged, deep kiss. John ejaculated between Matthew's thighs and drifted off into sleep again—and into Cal's arms again in his dreams.

Above all else the two were warm enough now.

John came further awake later in the night to find himself on his back and Hard. Matthew was straddling his pelvis, sheathing his cock in his channel, pressing the palms of his hands into John's chest, and rising and falling of John's cock.

"Matthew," John protested dreamily.

"Shush. I have gone with men before," Matthew murmured. "This is what I want; this is what I know you want. This is a path we can both take together for mutual pleasure and satisfaction. You invited me into your bed and showed me your real desires. No one need know but us."

With a groan of resignation, John gripped the lithe young blond's waist in his hands and began to help raise and lower him on the cock, at first slowly, languidly, but increasingly lustfully, jerking him up and slamming him down, faster and faster, with Matthew crying out at the total taking and both of them exclaiming to the ceiling as one, after the other, they ejaculated.

* * * *

By mutual connivance, the instruction and the roofing of the office—and then the reroofing of the cabin and of the shed, was drawn out during the day, while John covered Matthew and relentlessly pounded on his body on the bed at night. Neither spoke of by day of what they did with each other in the dark of night.

But after a couple of weeks John had to acknowledge that there was no more to teach Matthew of sums and all of the buildings had newly shingled roofs. John could tell as well that Matthew was hearing the call of the Northwest Territories ever more insistently. More and more wagon trains were going through. After Matthew had commented on the third one that had offered him room in the wagons for the extra rifle of protection, John swallowed hard and said, "You want to go, don't you?"

Matthew wasn't quick enough to say no, so John said it for him. "You want a new life—a new, different path—in the new territories. We've reached the end of our path together, I think. I think you should go. Go back and tell the man with the four wagons that you will go with him."

"But will you be all right?" Matthew said.

"I will manage," John answered. He stood and watched as Matthew gathered up his few possessions in his bundle and walked, with strong steps, toward the road where the wagon train had settled for the night. Then he saddled his horse and rode to Thad's Mill. He already knew that Thadeus was in Mount Solon that day. John had been invited to the citizens' meeting there, as well, where it was to be announced that he was to head the census collection in the region the next year. But he had seen Matthew talking with the wagon master and knew that Matthew was ready to move on, so he had stayed at the cabin to support Matthew in that decision.

Matthew had asked him if he would go on a different path now. John hadn't answered, because he knew he'd go on a new path, but no longer a different one. He'd made his decision about that.

Young Thad Wainwright met him at the door to the mill, with a smile and a quizzical look on his face. "My father isn't here. He's in Mount Solon today. I thought you would be there too."

"I didn't come for your father," John said. "I came because I knew he wasn't here today—that you would be at the mill alone. You knew when you told Matthew, the blond young man, about me what he wanted—why he was interested in me, didn't you?"

"Yes," Thad said, lowering his eyes, his blush betraying his own interest.

"I came for you," John said, "If you want me to cover you—to take care of your need and mine as well."

Thad didn't speak an answer. His answer came in taking John's hand in his, brushing his fingers over the rough callous of the wound on the back of John's hand, and leading John back into the darkness of the mill, toward the wheel room, as he began unbuckling his belt with his other hand.

Hunted

The rented Jeep Wrangler sputtered and died as Ben was approaching the base of the Vallecito Mountains northeast of Durango, Colorado, and, with a muttered "Shit," he guided the vehicle over to the side of the road. There wasn't any secret why the old Wrangler had died. It was out of gas. Ben had rented the car for the summer from a used car dealer down in Durango as soon as he'd arrived here. It had taken a while to figure out that the gas gauge was misleading. He'd fought with that all summer. Today, he'd been coming down from his uncle's place in the mountains to fill the Wrangler up, but he'd made a wrong turn, spent an hour getting back onto a road he recognized, and the gas hadn't held out.

With another curse, he grabbed the gas can from the floor in front of him, got out of the car, and, looking up at the hot sun and cursing that he'd come away just in jeans and boots and no shirt, he started the trudge down the mountain. He had no idea how far he'd have to walk on the side of the dusty road before he got to a gas station. He'd been filling up in Durango when he could and from his uncle's tank up on the mountain property most of the time, but he'd found out that morning that his uncle's tank was tapped out and wouldn't be refilled for a couple of more days.

Although well under six foot, Ben was built solid. He was in his second year in the football program at Penn State and had been sent out to his uncle Will's remote place in the

Vallecito Mountains for the summer to toughen himself up more, trim down a little, and help Will with the renovations of the A-frame hanging on the side of a mountain slope that Will had bought. That done, he'd gone on to put in a fence around a horse paddock. By late July he'd accomplished his mission. He was deeply tanned, with blond highlights coaxed out of his hair by the sun. Through hard work, as planned, his torso had been cut to perfection, and his thigh and arm muscles were bulging. He'd run nearly every day, clocked by his uncle, and had cut several seconds off his mile. Having gained muscle and weight while trimming off excess fat and running time, he'd return to Penn State as a perfect scat back—fast, agile, and with a low center of gravity. The house renovations were done and the fence finished and half painted.

He'd be leaving to go back East in two weeks, and it couldn't be quick enough for Ben. The summer workout had been great and his goals met, and the dry summer climate of southwest Colorado and the perpetual sunshine and semiarid scenery of the San Juan mountains had been invigorating. But the isolation of the mountains and the company just being him and Uncle Will day in and day out had been frustrating. Ben had needs and in State College an older man, a rich Penn State alumni who owned a string of car dealerships, took care of Ben's needs—both financial and sexual. Here there was only Uncle Will, who Ben wasn't sure about in the sexual department. Will was quite presentable, but he was Ben's uncle. So he was taboo, serving more as a source of frustration than a help in Ben's summer of doing without.

Ben was keyed up and more than ready to get back into the grove and into Chas Engleston's bed in State College.

It was these thoughts of sexual frustration and ticking off the days until he had a man who could get him off that were droning through Ben's mind as he walked in the heat down the dusty edge of the road in the direction of Durango, more than twenty miles to the southwest, with little promise of a gas station before that. At least Ben couldn't remember having seen one when he'd driven down to Durango before.

Ben was brought out of his reverie by a beat-up old blue and rust Ford pickup passing him from behind and pulling over on the shoulder ahead of him, kicking up rocks and dust.

When Ben reached the passenger door of the truck, it opened, and the man at the wheel straightened back up in the seat and turned his face toward the passenger door. He was dark skinned; bare-chested, like Ben; chiseled-bodied, with straight, black hair cascading down to his shoulder blades; and worn faded cut-off jeans, dusty construction boots, and a black leather necklace, with a turquoise-studded amulet dangling between two bulging pectoral muscles. He was tattooed, the most prominent one being the wings of an eagle stretching across his upper chest. He was probably pushing forty but not too hard. The squint lines in his face reflected many hours working outside in the sun. He had a slightly Asian cast to his face, and his smile was guarded.

"You stranded?" he asked as Ben came up to the open door, scrunched down, and looked into the interior of the truck, which was in a lot better condition than the bodywork was.

"Ran out of gas," Ben answered, raising the gas can to back up his claim.

"That your Wrangler back there?"

"My rented pile of shit, yes," Ben answered. "The gas gauge lies."

The man laughed. "Climb in. I'll take you to a gas station. None close by, though. Put the can behind the seat."

"Thanks," Ben answered, slid into the passenger seat after depositing the gas can and closed the passenger door. "Thanks, man. Hot out there."

"Yep. Not a day to be walking out of the mountains without a shirt."

"No, that wasn't smart of me," Ben said.

"Maybe it was. It got you a ride," the man said. "You're one good-looking, cut dude. My name's Ed." He rushed in getting the name in, as if, once having given a signal, he gave Ben an excuse to ignore it if he wished and concentrate just on the name exchange. Ben caught the signal and didn't want to ignore it. He was sexually charged, and the man was sexy and

26

gorgeous. There was an aspect of mystery about him—and danger. Ben had seen some Native Americans around this summer, and this guy could easily be one.

"I'm Ben. Just here for the summer, working for my uncle up in the Vallecito Mountains. Would you have stopped for me if you didn't think I looked good?"

The man turned his face to Ben and gave him a steady look. Ben returned the look. They were beginning to reach a mutual understanding of interests.

"No, probably not," the man admitted. He flashed a smile at Ben but then turned his attention back to the road, waiting for the next gambit, if there was going to be one.

Ben had been here before, done this before. "Nice country around here, but a little dull. I've been here all summer and haven't seen much action yet."

"Been down to Durango? That's about all the place there is for action around here. What sort of action were you looking for?"

"Well, clubs, bars. The sort of place a guy would go to be with other guys." There, Ben thought, it was out. It was up to this hunk to pick that up or not. After a short period of silence, he added, "But am I assuming badly? Did I say something that upsets you?"

"No, you asked just the right question . . . Ben. There's Colorow's down in Durango. That's a men's club. Just men. A hookup bar. I can vouch for that."

"Colorow's? What sort of name is that?"

"That's where the name of the state—Colorado—comes from. Colorow was a famous Ute chieftain. The name got corrupted into Colorado."

"A Ute chieftain? Is that what you are? Are you Ute? My uncle says there are a couple of big Ute reservations around here."

"Yes, I'm Ute," Ed answered. "The Southern Ute Indian Reservation covers most the territory south of here down to the border of New Mexico. I come from there. But I work on a ranch on the border of the reservation southeast of Durango."

"I've never been with a Native American before," Ben said.

"You mean you haven't been in bed with one before—a Native American man?"

"Yeah, I mean I've never been laid by one before." Might as well get the top-bottom issue sorted out, Ben thought.

"We have dicks just like every other man," Ed said. "In fact maybe bigger than most." Then he gave a dry laugh. He didn't follow that up immediately, as if maybe he'd gone too far—that maybe Ben wasn't signaling as clearly as Ed hoped he was and would ask him to stop the truck and would get out. But Ben didn't do that.

They drove for a while in silence.

"So . . . ," Ed said, trying to be nonchalant about it and staring straight out of the windshield and over the hood of the trunk, "So, you take dick, do you?"

"I prefer to bottom, yes," Ben answered.

"You know," Ed said, "When we do get to a gas station, it's going to be a long haul for you to get back to your Jeep . . ."

"But maybe you'd be willing to take me back?" Ben asked. "If you've got the time and I'll do you a favor in return? Do you top?"

"I've got the time," Ed answered in a low, guttural voice. "And I give cock—if a guy thinks he'd like to have cock from me."

"What's not to like?" Ben said. They rode on for a bit in silence before Ed spoke up again.

"You say you haven't seen the Ute reservation yet? I know where there's a really nice lake on the reservation not far from here. Maybe you'd—"

"Sure, I'd like to see that," Ben said.

"Gotta say I like what I see. I got hard just seein' you on the road."

"I had my hopes about you too," Ben responded.

Ed parked the truck in the shade in a stand of trees at the top of a hill overlooking a small lake. When he'd turned off the ignition, he moved an arm along the top of the seats behind Ben's head and turned his face to Ben's, giving him a tentative smile. His hand went to the back of Ben's neck, and he ran strong fingers up into the sun-kissed blond hair at the back of the young man's head.

They moved into the kiss together, Ed gently pulling Ben's head toward him, and Ben leaning in for the kiss. Ed's other hand went to Ben's crotch, finding him hard, and Ben moaned at the intimate touch of another man that he hadn't felt all summer.

When they came out of the kiss, Ed murmured, "I'd like . . . ," but Ben had anticipated him and was already dipping his head, working the older man's zipper, and pulling out a thick, hard cock. Ben's lips descended down the shaft, squeezing it tight, and Ed, moaning deeply, lay back in his seat, the fingers of both hands dug into the hair on Ben's head, as Ben gave him an expert, but not fully completed, blow job.

"You've done this a lot before," Ed murmured, with a deep sigh.

"Never with a sexy Ute before," Ben answered.

"It's not too—?"

"You're huge in thickness. Just the way I like them."

"You're a slut," Ed said, with a guttural laugh.

"At the moment, I'm your slut. Use me. Give it to me hard; be my daddy."

Ben sat on the cock in Ed's lap in the passenger seat, facing the dashboard and rising and falling on the shaft by the leverage of his feet, as Ed grasped Ben by his pecs, worried Ben's nipples with his index fingers and thumbs, and licked and nipped between Ben's shoulder blades.

With a groan, he pushed Ben off his lap, growling a "Not yet. In the back of the truck."

He pulled Ben out of the truck and virtually carried him around to the back. He lowered the tailgate, revealing a couple of sacks of feed in the bed of the truck. Inserting Ben's ankles into the loops at each corner of the truck chassis that held the tailgate up, he laid Ben on his back on the sacks of feed, pulled the young man's buttocks to the edge of the tailgate, grasped his hips, thrust inside him, and fucked him to a mutual ejaculation.

All the time, using his core muscles to rhythmically thrust his pelvis up to meet Ed's downward thrusts and to help establish the quickening pace, Ben egged him on, telling him how beautiful his body was; how masterful and big he was—and indeed he was what they called beer can thick; how powerful his thrusts were; how well he filled and worked Ben's channel; how deep he was getting, which was pure emotion, as Ed wasn't all that long; how far up into the heavens he was taking Ben . . .

At the moment of release, Ben already having beaten himself off, Ed held, as deep inside Ben as he was going to get, throbbing, and Ben clutched the older man's buttocks, digging in his nails, and Ed came down for a kiss, reaching for Ben's tonsils with his tongue. Ben trembled and Ed shuddered, releasing his ejaculate and filling out the bulb of his rubber.

This wasn't the usual fuck for Ben. This was intense, emotional—something special to think about. Someone special.

As the rust-blue truck pulled up to the side of the Jeep Wrangler an hour and a half later, and Ben gave Ed a grin and a last kiss and gingerly exited the truck, full gas can in hand, he said, "Colorow's in Durango, you say?"

"That's the place," Ed answered. "They'll love you there. Just be careful. Cowboys can be rough."

"You'll be there sometimes?"

"I'm there often enough. Always up for some sweet ass."

"I'd like you . . . again."

"Me too," Ed answered. "You're something special. I don't want to sound casual about it. You're something special."

Ben smiled, almost shyly. "Thanks, man," he said, raising the gas can in salute.

"No, thank *you*," Ed countered, turning his grinning face to the road, and raising dust and small stones as he pushed off.

* * * *

30

Will Lassiter stood there in the doorway of Ben's bedroom, somewhat confused, as Ben packed his bags.

"It's been great, Uncle Will," Ben said, "but we've finished with what I came here to help you with and spring football training is starting early. I might as well leave early."

"But your plane reservations," Will said.

"Have been changed already. I'll go into Durango for tonight and drop off the Wrangler. Then I'll fly out tomorrow, up to Denver, and from there, a direct flight to Philadelphia. No need for you to come into Durango to see me off. We can say our good-byes here."

And that was that. After lingering over lunch so that Will wouldn't think that Ben just couldn't wait to be gone— although that was the case, even if that partly was because Ben needed to resist temptation—they said their good-byes, and Will stood at the door of the A-frame cottage and watched Ben drive away.

Was it Ben's imagination, or did it seem that Uncle Will was particularly disappointed to see him go? Will had drawn closer to him over the last week or so, touching him more, leaving his hand to linger on his arm or shoulder or the small of his back more—like now, when they were saying good-bye and Will continued holding Ben's hand for longer than necessary. Was it because Ben had recently been so completely laid that he saw the interest and longing in Will's eyes now? If Will wasn't his uncle—and they'd rarely come in contact before, so it wasn't like they really felt related—Ben could have gone with Will. Ben preferred older men and Will was quite well put together. The rugged life of the Colorado mountains helped keep him in shape and he was a handsome man. But he *was* Ben's uncle—well, half way, as Ben's mother's mother and Will's mother weren't the same—so Ben wouldn't give into that temptation.

An hour later, Ben had entered the gates of the 1,700-acre Shadow Ranch southeast of Durango, snuggled up against the Ute reservation, the position that gave the ranch its name, and drove the half mile to the main house. He was met at the front door of the house by the towering figure of Jock Crane, decked out as the classic big ranch owner in flashy Western duds, sporting a leathery tan, a flowing gray mane, a large frame with enough meat on it for him to be considered overpowering without quite being fat, and a big welcoming smile.

A servant took Ben's suitcase out to the bunkhouse where Ben was to spend the last week and a half of his originally scheduled visit in the West, and, putting an arm possessively around Ben's waist, Jock Crane guided him into the master bedroom of the main house, tossed him onto the bed, tore off his clothes, and banged the shit out of him for an hour. Late in the hour, the gangly and wiry, but iron strong, ranch foreman, Sling, entered the room and tag teamed with Jock, banging the shit out of Ben himself and slapping him around, in turn, while Jock watched, tossed back scotch, smoked a cigar, and pulled on his cock. When Sling was done, Jock gave Ben another half hour of his cock, and the two left the young man there, panting, his legs still bent and spread, his mouth formed in a slight, satiated smile, when the dinner gong sounded and the two ranchmen went off to inhale their steak and potatoes.

This change in Ben's plans for the end of his summer vacation out West had come about three days earlier, when Ben, being sent down into Durango by Will Lassiter to bring in some supplies, had made a stop near the edge of town, within sight of the stockyards, to check out Colorow's, the gay bar the Ute, Ed, had told him about.

Ben found the bar in the early afternoon. In keeping with the pace of work in the area, the place was nearly deserted when Ben went in and bellied up to the bar. He ordered a beer; was carded, and, to the barkeep's surprise, passed; and was barely getting around to asking the barkeep about business and gay nightlife in Durango, when two men entered the bar. The one taking the lead was a tall, older, commanding-figure man decked out in Western wear. The guy following in his wake was a thin, wiry, slightly younger man in the serious ranch working gear of a tartan plaid shirt, worn jeans, scruffed cowboy boots, and a worn Stetson hat.

Seeing Ben at the bar, the two whispered briefly to each other and then approached, the older man settling onto a

32

barstool in the direction in which Ben was facing, and the wiry one saddling up behind Ben.

"Can I buy you a drink, son?" the older man asked in a confident, overloud voice.

"I've already ordered a beer," Ben answered.

"I'll cover it," he said, nodding to the barkeep, who nodded back. "Howdy, Clyde," the man said to the barkeep, thus establishing himself as a regular here.

"Howdy back at ya, Mr. Crane," Clyde answered. "The usual?"

"Right," Crane answered. "And whatever Sling wants. And this good-lookin' young man is on my tab now too."

"That OK with you, sport?" the bartender asked Ben in a "Do you know what this signified?" voice.

"Sounds good to me," Ben answered.

Scotch on the rocks was presented to the older man and a beer to the man standing behind Ben, the older men served before Ben.

"New here, son? I don't think I've seen you in here before." Crane looked at Clyde, the barkeep, who nodded a signal that Ben was legal.

"Yes, my first time," Ben answered, impressed by the size and bearing of the man. "Just here for the summer—two more weeks. I go to school in Pennsylvania—college." Adding that it was college was his way of signaling he was legal. Ben had entered the bar prepared for some action.

"You know what kind of bar this is?" Crane asked, eyeing Ben pointedly.

"Yes sir," Ben said, giving Crane a level stare back. "I asked around to find out where someplace like this was in Durango."

"So, you know that young, good-lookin' guys like you come in here to get laid."

"Yes, sir," Ben answered, without batting an eye. "That's what I came here for."

"You're not at all shy, are you?" Crane asked, with a big smile.

"No, sir. You don't mince words either. Does it put you off that I don't tease?"

"Not in the least," Crane said.

That's when Ben felt the hand of the man behind him. He'd taken hold of Ben's belt in back. Ben knew he wasn't going anywhere now without effort. He hadn't come in here to back away from an encounter, though, and the man facing him looked rich and he looked like he knew what to do with someone with Ben's needs. He also looked like chances were good he was hung and masterful—not just from his size but from the cocky way he carried himself. Ben wasn't that sure about the guy behind him, holding onto his belt, though.

"And you get that old farts like me come into places like this to find young guys like you to lay."

"Yeah, I can understand that, I guess."

"You can take a big cock?"

"Aren't they the best kind?" Ben answered.

"You got family here? Or a man of your own? Anyone know you're in this bar—or in Durango?"

"No," Ben lied. "I'm here all alone. Closest one who knows me is in Pennsylvania and there aren't many there who know I'm doing the West this summer." It was a strange question, but Ben wasn't giving it much thought. The older man, Crane, standing in front of him, was feeling up his crotch now, and the other guy—did the man call him Sting or Sling, or something?—was feeling up Ben's butt as well as hanging onto his belt.

"Does going with two men put you off?" Crane asked.

This too seemed a strange question, Ben thought. Two men were feeling him up now and he hadn't flinched. "No, sir."

"I'll give you $100 for the use of your ass for an hour—and $50 for Sling here to have you afterward for a half hour."

"Just like that?" Ben asked, impressed and aroused that it was put out there just like that—that he was offered money at all.

"Yep, just like that. They got rooms upstairs here. I'll pay for that too."

Once upstairs, Crane commanded Ben to take off his clothes, and as he stripped, so did Crane.

"Pose for me," Crane said when they were both stripped and he was sitting on the foot of the bed—Sling was leaning up against the door, as if to stop Ben if he chose to try to bolt, and leered at Ben.

"Turn around . . . slowly. Again. And flex for me." Ben did so, as Crane spread his thighs and took his cock in his hand. As Ben had thought would be the case, the man was hung—thick and long. He was chunky without being fat—solid and muscular.

"Not tall, but an athletic build," Crane said. "What sport?"

"Football—and tennis," Ben answered.

Crane snorted. "I don't consider tennis a sport. Sturdy legs, though. Can you run?"

"I play scat back on the university team," Ben said, with some pride. "I run every day out here and have taken two seconds off my mile time."

"You'll find that useful. Nice dick. Work it up for me." They squared off, each working his own dick, each eyeing the other's dick.

"How old?"

"Nineteen," Ben answered.

"You sure about that?"

"Yes. Want to see my license." Both Crane and Sling laughed, and Ben looked around to see that Crane already had his billfold and was rifling through it. Sling nodded to Crane.

"Turn, bend over, and spread 'em—the cheeks," Crane specified. And when Ben had, Crane said. "Spread the hole with your fingers. Ah, you open right up. You've been used."

"Yes," Ben answered. He thought he probably should be irritated or embarrassed by this, but it aroused him. The man was hung. Ben was going to get a good fucking. That's what he'd come to this bar looking for. He even was going to get paid for it.

"Recently? How recently? Was he hung?"

"Three days ago. He was thick."

"Good. You'll want to open up well. Face me again. Work your cock up with your hand. No, not standing. Go down here. Go down on me."

Ben gasped and choked as Crane made him deep-throat his cock, holding the young man's head against his crotch until he heard Ben gag. Ben sputtered when his mouth was released. He was concentrating on getting his breath and he barely heard Crane say, "OK, spike him Sling."

The next thing he knew, the other man had soared across the room, grabbed Ben by the hips, lifted him from his knees, and slammed him down on the bed beside where Crane was sitting. Ben hadn't seen it, but Sling had stripped, had gone hard, and had sheathed himself. He grabbed one of Ben's wrists and bent one of Ben's arms behind his back and painfully upward. He grabbed a handful of Ben's hair with the other hand. He cruelly thrust into and up Ben's channel with a godawful long cock and pumped the young man hard, shaking the flimsy bed and banged the brass headboard against the wall.

"Too rough for you?" Crane called out.

"No, sir," Ben answered in a slightly pained voice.

Sling pumped Ben for a good fifteen minutes before coming. He'd forced Ben to go up on his knees on the bed, and Crane reached under the young man's belly and milked his cock, with Sling not shooting off until Ben had.

Sling rolled off Ben and Crane took up the position he'd left, working a thicker cock inside Ben than Sling had had. He established a slow-to-fast rhythm fuck, his hands grasping Ben's hips to hold the young man in place. Ben didn't object to this in any way. He'd come to the bar looking for a rough fuck. He was getting a rough fuck.

Sling moved to the bed above Ben, grasping the young man's wrists and holding him in place, while he waved his cock in Ben's face until Ben got the idea and sucked his cock while Crane was riding his ass.

Afterward, Ben lay in place, belly to bed, moaning and nearly purring, as the two men used the bathroom to clean themselves.

When Crane came out of the bathroom and while he was dressing, he said. "You say you're here for two more weeks."

"Not quite. Two days less than that," Ben answered, his voice subdued, half wanting one or both of them to come behind him and fuck him again.

"And you say you're here alone."

"Yes, I'm here alone."

"I have a ranch east of town. I'll pay you $2,000 to come stay at the ranch until you fly out, for you to take whatever Sling and I give you during that time. Think about it. You have until Sling comes out of the shower and dresses to decide."

So, three days later Ben drove down from the Vallecito Mountains to the Shadow Ranch, knowing what he'd find there, wanting what he'd find there, and getting fucked royally as soon as he arrived.

After he'd cleaned himself up a servant showed him out of the house and to an outbuilding, where the staff ate its meals. There were about a dozen men eating at a couple of long tables. To the surprise of both of them, one of the men was Ed, the Ute hunk from a few days previously.

"You work here?" Ben asked.

"What are you doing here? You don't want to be here," Ed said, as he motioned Ben to sit. He looked around the room and must have decided he didn't like who was observing them, because when Ben asked him why he shouldn't want to be there, he clammed up and didn't speak again until after Ben had finished eating. He then motioned Ben to follow him outside and headed for the door.

"Mr. Crane paid me to be here until I flew back to Pennsylvania," Ben said.

"Crane? You didn't—?"

"Fuck him? Yes, and the ranch foreman too. I ran into them at Colorow's, in Durango—the bar you told me about."

"Listen, I didn't tell Crane about you—that you were randy and would put out. I didn't tell him anything about you," Ed said, his voice nervous.

"I never thought you did. What's the matter?"

"Probably nothing. Listen, don't act that we've ever met before. You sleeping in the big house?"

"No, I don't think so. My suitcase has been taken to a room in the bunkhouse, I've been told."

"Good. I'm in there too," he said, and then he was standing, looking around nervously, and he was gone.

He wasn't gone forever, though. Late in the night, Ben heard the door to his room open. Even though they weren't big, there were separate rooms in the bunkhouse for the living-in workers. The hall light was on and Ben was able to recognize Ed, so the young man didn't challenge him or anything—Ben just moved the covers off his body, revealing that he was sleeping naked, and turned onto his back.

Ben opened his legs to the Ute hunk, as he came done on top of him, spreading his legs, bending his knees, and pressing his pelvis up to Ed by leveraging his feet on the mattress. They kissed, Ed embraced Ben closely, entered him deeply, and took him swiftly.

Afterward, still lying on top of Ben, although taking most of his weight on his knees and elbows, still inside the younger man, Ed urgently whispered to Ben. "I was serious at dinner. There's some bad shit going on here. In the morning, you need to get back in that Jeep and ride the hell out of here."

"I don't know that I can now that I've found you are here." Ben ran his hands over the Ute hunk's hard body. Ben knew Ed wanted him again. Ben knew he wanted Ed again.

"I'll give you my number. I'll meet you somewhere else. Anywhere else. Just not here. You need to get out of here."

"Not just this minute, though," Ben said, still trying to take this lightly—assuming that Ed was jealous that he was letting Crane do him and that the ranch foreman, Sling, was taking a piece of him too. Ben wasn't sure himself that he wanted to just be giving it to Ed. "Not just this minute," Ben repeated. "You're hard inside me again. You're going to fuck me again."

"Yes, I'm going to fuck you again," Ed growled. And then he did.

* * * *

Ben got to breakfast in the staff dining building late the next morning. Ed had been in his bed when he went to sleep, exhausted by the virile attentions of the Ute hunk, but he was gone when Ben woke. And he was on a horse, with a couple of other ranch hands, ready to go out on a fence-mending job when Ben emerged from the bunkhouse.

"Remember what I said," Ed called out to him. "This morning."

"Yes, right, this morning. After breakfast," Ben said as he walked on to the dining building.

He wasn't sure whether he'd really leave right after breakfast or not, though. He wasn't one to sneeze at the $2,000 Crane had offered him to be here for the next week. He'd have to mull that over breakfast. As it turned out, Ben hadn't even finished his breakfast when Sling was coming into the dining building looking for him.

"Wolf that down and get your tail out here," Sling said, coming up beside Ben and making plain that if the young man didn't rise for the table himself, Sling would pull him up and hustle him out. "We're going hunting today."

"Hunting? I don't hunt," Ben said. "Don't know the first thing about it."

"No one gives a shit whether you can hunt or not," Sling said. "You can fetch and carry, and Mr. Crane wants another set of muscles for his hunting trip up into the mountains."

When Ben came out of the building, Sling possessively bundling him along, he saw that four horses were prancing around in the dirt courtyard between the buildings. Crane was on one horse already, there were two horses saddled for Sling and Ben, and there was a loaded pack horse.

Ben could tell which horse was his. There were rifles hanging in holsters off the saddles of Crane's and Sling's horses. There wasn't one on his horse. The packhorse was carrying quite a load.

"We're taking all that?" Ben turned and asked Sling. He was gesturing at the pack horse.

"We hunt until Mr. Crane is satisfied. If that takes a couple of days in the mountains, he still wants to be

39

comfortable. Now get on that horse and don't hold us up. And don't tell me you don't know how to mount and ride a horse."

"I know how to mount and ride a horse," Ben shot back, not too politely. Sling fucked great but he was an asshole otherwise.

"Well, Mr. Crane and I know how to mount and ride you—and we're gonna be doing a lot of that on this hunting trip—so don't give me none of your lip."

Ben buttoned up his lip and concentrated on not making a fool of himself in mounting his horse, pointing it toward the mountains on the south side of the ranch, and keeping up with the other two men as they rode out onto the range.

All thought of getting in his Jeep and escaping the ranch had drained completely from his mind.

* * * *

This was Ben's first summer in the mountains of Colorado but it wasn't his first experience of riding horses. His uncle had horses and Ben rode them regularly, but other relatives of Ben's had ranches or farms and horses too. So, he had no trouble keeping up with the other two as they road up into the mountains at the south end of Shadow Ranch. Crane told him they were still on his property and would remain on his property, so he didn't fuck what the hunting regulations or licensing requirements were.

"What are we hunting?" Ben asked.

But the only answer Crane gave was, "You'll see." Sling said little or nothing himself. He just rode close enough to Ben and kept such a controlling eye on him that Ben thought the man was more his jailer than Crane's ranch foreman. One thing had been made clear to Ben—well, two things. He was along to fetch and carry, but, more important, he was along to provide the men with a fuck toy.

At noon they stopped by a mountain stream, and Crane commanded Ben to strip and cavort in the stream for his viewing pleasure while Sling set up lunch. This, of course, didn't surprise Ben, and he stripped down and did as

40

commanded. This was what he was being paid $2,000 to do. After they'd eaten, with Ben told to remain naked and Crane watching him move around and fisting his cock while he watched, Sling took out several lengths of leather strips.

"Go over to the fir tree over there," Crane said to Ben.

As soon as Ben realized that he was going to be bound in the tree in such a way that his arms were bound with the leather straps over his head and his legs spread and his ankles bound on other branches so that he essentially was in the same sling fuck position that Sling had taken him in Crane's bedroom back at the ranch the previous day, Ben half objected. "You don't need to do this."

"I want to do this," Crane answered. "Remember, I paid you for your ass for however I wanted to take it."

And take it both Crane and Sling did, stripping off their jeans and briefs and coming in between Ben's legs, grasping his hips, impaling his channel on their hard cocks, one after the other, and fucking him to their completions. The boughs of the fir made a swishing sound as the men pulled his channel on and off their cocks, Crane being thicker and more demanding on Ben's channel walls and Sling longer and more demanding in reaching up into Ben's intestines. It was OK with Ben, though. Both men slapped him around a bit, but it only added to his arousal, and he arched his shoulders and head back and gave the men the responses of being taken gloriously that he knew they wanted to hear. Ben was beginning to get a glimmer of what the two were hunting.

The afternoon ride was rougher on Ben. Not only was the ground rockier and the incline steeper, but his ass was more painful—not just from the fucking but also because Crane had made him hold in a big butt plug. "I want you open for me for later," Crane had said.

Later came in the twilight, after a ride along the tree line near the summit of the mountain, settling down in a glade in a hollow, the men putting up two tents, Sling fixing supper, and then Crane commanding Ben to strip again. This was when the two men doubled Ben. He'd never taken two at the same time before, but the butt plug, indeed had kept him open, and, with Crane standing in front of him, crouched, with Ben's thighs resting on Crane's thighs, and Sling standing behind him, grasping his waist and controlling the rise and fall of Ben's body, the two men both drove their cocks up inside Ben's channel and fucked him to a three-way ejaculation.

Afterward, Ben completely cowed and submissive to any manipulation, Sling draped the young man, belly down, over a saddle resting on the ground, tied off his wrists around the trunk of a small tree above his head, spread his legs, and staked out his ankles. During the evening, while they were sitting around the campfire and drinking whiskey, Crane and Sling, as the mood struck them, mounted Ben's ass and fucked him again.

After dousing the fire, they simply covered Ben with a blanket and went to their separate tents to sleep.

Ben woke the next morning to the pain of being kicked in the side. He opened his eyes to find both men already dressed, grinning, and resting their rifles, business end pointed to the ground and standing on either side. Sling pulled the blanket off Ben. While he was unbinding Ben and Ben turned over and sat on the ground, rubbing his wrists to dispel the numbness, Crane laughed.

"You asked what we were coming up here to hunt. We're here to hunt *you*."

That didn't surprise Ben, until, with a laugh, Crane continued. "With our rifles. We like our game to have some intelligence. It's a good thing for you that you've shaved two seconds off your running time this summer. It's time to take advantage of that. Run. In any direction you want."

"Wait. You can't . . . you can't just—" Ben muttered, scared and confused, but then he yelped, as Sling gave him a swift kick in the bare buttocks.

"You agreed that we could do whatever we wanted to you," Crane said. "This is what we want to do to you. We want to hunt you down and shoot you. You should have asked for more clarification." He laughed.

"You heard the man," Sling growled. "Run. There's no sport in shooting you here, but we'd do it piecemeal for the pleasure of it, if that's what you want."

"No, wait," Ben said, but he'd come up into a crouch.

"It's sport. You'll get a head start," Crane said, nudging Ben's shoulder with the barrel of his rifle. Then, when Ben didn't take off, he fired the rifle close to Ben's bicep, kicking up stones that cut into Ben's shins. Ben went up like a jackrabbit then and headed for the densest section of trees, downhill from the camp. When he reached the fringe of the foliage, though, he turned around, looking panicked, and cried. "No, you can't do this."

Sling laughed, raised his rifle, and fired. The pain on Ben's arm, although it was only grazed by the bullet, was searing and a shock that mobilized him to turn and stumble through the undergrowth in a zigzag pattern. He heard two more shots, but he kept running, using whatever he could as cover in his fight for evasion and survival. The ground was rocky, but they'd let him keep his athletic shoes on the previous night. Now he knew why—it was more sporting. It might prolong their hunt. His panic carried him swiftly downward. He had to reach the ranch. It didn't matter that it was too far away to get to in time or that he didn't know if anyone would help him even if he got there. He knew know why Ed wanted him to clear out. He knew too why Crane had asked him all those questions about if he were here alone. He hadn't mentioned his uncle, but that didn't matter anyway. His uncle thought he already was back in Pennsylvania.

He moved around for some twenty minutes, getting better and better at not making noise. From time to time, he knew someone else was out there—that he wasn't alone. And once a shot had come very close, but Ben had dived into the underbrush and scrambled away on his knees and elbows.

Another time he heard a shot, but it wasn't close by. The shot was misleading, though, because it made him think that they were getting farther away. He hadn't given a thought to the possibility that they had split up, but obviously they had. He tripped on a tree route and sprawled onto the ground on his back. He went up on his elbows but he found that he was looking into the barrel of a rifle. Crane was at the other, stock, end. He was grinning.

"Say good-bye, son. You were a great lay. You're even better blood sport."

Ben shut his eyes tight. He was too exhausted to fight it anymore. He had always thought that the shot that got you would be something you didn't hear. He was wrong about the shot this time. It rang in his ears. He opened his eyes. The expression on Crane's face was one of great surprise as the spot of red in the middle of his chest blossomed like an opening rose and he crumpled to the ground.

* * * *

Ben held Ed inside him, clutching the Ute's buttocks and comforted by the weight of the man's body on his, until Ed's legs were cramping and he rolled off to the side. Ed cupped Ben's chin in his rough, calloused hand, the manly texture of it sending a chill up the young college student's spine, and kissed him tenderly on the lips.

"How did you know? You warned me," Ben whispered.

"I didn't know for sure. Young men have been brought to the ranch to service Crane and Sling and just not been there anymore after the two had gone on hunting trips up into the mountains. When I returned to the ranch last night, they were on another hunt and you weren't there. But your Jeep was still there. It took me most of the night and the rest of the day to track you up to the top of the mountain. This is my people's land. I know it better than Crane did."

"What now?" Ben asked.

"Now you stay here until your flight leaves and we'll drive down into Durango and leave off the Jeep, just like everything is normal. Then you'll be out of it. No one but Crane and Sling knew where you'd come from—or care. They'll look for them and eventually find them, but there won't be anything linking them to anybody. I'm known to be up here tonight at the reservation. No one here will say anyone else is here. They'll hide you until the day of your flight. The Jeep is in a barn nearby. No one will connect it to the men's disappearance."

They were on the Ute reservation south of the Shadow Ranch—in the compound of Ed's extended family. They had

44

come down the mountain and, at night, Ed had gone in and gathered up all of Ben's gear and they'd driven away in Ben's jeep, with Ed's horse tied to it. Everyone else on the ranch had been celebrating the absence of the rancher and foreman and all were dead to the world after being drunk on their tails. On the way to the reservation, Ed took his rifle apart and they stopped and buried pieces here and there. The rifle that killed Crane and his foreman would never be found.

Ed rolled over and sat up on the side of the bed.

"You aren't leaving me, are you?" Ben asked.

"I have to. I have to go back to the ranch and act like nothing's happened. Someone will get you to the airport if I can't."

"I understand, but try to be there," Ben said.

"I'll do what I have to do," Ed answered. "You understand that this is it for us. For your protection, you have to go back wherever you came from—I'll forget where that is—and live your life. Just be more careful who you sleep with from now on."

"I want to sleep with you. I've never had anyone who—"

"Try to forget me," Ed said, leaning over for one last kiss, and then he was gone.

But forgetting wasn't that easy for Ed, either. The night before Ben was to fly out to Philadelphia, Ed returned, climbed into the bed, and made totally possessive love to Ben, pinning him to the bed and fucking him again and again throughout the night.

He wasn't there in the morning, and didn't take Ben down into Durango—two of his brothers did that, using another Jeep in addition to Ben's for them to have a way to get back to the reservation. But when Ben opened his carry-on bag for inspection at the airport, he found a slip of paper with a cell phone number on it. He carefully inserted it into his wallet, knowing that someday—not soon—but someday, he'd call the number.

Oversexed

I let out my breath in a dissatisfied hiss as Pete pulled out of me, went down on his back beside me in the bed, jerked the condom off his cock, and masturbated himself to a quick ejaculation. I turned onto my side, facing Pete, and finished myself with my hand after I'd watched the cream burble out of his cockhead. I'd still been grinding against him, taking him deep, still building up to my zone of Nirvana, when he'd left me.

I think he'd done it on purpose. He knew I needed a long buildup and wanted to luxuriate in the zone with my partner for a while before I came. The zone came faster the second and third times. I wanted it repeatedly. Pete could do that if he wanted to. He'd done that well enough for long enough that we'd melded enough that, though not married, we'd become one in everything else. We owned the house in Philadelphia together. We worked together—I in front of the camera and he behind it in TV commercials—we shared a closet. We even shared an underwear drawer—and the briefs in it. It made me feel extra sexy to wear Pete's briefs, feeling his intimacy close to my skin.

I lay there, on my side, toying with my cock, wishing I could lure Pete back into the bed, back inside me, so that he could complete me—would take me into the Nirvana zone and let me ride on the clouds as I rode his cock. But he was having nothing of that, pulling clothes out of closet and drawers and consulting on what I wanted to keep and what he could take. All the time he was talking—very reasonably, much too reasonably—about how to divide everything else, saying he'd enlist a Realtor to get the house sold and would send me half— when I could give him an address. Clearly he didn't want me to stay in the house or even discuss the possibility of the two of us keeping it, together. He clearly was finished with together.

I didn't give a shit about the clothes or the house or the dishes. I wanted him on top of me again, possessing me with his hard cock, pumping me interminably until I could reach the Nirvana zone, dancing me on the clouds, coming, and then, after a cuddle, being inside me again, riding me hard and long, coming together with me that time.

But that was the problem. He said I was exhausting him—that I couldn't get enough, often enough. Couples settled down, he said. They mellowed and other aspects of life together became as important, as meaningful, as the sex. He wanted a relationship that went beyond him keeping his cock hard for me as I luxuriated in the Nirvana zone.

We had merged in all ways except for cars. We didn't share cars. He had his Dodge Ram truck and me my Mustang convertible. If we'd come to share even that, maybe I wouldn't be standing at the upstairs bedroom window, still naked, still hopeful, and pulling on my cock, as I watched him drive away in his Dodge Ram.

* * * *

The season was over on the beach north of Ocean City and, save for a two-hour slice of time in the early afternoon, the wind was too raw to lay on the beach. Forget about going into the water. The ocean's resentment at the end of the beach season had been translated into angry surf. I had finally given into Pete's relentless e-mails to get out of the house, brought to the head by a signed sales contract, and had booked the cabin on the beach on impulse. It was clear that it was over with Pete. I hadn't had sex since he left me, hoping against hope that he'd be back, and I was crawling the walls.

47

I had decided to go cold turkey on sex, though. I had decided that it was me—that I was oversexed and had indulged to the point of not thinking of, caring about, the needs of my partner. Pete had been a good thing, compatible in every way, a good help-mate and capable of taking me to and holding me in the Nirvana zone long enough for me to melt. I clearly had taken advantage of that and not cultivated the needs he had. I decided that I needed to train myself to want and need less. Surely as I aged, my overweening need for prolonged sex—my satyriasis, the male version of nymphomania—would lessen and maybe even go away. Maybe I had just found Pete at the wrong time of my life. Maybe I needed to push myself to that time of life.

The cabin had no WiFi. I had purposely booked it for that reason—not just because it was tiny, unheated, and cheap for out-of-season beachfront. I was denying myself access to the Internet—to sex videos, dating services, and dirty stories. I also denied self-gratification to the extent I could. The nervous energy this gave me, though, was having me bouncing off the walls of the beach cottage.

I took to walking the beach in the morning and the afternoon and at twilight. In season, there would be eye candy to ogle and to flirt with and signal to. I knew all about identifying prospective tops and flirting and signaling. And, as a male model, I had no trouble being successful with that. But it was early October. The beach eye candy was long gone. At the most there were joggers, serious muscle builders, pounding up and down the surf line, taking advantage of the hard-packed sand that the surf was still saturating.

I walked farther up the sand, giving the joggers their space, but staying within ogling distance of them.

It was late in the afternoon, within an hour of twilight. The beach seemed deserted, as did the houses—mostly '50s-style cottages, like mine, with the occasional more recent McMansion pushing in—lining the beach. I had never felt as alone—as jittery sexually—and was about to go inside, frustrated by the aloneness and contemplating going out to try to find a gay bar that hadn't closed for the season, while recognizing I wouldn't find one.

I saw him jogging up the beach from a great distance, moving quickly, legs pumping in his baggy athletic shorts, his torso covered with a loose hoodie. He was my age or a bit younger, obviously a bodybuilder, a serious muscle man. As he came closer I could see that he probably was a boxer too, his face showing the scars of combat. His arms were pumping and he was concentrating on his run. At first I thought he hadn't seen me at all—that he was completely absorbed in himself and his workout. But as he came closer, coming at me, we made eye contact and he smiled. I smiled back, and nodded. He continued on up the beach.

He was behind me now. I turned several times to watch him run, my cock hard from the need of someone being inside me and with him being more than satisfactory in my fantasies of being pumped. One of the times I looked around, I found that he had too. He knew I was here. He was interested in me. But he was behind me, still running, probably running out of my life.

But then I heard him coming up behind me, on his return up the beach. He was puffing but not straining, just setting a rhythm of breathing as he ran. Passing me, he turned and ran backward a couple of paces, smiling at me, his hand going to his basket, giving me both a signal and a question. I smiled back, my own hand instinctively going to my basket, signaling my own interest.

There, up ahead, as he continued to run, I saw him pull off his hoodie, showing a muscular, hairy chest, and stuffed the hoodie in the back waistband of his shorts. I pulled my own sweatshirt over my head, so that, as he ran back to me, he could see my model's body, my own trim but well-defined blond musculature. I pulled my shorts down so that he could see the curves at the top of my legs and below my hard belly, teasing him with what lay just a few inches below my low-rise waistband.

He took control, just as I wanted him to, as he reached me, taking a last look up and down the beach and then pulling my body into his, taking my mouth with his, stuffing his hand down my belly, under my waistband, and assuring himself that I was hard for him.

He fucked me, raw, belly down on a plastic garbage bin next to a deserted cottage just above the sand line from where our body's had collided. There was little preliminary. He was close behind me, bent over me, one arm around my neck and the other around my waist, holding me in place, while he pumped me hard and fast with a cock that hadn't been all that long when I had it in my mouth, but was jaw-unhinging thick. I tried to fuck him back, attempting to move my pelvis to meet his thrusts, but he had no interest in that. He held me close, fucking me like a dog, all his own need and want.

He wasn't long enough to work me deep, as I preferred to build to the Nirvana zone, but he had me groaning from the thickness of him and the lack of preparation to open fully to him. And he was long enough to reach and work my prostate, which his bulb was rubbing vigorously. I was beginning to build, beginning to reach for Nirvana.

But then it was over. He had taken me quickly, deflating me when I felt him tense, release, filling me with his cum, coming within minutes, and then pulling out of me and holding me there only briefly, both of us panting, me panting—unsatisfied—harder than he was.

"Again, again," I mumbled, but he either didn't hear me or didn't care. He already was pulling off me, readjusting his clothes.

"My cottage is just up the beach. Come back there with me. Do me again," I murmured as I felt the tension leaving him, his grip on me lessening.

"It was good, but I don't think so," he answered. Then he pulled out of me, put his jock back in place, pulled his shorts up and his hoodie on, and was jogging back down to the surf to resume his run, uncaring that I was still draped over the garbage bin, unsatisfied.

So this was how Pete felt after I had used him and not given enough back, I thought. I trudged back to the beach cabin. Suddenly the walls were too close on all sides, the cottage was too cold, the future was too dreary—and there was no WiFi to give me any chance of pushing the encounter of reality to something more satisfying in fantasy.

I knew that an off-season cottage on the beach wasn't the answer.

* * * *

Trying to go cold turkey on satyriasis wasn't working. I hadn't suppressed any form of want or need; I'd just frustrated myself in the attempt at self-denial. I didn't know what to do, where to go, other than the cold cottage on the beach and the sense of loss and rejection. I went out on the beach the following day, at the same time, and the bodybuilder jogged by me again. I hadn't asked for or gotten a name from him. I'd introduced myself—Chris—to him and only gotten a grunt in return. Even then all he'd been interested in was the hookup, the fast fuck, and the quick "so long."

I stood, smiling, expectantly, willing to have no more than he'd given me before, willing to give up most of my own need just to have a dick inside me again. But, although he smiled, he jogged right on past me and didn't look back.

I returned to the cottage at a complete loss of what to do, where to go. Luckily, I had a letter waiting for me from the Realtor for Pete and my house. The house had sold quickly. I would be sent my share of the profit right after settlement. It was enough for me to hole up somewhere and reassess my life for several months.

I called Max at the modeling agency, saying I needed a sabbatical and then we discussed me being put on jobs where Pete wouldn't be behind the camera.

"Pete's already made that request," Max answered. "What's up with you guys? You seemed so good together."

My unreasonable demands were what was up with that, I thought, deflated that Pete had already requested the separation. How much blame did I need to have flung in my face. And why couldn't I do anything about who I was, what I wanted and needed? What was wrong with me and how could I fix it?

I guess I knew what was wrong with me—I was oversexed. I just didn't know how to fix it. Abstinence hadn't worked. Maybe controlled self-regulation would have to work. I decided to move on, to try something else.

The jogger was back the next day, waiting for me when I came out of the cottage. He pushed me back into the cottage and to the bed, giving me no more preliminary time or preparation than he had before. I opened my legs to him and took him inside me gladly, prepared to be satisfied for whatever I could get, feeling vindicated at least that he'd come back for more. He fucked me fast and hard, came, and then left. I lay on the bed, on my back, legs parted, and jacked myself off. This hadn't been anywhere close to the Nirvana zone. But it didn't really matter; I'd already decided to leave.

* * * *

I found a small stone house to rent on a remote hillside of an estate near Chadds Ford, Pennsylvania. I needed to have a retreat where I could hide when I needed to and have all to myself but that was within a reasonable drive of the big city. Philadelphia was a forty-five-minute drive northeast and Wilmington, Delaware, a half hour to the east. Less than an hour and a half would get me to the Baltimore inner harbor and two and a half hours to Washington, D.C. New York City wasn't an unreasonable distance away either.

The house was in a picturesque setting in a wealthy, rolling hills county of estates within a doable commute of cities. The particular estate I was on was owned by a New York ad agency CEO who commuted back to Chadds Ford on weekends and thus afforded me privacy. I knew her slightly, as I had done commercials for her agency. She was happy to rent me the cottage at a reasonable price and not ask me questions or intrude on my life. She knew I was gay.

The side of the estate my cottage was located on was abutted by the Brandywine Battlefield Park, which included walking trails I could use for exercise. The house itself was small and was built into the side of the hill. The entry was on the upper level, with a living room on one side and a dining room-kitchen combination on the other. On the walkout level below it, a larger room I used as an office and exercise area was under the living room, and a small bedroom, accommodating a double mattress and not much else and a bathroom and snug laundry room were under the dining room kitchen combination. I had rented it mainly because, unlike the beach cottage, it had reliable WiFi and because I could play music as loudly as I wanted to as I exercised hard and abused my body physically and sexually to work off my frustrations.

For the first three months, I was on the Internet constantly, running through the gay porn sites and getting myself off as frequently as possible, trying to take care of being oversexed on my own. I also played the gay dating sites hard too, being willing to drive to Philadelphia, Wilmington, Baltimore, or even New York or Washington, D.C., in search of a man who would stay inside me, hard, long enough to take me into the Nirvana zone and hold me until I melt—and then do it again.

All the time I held the men at arms' length, not telling even the ones who wanted to continue in a relationship where I lived or how they could contact me. I even avoided telling them my true name if I could. I needed the retreat. I needed my isolated cottage in the woods. I was trying to come to grips with myself and lessen my need for constant, consuming sex.

I didn't find the man of my dreams from the Internet. No one who came even close to what I had had and had lost in Pete. I only found repeats of the bodybuilder who had used me and tossed me away on the beach north of Ocean City.

That is until the first warm day of the spring, when, just in shorts and running shoes, I took to the walking trails at the Brandywine Battlefield Park.

He was tall and muscular without being overbuilt. At first I thought he was black, but his skin was milk chocolate in hue and his facial features had only a hint of the Negroid. I marked him as Hispanic, possibly Cuban. He was probably over forty, but very well preserved. His hair was cropped close but was black and curly and he had one of those fastidiously kept five o'clock beard and mustache combinations. His eyes were blue, which was an inconsistent shock. An elaborate, colorful tattoo of a swirling pattern covered his left pec, ran over his shoulder, and went down below his bicep, emphasizing the hard bulge of both the breast and the bicep. His aureoles were prominent, thick, and black. The right one had a gold ring in it, as did both his ears and his navel. He jogged past me on the path in the park, his eyes taking me in as soon as he came up over the rise. His smile was instantaneous and easy, his teeth white and perfect. He, like me, was in low-rise silky shorts, cut high up the side, and running shoes.

He was there and gone in an instant, the pathway being hilly and the foliage close on both sides. I drew in my breath and didn't let it out until he was well past me. He had been gorgeous, and the presence had been so fleeting that I would have believed he had been a mirage—subject to the wishful thinking I was engaging in as I walked the path—if he hadn't left his musky scent in his wake.

I shook my head and continued on. The trails here were convoluted and folded back on each other. It was that fact that I latched onto when, not more ten minutes later, he approached me on the path again, once more coming toward me. The same smile on his face, but this time also a query in his eyes, signaling interest that I clearly recognized. One of his hands, with long, sensuous fingers, was spread out on his flat belly, the tips of the fingers running below his waistband in front. His eyes were boring into mine, but he didn't miss, I'm sure, when I palmed my belly in the same way. He slowed as he came upon me and smiled and inclined his head in the direction in which he was jogging, his rhythm that of a dancer's, covering the path lightly rather than in a trudge. His eyebrows went up in a query and an invitation. And then he was past me.

I felt myself panting, going hard. I stopped and turned. He already was over the rise in the path behind me, but almost involuntarily I started moving in the direction, the direction in which I had come from. In addition to the signaling, he obviously needed this statement of submission to him—reversing my direction and coming to him.

He had stopped not far down the path behind me and was half sitting, half leaning on a low-lying branch of a tree. His arms were spread, his hands grasping the tree limb on either side of him, but the waistband of his athletic shorts and his jock had been pulled down and were hooked under his balls. His cock, what looked to be nearly a thick foot long—a veritable black snake, blacker than the tone of his skin—was exposed and projecting directly out between his spread thighs. He was half hard, and he was smiling at me. His black, curly pubes were closely and neatly trimmed. His balls were huge and hairless, nearly as black as his cock.

I stopped in the middle of the path when he came into view, gasped, and heard a low, rattling sound come up from deep in my throat. I'm sure he heard it too. When he was sure I was there, motionless, and staring at him, he gave a low laugh. His eyes went to my crotch and he could see that I was hard as well. One of my hands had involuntarily snaked to below my waistband in front. There could be no question what either one of us wanted, was willing—anxious—to do.

"Come," he said in a low, rich baritone voice and stood and walked off into the woods beside the path. I followed him. He found a fir tree with thick, low-hanging branches and positioned himself much the same as he had just off the pathway.

Neither of us said anything. He just projected his pelvis toward me from where he was perched and put his hands on my head as I came to him, knelt between his thighs, and took his cock in my mouth. He used his hands to guide my head, forcing me to take him deep and releasing me when I started to gag, only to pull my throat back onto the cock as it got harder and harder.

This was going to be a rough fuck. That was fine with me.

When he pulled me up onto my feet in front of him, he took my mouth with his in a deep, possessive kiss, while he pushed my shorts and jock off my hips. I let them shinny down my legs and stepped out of them.

"I'm Luis," he said, after he'd freed me from the kiss, if not from the gaze of his incongruously blue eyes.

"Chris," I automatically answered. I rarely gave a man my name, and never my real one—at least not before now; not since Pete. That I'd given him my name somehow bound me to him. To that point, some part of me had wanted to pull away and escape, even though this was the type of encounter I dreamed of and had entered before, only to be disappointed in the domination of the man and his insistence on a fast fuck centered only on his own need. Once I'd given him my name I was bound to him, though.

"Do you live near here? Is here someplace we can go?" he asked.

My home, nearly within sight of where we were, was my private retreat. I had decided it was sanctuary, no matter what. I instinctively answered, "No, sorry."

I immediately was afraid this would change everything, that it would put him off. But it didn't. He merely stood, lifted me—being taller and heavier than I was—lowered my back onto the fir branch, and took me there.

I grabbed the branches over my head and swayed in the branch my back was lying in, as he wishboned my legs and attacked my cock and balls and hole with his mouth until he had me hard, open, and begging for his cock. He'd gotten protection from somewhere and somehow got it rolled onto his monstrous snake of a cock and hunched over me, still wishboning my legs, his face close to mine, his eyes boring into mine, holding me in thrall and controlling me, as he entered, entered, entered me and penetrated me to a depth no man had reached before.

When he was fully inside me and I felt his balls against the tender skin of my inner thighs, he held, as I gasped, close to hyperventilation and eventually whined, "Fuck me. Fuck me hard."

As he pumped me then, big balls slapping rhythmically against tender inner thighs, I felt myself slowly rising to the Nirvana zone. He continued, a slow, steady, deep thrusting and I was there—in the zone, where I hadn't been since the days when Pete and I were clicking along on all cylinders, early in our relationship.

"Yes, yes, like that. Don't stop. Take me higher," I whined, gasping and melting to him. He didn't stop. He was a veritable fucking machine, pumping me interminably. "Stay with me deep," I whined, and, as if he understood exactly what I needed, he moved deep inside me and held there, as I went to

Nirvana, exploding again and again on his rock-hard shaft holding steady deep in my gut.

I went from happy to melting to melted and shimmering, firing off twice while he was still inside me in that position, burbling meaninglessly, crying, sobbing, begging him to finish me, and, after he had, begging him to stay inside me. Begging him to finish me again, and, when he had, purring and sobbing at the same time. I went soft and vulnerable for him. He conquered me, tortured me, slayed me, giving me no mercy, taking me more completely than I'd ever been possessed before—and forever, fucking me in waves and waves of surrender and pleasure—a death by cock.

I knew when he came, as it was with his body tensing and shaking, and his cock thrusting up deeper inside me then it had ever been. He didn't withdraw, though. He pulled my legs into his side, causing my shimmering channel to sheath his throbbing cock closer, and he leaned down and kissed me—on the lips, all over my face and throat, on my nipples, to return eventually and fully possess my mouth. I was clutching his shoulder blades with my hands, digging my fingernails into his back. But he didn't complain.

I felt his going hard again and tore my lips away from his, and cried out, "Fuck! Shit! Yes, yes!" as he turned me on his cock, face down into the needles of the fir branch and took me into the Nirvana zone—and beyond—again.

When he pulled out of me this time, I was barely conscious. I was dancing on the clouds and barely aware that he had withdrawn and was standing and pulling his jock and shorts back into place.

"I hope you're OK, that I didn't hurt you."

Of course you didn't hurt me. You fucked me like no one has fucked me before. That's what I wanted to say, but I was in no condition to say anything. I was still moaning deeply—still in the Nirvana zone even though his cock no longer was inside me. I tried to vocalize that I was lost to him but nothing came out but drool and whimpering.

"Pity there's no place for us to go," I heard him say. "I'd like to do you again. You're a sweet lay. It just isn't safe here. They patrol the park."

I wanted to scream that I lived just over the hill—that I'd take him there—that I'd open my legs to him all night, all weekend. All month. But, by the time I was able to form the words, "No, wait," I was alone. I walked the entire system of Brandywine Battlefield Park paths, but I didn't see him again.

I dragged myself back to the cottage. It had been wonderful while it was happening, but it left me bereft. I hadn't been wrong. I was capable of being fully satisfied by a man. And the yearning was still there—now more than ever. Nothing I'd done had been able to change my need and want. I couldn't handle this alone. It almost would have been better to have decided I couldn't be satisfied fully.

The next day, I started calling around for a recommendation of a shrink to go to to help me do something about this craziness I had. I got a referral and called for an appointment. I would go into Philadelphia the next week.

* * * *

I had signed up for Dr. L. Phillips's last appointment for the day. I would take advantage of already being in Philadelphia to hit the bars and hope for a hookup that would be satisfying, but after Luis in the park I didn't think any man ever again could satisfy me.

I did a double-take when I was ushered into the therapist's office. I could swear that . . . but he wasn't showing any recognition, so maybe . . . He didn't have the earrings and was quite professionally dressed, so maybe it was just the familiarity and me remembering a man who wasn't really that similar. I wasn't paying all that much attention to Luis in the park after he'd begun fucking me. Just the eyes. The therapist had glasses on—with yellowish lenses.

I certainly wasn't going to say anything if he didn't. I wasn't going to be the one to suggest that he was the man who . . . who had fucked me so fully, totally manhandled me and conquered me. Who had made me his willing, malleable slave, if only for an hour in the woods.

"Come, lay down on this couch over here and tell me what's bothering you, Chris." The voice. A smooth, low

58

baritone. And he called me Chris. But he would have known that from his appointments book. I wouldn't be the one to make the connection if there was one to be made. Phillips. That wasn't an Hispanic name. But blue eyes. There would be some sort of mix there.

I stretched out on his couch. He was standing beside a wing chair that was a good ten feet away from the couch and pointing to the side. A therapist's positioning, I guessed. The therapist could be there but not directly connected.

"Tell me why you have come to me," he said. He wasn't sitting in the chair yet. Shouldn't he be sitting in the chair with a pen and a notebook?

"It's about . . . it's about . . ."

"It's about sex, isn't it?" he asked, his voice low.

"Yes," I answered. "I can't be satisfied . . . well, other than once, recently . . . I'm oversexed. That's what my last partner said. I thought we could make it work, but he said that our problem was that I could never get enough . . . that I was oversexed."

"Being oversexed is a condition, Chris. It's not a problem. Or it doesn't need to be a problem."

The voice was coming from farther away. I turned my head and saw that he was at the door, turning the lock. Then he was walking toward me, unbuckling his belt, slipping his trousers off his hips.

"The answer to satisfying being oversexed is to match up with a partner who also is oversexed," he said as he pulled his trousers off his legs. His cock, hard, black, thick, and long poked through the part in his dress shirt.

Luis. Luis of the park. It was Luis from the park.

He was standing at the foot of the couch, rolling a condom on his cock, slipping my loafers off, reaching up and undoing my belt, unzipping me, pulling my trousers and briefs off my legs.

I was frozen to the couch, already moaning. He climbed onto the couch, hovering over my body. Grasping my ankles and hooking them on his shoulders.

"Being oversexed is a gift, Chris. An oversexed submissive is a rare gift for an oversexed dominant. It isn't a problem. It is a glorious gift." He reached up, taking my wrists in the grip of one of his strong hands. His other one was fingering my hole. I winced and gasped as he entered me with two fingers and then a third.

"I lied," I whimpered.

"How so?"

"I did have someplace we could go. My house is next to the park. This weekend, you could—"

"Of course. But we may be here through the weekend," he said. Then he gave a low laugh.

I moaned as his fingers withdrew and then gasped, arched my back, and cried out as he entered me, going deep with a strong, fully possessing thrust, holding there, waiting for me to adjust to him before he took me to the Nirvana zone, still hard and deep inside me, motionless until I had exploded on the hard cock again and again, and then he would start taking his pleasure of me.

I wouldn't be barhopping in Philadelphia tonight. I wouldn't be in the condition to bar hop anywhere for some time to come.

The Capitol Limited

I don't know how long he'd been sitting there, across from us, in Washington, D.C.'s, Union Station waiting room before I saw him. Denise was off, checking out the shopping concourse because she couldn't sit still for the two-hour wait before we could board the Capitol limited bound on an eighteen-hour, one-night run to Chicago. The senator was pacing an eight-foot path between the banks of benches in this row like a caged lion. The pacing wasn't the only leonine aspect of the six foot six, powerfully built politician with a mane of gray hair and a commanding presence that had sent him to Congress four times. Neither of us had thought it wise to let Denise, seven months pregnant, go off on her own. In fact neither of us had thought she should be taking this "check with the constituents" quick trip back to Chicago at all. The senator had certainly done everything he could to cry her off on the trip. But no one successfully told Denise what to do—not even the senator.

He was dark—swarthy—and muscular, the man who caught my attention and who kept looking at me. He was dangerous looking, with an olive complexion, long, black hair gathered in a ponytail behind his head, a close-cut beard and mustache, and steely black eyes. His mouth was set in a cruel, knowing smile, which made me feel that he could look through my Joseph A. Banks congressional aide clothing and look into my soul, discern my deepest hidden desires—know what I wanted, what I would do for a man like him.

Involuntarily, my hand went over my shoulder onto my shoulder blade as if I were trying to scratch and itch there. But it wasn't an itch I was searching for, and what I was searching for had nearly faded away. It had been a week.

It wasn't just the aspect of danger and cruelty about him that had attracted me or the way his intense gaze kept coming back to me and that cruel smile. It also was the black leather he was wearing: a form-fitting black vest, emphasizing his muscular torso; a thick, many-stranded belt, with the ends of the strands hanging down at his side in a tassel; and black motorcycle boots, with heavy silver buckles. The total package looked arousingly devilish.

Black leather. A smoky room, men swirling around, in black leather. Black painted walls and ceiling and floor; raucous noise, catcalls, dares, and challenges; macho posturing; a spotlighted X frame. And me, naked, willingly being tied to the X frame. A whip. The delicious sting of the black leather strands. Going hard . . . knowing I was going to be fully used . . .

"I found this beautiful cashmere shawl in a shop right over there. Feel it, Chad, isn't it the softest you've ever felt? I wanted something for the train. I get chilled so easily of late."

She put a hand on my back, and I started to wince but then realized that the hurt had faded away.

"You're not cold, are you?" I asked, coming quickly out of my reverie to respond to Denise now that she was back from the absence that had had both the senator and me on edge. As charismatic as the senator was, Denise was always the center of attention wherever she was.

"No, I feel fine. I . . . oh, oh my."

"What is it Denise?" I asked, in a slight panic. I still thought she should have stayed here in Washington. We only planned to be gone for the long weekend. If the senator would fly, we'd just be gone for a few days. But the senator wouldn't fly.

"Denise?" This time it was the senator, turned back to us, a look of slight concern mixed with not-so-slight irritation floated across his face.

"No, it's all right," she responded. "He kicked. Here, Chad, feel my belly. Can you feel him kick?"

Tentatively, I placed a hand on her belly. I didn't feel a thing, but I said, "Yes, maybe," as I knew that was expected of me. Denise was holding my hand to her belly and giving me a look that I hoped the senator didn't see. My eyes went to the man sitting across from us. He was still staring at me, knowingly, a slight smirk of amusement on his face—amused at my embarrassment.

Almost anyone else in the waiting room who viewed the tableau of Denise and me, me with my hand on her pregnant belly, would, I'm sure, think we were a couple. The man sitting across from us knew otherwise. He knew what I wanted, what I would do for a man like him.

The knowing look, and the amusement at my embarrassment. Ever so briefly the scenario ran through my mind and imagination of being restrained, wrists to ankles, and that man, naked as I was save for a black leather chest harness, hunched over me, his body between my spread legs, inside me, filling me and working me cruelly. Black leather gloves on his hands, his hands on my throat, choking me in rhythm to his thrusts inside me, while I writhed under him and cried out in a passion that knew I shouldn't feel but had no control over.

"You, Daniel? Do you want to feel your son kick too."

That should give any others who overheard her pause, I thought—that it was the senator, not me, who was the father of this child.

The senator just gave her a disgusted "What? Here? a senator, with everyone looking" look and said, "There will be other, more private and dignified opportunities for that, Denise." He turned and strode off a couple of paces, as if he wasn't part of this family setting—me still with my hand on his wife's belly, although I removed it, somewhat forcefully, as soon as I realized that. Denise was his third wife, hardly older than his oldest daughter. It was quite evident to me that he hadn't planned on raising a third family.

Denise was preparing to give him a sharp retort, which came easily to her, but changed gears and gave me a warm smile instead. I moved a bit away from her and turned my eyes toward the man sitting across from her. Denise hadn't been shy with me. I had gotten the impression ever since the senator, for whom I was a legislative assistant, had married her that she would have been pleased if I had been the father of her baby. But I wasn't. If the senator wasn't the father, I had no idea who was. My preferences were elsewhere.

When my eyes went to the man in the black leather sitting across from us, he still was staring at me. I knew that somehow he had deduced what my preferences were—and was willing to fulfill my fantasies, given the opportunity. Even as I watched, he widened his stance and dropped a hand to hanging down over his bulging basket. Having gotten my attention, he moved his hand to take hold of the strand of leather hanging down from his belt. The fading welts on my back twitched. I looked up into this eyes—that knowing smirk again.

Soon thereafter an Amtrak official approached us with a porter and a cart in tow and addressed the senator. "Perhaps you'd be more comfortable boarding now, Senator Dobbs," he said. "The Capitol Limited is in early and ready. We could board you before the others."

"That would be fine, James," the senator answered. He was a regular VIP passenger on this run. It took him back to his constituents. Amtrak officials knew who to curry favor with.

As I helped to gather together our suitcases and carry-ons to pass over to the porter loading his cart, I looked across the aisle to where the leather man had been sitting.

But he was gone.

As we moved toward the train, the senator was moving deliberately and at a quick pace, with the Amtrak official sweating in his wake. Denise and I brought up the rear. Denise laced her arm through mine, controlling my pace and, with a coy smile for me, giving me the impression that wasn't the only thing about me she'd like to control. "You know, you remind me a lot of Sean Barkley—same sweet, 'oh my gosh' good looks."

If I hadn't already thrown my guard up when she took my arm, this was enough to do it Yes, I remembered Sean— the senator's spokesman, held over from his recent campaign. Sean had suddenly disappeared from the staff roster four months ago—about the time that Denise's pregnancy would have become obvious.

"Do I?" I asked noncommittally.

She swerved in her line of thought. "Wasn't Daniel thoughtful to have specified three separate bedroom compartments on the train? He's self-conscious about his snoring, you know. Besides, I couldn't see him climbing up to the upper bunk—and I certainly couldn't be expected to sleep up there. It's nice that I'll have a compartment all to myself."

But it wasn't really a change of thought, I realized. I answered with only a clearing of my throat, looking up and down the platform now that we had reached the train. I only briefly wondered how a man went about fucking a woman who was seven-months pregnant. It wasn't like I had any experience in such matters.

I looked around again with a different interest, but I didn't see the leather man anywhere. I wondered what train he was taking—where he was headed, who he'd be fucking tonight. Who he'd be cruel to tonight.

* * * *

The light was dimming outside the train and we were nearly clear of Pennsylvania as I drifted off from the monotony of the blurred landscape, the rocking motion of the observation car, and the clickety-click of the wheels on the rails. Thoughts of the leather man I'd observed in the Union Station waiting room floated into my half-conscious brain and my thoughts went to that night at the DC Eagle in Washington and, afterward, at the nearby Rocky's hotel, a gay-insistent flea bag with thin walls in the rooms but no cares about the sounds the walls didn't trap. Nor did they care how many men piled into one of their rooms. Six or seven men, all leathered up, the hotel obligingly providing the sling, where I was trussed up, wrists and ankles bound high on the chains, as, one after the

65

other, with one guy always holding my head and waving poppers under my nose, the men whipped and fucked me, some with condoms, some without.

I'd been drunk, but not too drunk not to have gone willingly with them and having the experience lodged into my brain as a want—and, increasingly, a need.

Taken out of the sling and rebound to the chain, high up, by my wrists, given a taste of the whip on my back, buttocks, and thighs before another round of fucking. And I was aroused by and melted to that as well.

A laugh across the aisle from where Denise was sitting beside me and the senator across from me, a table between us, drinks on the table, brought me back from my reverie, and I looked out into the aisle—in time to see the leather man passing by. He'd had his eyes drilling into me, a cruel little smile on his lips, even before I looked up. When I did, and we made eye contact, I flinched but didn't look away from him. As he passed, I swiveled my head around, and sucked in breath. His belt, the strange bunching of stands of leather, wasn't really a belt. I could see now that he was showing his back to me that it was a whip, gathered and wound around his waist. The black leather handle of the whip was at the small of his back.

"Excuse me," I murmured to Denise, rising. "I have to use the restroom."

As I moved across her to reach the aisle, one of her hands was inserted between my legs, high on my thigh, and she smiled up at me. It was probably a knowing smile, as she surely could tell that I'd gone hard. She didn't really "know," though, as it wasn't for her that I'd gone hard.

"I think there's a book in my compartment I want to have. So, maybe I'll go back with you to fetch it."

"Isn't that the book you were reading?" I asked, pointing to a Donna Leon that was wedged between her rump and the side of the bench.

"Why, yes it is," she answered, her voice sounding a bit chagrinned. "I think I also need—"

"The senator shouldn't be left alone," I said, turning her attention to him across from us. He'd drunk a bit too much. Indeed, someone needed to be here to make sure he didn't make a scene that would be memorable enough to make the papers in Illinois. There already had been some rumblings about his drinking and not showing up for many votes in Congress if they were taken in the morning.

"I'll just be a few minutes," I said. "Then I'll sit with him and you can fetch whatever you need from your compartment."

I didn't wait to see the disappointment and ire on Denise's face, but already was pushing to the end of the car and through the connector compartment between this car and the sleeping car.

The leather man was near the end of the car. He had turned and was looking at me, expectantly gesturing with a hand at the door of a compartment, which I took to be his. Indecision caught up with me. This was dangerous. I couldn't let it be this easy. I couldn't even be sure that I was reading the man right. Instead of walking down the corridor to him, I turned right and went into the lavatory just inside the door into the compartment. This, after all, was where I had said I was going. I just didn't think I was ready to fall over the edge yet— not without some second thoughts.

But I didn't lock the lavatory door.

The door opened, and there he was, entering and locking the door behind him. He grabbed me and pulled me into his chest with one strong arm around my back, his hand gripping the back of my neck and pulled my face into his for a possessive kiss. His other hand went directly to my basket, assuring himself that I was hard for him, which I was.

Pulling his lips off mine, he growled, "You want it." It wasn't a question.

"Yes," I murmured.

"You want the whip too."

"Yes," I whimpered.

"Hands on the wall high over the toilet, butt jutted out to me," he growled.

As I turned, with a moan, he pulled my Polo shirt over my head, and I palmed the wall over the toilet and jutted my buttocks back to him. The space was so confining that there barely was room for him to fit behind me. He jerked my trousers and briefs down to my ankles and went down behind me, attacking my hole with his mouth, and my cock and balls, which he pulled back between my spread thighs, with one of his hands. He was palming my belly with the other hand, holding me steady as the train car swayed.

Standing and leaning back so that his shoulder blades pressed to the wall opposite the toilet, he found just enough room in the back swing to give me a little sting when the leather strands of the whip kissed my back and buttocks. He gave me just a taste of that before he cupped my chin, forcing my head back, and arched my torso painfully back to him. I cried out as he invaded me with the fingers of a hand—one, two, all four, up to the knuckle, and spread them, forcing me open for him—for which I was grateful when I learned how thick he was. He penetrated me to the depth of only an inch or more with the bulb of his throbbing cock. He gave me a few lashes on my back and buttocks with the whip.

Near to sobbing, I begged him, "Fuck me. Please fuck me."

More lashes, none cutting deep, all asserting control and mastery, and then the whip was gone, his arms were snaking around my sides, his hands were palming my pecs, fingernails digging into the flesh around the aureoles of my nipples, and he plunged his cock deep inside me and plowed me. I had opened well to him and took the fucking with sighs of appreciation and encouragement. He was thick and long— and cruel in his thrusts. I uninhibitedly voiced my testing, confident that the noise of the train covered my cries unless someone had an ear pressed to the door. The train wasn't crowded; I thought nothing of giving him the surrendering acknowledgement that he was gloriously torturing me.

When he was in deep, I realized that he had a leather studded cock ring circling the root of his cock that both kept him rock hard and punished my rim. He took me in powerful thrusts, and I felt myself go soft and spongy inside for him, fitting my walls to his thickness, feeling his entire circumference as he worked the muscles of my walls. I cried out for the lash again, but even in this he was cruel, denying me the exhilarating sting of the whip with a guttural laugh and a "later; more later."

He wasn't sheathed and I knew the instant that he tensed and came, spouting forcefully deep inside me, giving him even more friction as he continued to thrust for nearly a minute. I'd already come, to the stroking of one of his hands. I whined for more and for another taste of the whip, but he was finished—"for now," he said. "I know which is your compartment," he said. "I know you are alone in it."

"Yes, yes, please," I murmured, only later having second thoughts about what he'd do, given more privacy and time. "I won't lock the door."

As if he anticipated my thoughts, he growled. "You will suffer. You want to suffer."

I couldn't say he was wrong.

I took a few minutes to pull myself together after he'd come, pulled out of me, and slipped out of the lavatory, with a muttered, "Later. I'll do you royally later," which made me shudder and my expectations soar.

When I returned to my seat, Denise was gone, having left the senator to lean over in his seat, head against the vibrating window of the carriage, and snoring loudly.

I looked at my watch. I'd been gone less than twenty minutes. It seemed like an eternity. And I was both satiated and tied up in knots. I knew what I wanted. But I also wanted my job in the senator's legislative office, and there was no one in Congress more aggressively antigay and down on perversion than Daniel Dobbs was.

* * * *

The dining car was nearly full by the time Denise had gotten herself together and joined us in the club car before we went in to dine. The senator used the time to imbibe a couple more scotches on the rocks. He had gotten his second wind, though. The nap had done him well and, apparently, opened up the hollow leg where the liquor was going rather than to his brain. There were no empty tables in the dining car, but there was one with just one guy at it, and the waiter slid us right in beside and across from him.

He was a college basketball player, Christopher Somethingorother, on his way back to Chicago to attend Loyola University. He was a good-looking kid, which wasn't lost on Denise, and I was happy to see her transfer her charm to him. After dinner we went back to the club car, with Denise dragging Christopher along, and Christopher and I got roped into a poker game, with Denise looking on and rubbing Christopher's shoulders and who know what else. The senator sat to the side, went through some papers in his briefcase and chugged more scotch.

Christopher and Denise were the first to disappear— together. I had little doubt where they were going, and I wondered whether Christopher had learned the knack of fucking a seven-month-pregnant woman. If not, I'm sure Denise would be able to guide him. I'd already heard from her how it could be done with her sitting in my lap and me palming the baby, lifting her belly enough to get my dick inside her—no hard thrusting, of course.

I was just glad that he was there to do the honors and to keep her off my case. I was busy trying to spot the leather man. I hadn't seen him in the dining car for the supper service, and I was getting antsy. I kept telling myself that I wouldn't put myself in his hands again on the train—that it was too dangerous to do that here—but I knew I was just kidding myself. I wanted more than the taste he had given me. I wanted to feel the sting of the welts on my back and buttocks. He had been too gentle with me. I wanted him deep inside me. I wanted to know if I could take his fist.

At last, there he was. The leather man walked through the club car toward us, from the direction of our sleeping car. I saw him as soon as the door slid upon, accompanied by the increase in the decibel rate of the train sounds until he'd slid the door shut again. He looked around until he saw me and then did "the stare" as he walked the length of the club car and went into the next section, a coach car. A few minutes later, he came back. He didn't look at me this time, although he could have demanded eye contact. I was sitting with my back to the side of the carriage and had a sweeping view of the club car. But as he passed, his hand went to the small of his back, and he stroked the handle of the whip he was using as a belt. I had already gone hard at his appearance, but I felt myself shudder and moan and had to quickly look at the others at the poker table to ensure that they hadn't heard me. They were making noises of breaking up the game, though, which was just fine with me.

I heard the senator snort as the leather man reached the far end of the carriage, looked around, and this time captured my eyes with his for a fleeting, but understandable moment. The senator's papers went back into his briefcase and he stood, said to me, "I'm for turning in," and headed for the sleeping car in the leather man's wake.

I was in panic. How long could I wait before I followed? Would the leather man be gone, assuming I was choosing not to follow him, when the senator had cleared the corridor and was safely in his compartment? Did the leather man really know where my compartment was? Was he being cruel and just teasing me and wouldn't be there? How long did I have to wait before I checked the lay of the land out?

He wasn't teasing me. He was the only one in the corridor of the sleeping compartments—and he was standing by the door to my compartment. His smile was cruel, knowing. And he'd taken the whip from around his waist and was holding it at his side, flicking it against his leg. A black leather gym bag sat on the floor of the corridor beside him.

I trembled as I approached him. When I did, I was shocked to see that the door to my compartment was slightly ajar. The man had a key to my compartment. It meant nothing but a signal of my submission that he hardly had needed that I told him the door would be unlocked. I had no defenses against him. He could come and go in my compartment as he wished.

We stood close together, facing each other, for the longest moment, until, suddenly, he grabbed me roughly by the arms, spun me with my back to the door to my compartment, and propelled me into my compartment. So explosively did he push me that I went down on my back on the compartment floor where the space was so confined that I was closed in on all sides. He fairly flew into the compartment, coming down on top of me. He kicked the door closed with a boot as he descended on me. The breath was knocked out of me, and before I could regain it, his hands were on my throat. He bounced my head off the floor of the compartment a couple of times to daze me. The floor was some sort of rubberized padding, so it did minimal damage, but I was frozen by shock.

He took my mouth, brutally, with his, and when I adjusted to hungrily falling in with the kiss, he bit me on the lip. I yowled. Holding my throat in the grip of one hand, he worked my belt, waistband button, and zipper with the other and jerked off my trousers and briefs. Spreading my legs, bending my knees, and planting my feet flat on the floor, I raised my pelvis to him to give him a straight-angle shot, and he forced himself, brutally, inside me and immediately began pumping me.

I was dry and not open enough to take him comfortably, but I hungrily took him inside and counterpunched his thrusts, taking him hard and deep.

When he'd come, we lay there, entangled, both panting hard. I was open to him now and wet inside. He hardened again quickly and I begged him, "Again. Please, again," and arched my back, taking him deep again, working up to my own ejaculation.

* * * *

I was strutting on the clouds in excruciatingly alive pain and pleasure. Not only was my skin tingling from the slash of the lash and my nipples tingling and searing from the clamps joined by the chain that he occasionally was pulling on, my balls aching and screaming for attention by being distended by the weights, and my arms cramping from being bound to the frame of the bunk overhead and my legs from the thigh separator, but I also was getting a jolt of pain from rubbing against restraints and bumping against the frame of the lower bunk as the train carriage swayed and I tried to maintain my balance. My hearing was ultrasensitized, zoning in on all of the sounds of the luscious torture: the clacking of the wheels on the rails, my muffled groans from the sting of the lash and his fingers twisting in my channel, the swish of the whip, his heavy breathing and low growls.

I bit into the rubber of the ball gag and let out a cry of ecstasy as his cock thrust up into my channel, lifting my feet off the compartment floor and causing me to bang my head on the frame of the top bunk. He thrust up again and again and again, reaching around and milking my cock. I was naked. He was only in leather—a torso harness dipping down to grab and gather his balls at the base of his hard cock. Black leather gloves and the black leather boots.

I came for him and he stepped away from me and struck me again with the whip, again and again and again. I writhed in ecstasy to the swaying of the carriage. He was inside me again, fucking me in earnest this time—taking me to his ejaculation and another, weaker one from me. My balls ached from the draining and the distending, and I hung there and whimpered as he ran his gloved hands over the welts he had raised on my back, buttocks, and thighs.

I had never been dominated and fucked—and drained—so fully before.

He was dressed before he released me and handed me my trousers, steadying me with his hands, as I fumbled to pull them on my legs, all of my limbs feeling like rubber, sensation only slowly pushing out the numbness, the pain slowly dissipating—but with it the regretted cessation of the peak of sensitivity, the glorious feeling of being completely possessed and taken—the ecstasy of total surrender.

I stood there, dumbly, clinging to the frame of the upper bunk for support as he pulled on his own clothes and put his toys back in the black leather gym bag.

I hadn't said anything since he'd released me from the ball gag. I was afraid that if I asked him if he was finished, he'd say he was. But then, it was just an overnight train trip. When would I be worked over this gloriously by someone again? I knew I should be angry, resentful, embarrassed at having given it all to him. But he had known I wanted it. There wasn't anything else to say. "Thank you" or "don't leave me" or "do me again" would sound so needy and pathetic.

He went to the door and now I did speak. "Your bag. Don't forget your bag."

"The bag stays," he growled. My spirits soared. The implements of his torture stayed here. There was time left in the night.

But then he was at the door, opening it, and stepping out into the corridor. I was drawn to the door too, not wanting him to leave, wanting him to possess me fully, not wanting the night of divine taking to end.

I was confused. Someone else was in the corridor, standing at my door. The senator. I was undone. He could see what had happened. I was bare-chested. I dare not turn my back to him or he'd see the welts. My mind raced. How was I to get out of this?

"Thank you, Paulo," he was saying. He was speaking to the leather man. "I had to be sure he'd take it. I'll take over from here."

"The bag of tools is in there," the leather man—Paulo—was saying.

My ears were buzzing, not yet recovered from Paulo's taking. I felt sluggish, like I was underwater—not quite catching up to the action.

Paulo was moving down the corridor. The senator was pulling his shirt off. Underneath, his chest was criss-crossed with a black leather harness. He punched me in the stomach and I fell back into my compartment, onto the floor. He entered the compartment and slammed the door behind him.

Panting, I looked up at him with slitted eyes, going hard again as, pulling his trousers off his legs, he showed me that he already was hard. Paulo had passed the whip to him as he left, and Daniel stood over me now, raised his arm, and brought the thongs of the whip screaming down onto my chest as I cried out in painful pleasure.

The whistle of the Capitol Limited sounded off and the train rushed on in the night.

The Agent's Third Secretary

The three of them were sprawled out on the richly patterned Oriental carpet on the rise of the sand dune with the vista of the pyramids of Giza stretching out before them—and beyond that the Nile and beyond that yet the teeming city of Cairo, the sun shining on Cairo, giving it a false sense of cleanliness and purity. Below the dune behind them buzzed a phalanx of Egyptian servants, packing up the boxes from the meal the three had just eaten, holding the horses in check, and pretending they weren't watching the *effendis*—the foreigners—being outrageous.

The popular German courtesan, Claudia Beck, lay stretched out on her back, her ample breasts exposed and the silk panels of her riding skirt evocatively folded back to reveal her prominent and famous mons Venus and the trimmed triangle of strawberry blonde curls above it.

Sitting beside her, with one hand languidly stroking and patting her mound, the thirty-something dark and sultry Lebanese artifact dealer and rake, Philippe Bey Karem, dressed in the sparkling white thwab of the affluent Arab population, spoke in light tones with the young blond gentleman sitting at the other side of the carpet and sketching the pyramids. Gavin Barnett, third secretary of the British agent and counsel-general—and de facto administrator of Egypt at the time—Edward Missert, was Karem's excursion guest for the day. He incongruously was dressed in dinner kit, although his thin, boyish body helped negate the effect of the sun on Western costume. Each was overdressed for an excursion into the desert as the trio would be going straight to an evening at Shepheard's Hotel from the picnic.

Barnett, barely of age and recently come out to Egypt to train in the British foreign service, also, not incidentally, was the son of Missert's sister and the son of a lord. Karem, son of a French mother and a leading merchant and politician of an old Levant family father, had only recently come into contact with the young, handsome, and willowy English youth and was cultivating him for his influential contacts.

By degrees, Karem was pulling Barnett into his jaded world of pleasure and excess, and Barnett, although he so far had politely declined Karem's offers of directly imbibing of pleasures that would be unspeakable in London but were openly available to the rich and well-connected in Egypt—most easily if they were foreign—had not shrunk away from Karem or his international set. Instead, he had followed along on a series of debaucheries as voyeur without having become embroiled in them himself.

Karem quite definitely had other plans for the young Englishman, though.

"Would you like to fuck her?" Karem asked, indicating the red-haired beauty lying beside him by burying two fingers between her folds as she arched her back and purred for him, her eyes slitted from the drugs she had indulged in. Claudia was from one of the best houses on Sharia Wagh el Birker Street in Cairo, the brothels there able to operate almost openly for those with the means to attend them as each was protected by one of the foreign consulates in the city. Although Egypt ostensibly was ruled by Egypt's Khedive, Ismail Pasha, on behalf of the Ottoman Empire, the Khedive had run the country so far into the ground that the British had taken over all of the administrative controls. In the wake of this, the foreign government concessions in Cairo had become almost autonomous from any Egyptian control, and the British were too busy with possible revolutionary movements to provide and enforce a moral standard there.

"I would like to get this sketch done before the sun goes down. But thank you." Barnett's answer was a polite one, not showing any surprise or censure for the offer. But as yet Karem had not found the young man's vice. Karem's modus operandi was to discover a man's vice, feed it, and then milk it. But he would keep on trying to ferret out the young man's fetish. No one that handsome and sensual could be without a vice. It wasn't champagne, Karem had already found. Though Barnett joined him in swigging the bubbly from the bottle, he didn't drink in excess. It also wasn't drugs. Most of what they had brought on their desert picnic had gone into the German whore.

"Well, if you wouldn't mind then," Karem said.

"No, no, don't mind me," the young man answered, turning his attention back on the pyramids. "I'd like to catch this while the light is just right."

Brushing the hem of his Arabic robe up to his chest to reveal his masterful musculature, jet-black pubes and an up-curved erection, Karem lifted and turned Claudia onto his lap, impaled her on his cock, and raised and lowered her body rhythmically on his staff as she sighed and hummed and he continued talking with young Barnett about what life had to offer a handsome young blond European in the city.

Gavin murmured polite interest in every taboo and fetish mentioned, but nothing made him ask for a further description of the decadence. Philippe avoided telling him that young men like Gavin went for a premium among Egyptian men who preferred men, but that certainly was in his mind. Philippe's own sexual interests were universal and he was close to exploding inside the German whore's well-used passage. And then he did, afterward gently lowering Claudia's back to the ground in front of him, his cock still inside her. He reached over her belly and squeezed her breasts and thumbed her nipples as she purred in her drugged-out world and Gavin continued with his sketching.

Later, Karem raced across the desert for the Nile crossing to the city on his blooded stallion, as Barnett and Claudia Beck did what they could to try to keep him in sight. Gavin could have kept pace with him. He was an expert horseman. But he also was a gentleman. Servants on slower horses were doing what they could to keep the German prostitute in the saddle of her mare, and Gavin stuck with her to ensure her safety.

Once across the Nile, having left the horses on the west bank, they transferred to Karem's Wolseley-Siddeley Tourer motorcar for the run to Shepheard's Hotel, the Mecca of European society in Cairo, where the evening already was in full cry. Most of the foreign diplomatic corps and non-Egyptian merchant class were there. Claudia had sobered up enough not to be out of place—and would not have been out of place anyway, as half the male dinner guests—and some of the women as well—had indulged in her charms during her reign on Sharia Wagh el Birker Street, which promised to be all too short. Courtesans were welcomed at Shepheard's as long as they were Europeans. Almost anyone was welcome at Shepheard's if they were rich and/or well-placed as long as they weren't Egyptian.

This membership restriction was illustrated on this evening when the Khedive's own principal adviser, Ahmed Aziz, was turned away at the dining room door. He had, in fact, received an invitation to attend from the British Agent's office and had shown up, assuming that the "No Egyptians" rule was being relaxed, but the invitation had been sent in mistake. He had been anxious to attend because he had a liaison to set up, but it was not to be. The best he could do was to consign a note to an embarrassed Egyptian waiter to be delivered for him.

The various societies within the international society in Cairo took up separate stations in the Shepheard's dining room. Philippe Bey Karem was the center of the racy set, and Gavin Barnett initially went to the section of the room where Philippe was holding court, but he soon gravitated to the more stalwart administrative section, where his uncle was the focus of attention. Although Karem watched Gavin drift off, still a little perplexed that he hadn't found the young man's vulnerable sin, he was content to work on that another day. He didn't want the Agent's third secretary to incur the wrath of his uncle. He certainly didn't want Barnett to be sent back to

England in disgrace with his tail between his legs. He wanted to suborn and use the young man to his own business and political power advantage in Cairo.

Gavin didn't stay long with his uncle's group either. Having checked in and played court to Missert until the next supplicant snuffled along, Gavin drifted into the shadows of the room and, eventually, left Shepheard's and walked slowly into the Arab quarter, with its close alley-like streets, still alive with vendors, food merchants, hashish hawkers, and women of the night plying their trades. Gavin was a golden-haired sensation wherever he walked. He had been in Cairo long enough to know how alluring a well-proportioned young blond—male or female—was to the Egyptians. He had many an offer as he walked the alley, but he was official-looking enough—and known by many to be related to the all-powerful British Agent—that he wasn't accosted physically. He walked in a cleared space bordered by appreciative onlookers no matter how crowded the street was. Once or twice he extracted a slip of paper from his pocket and looked at it to check where he was going. He had a goal.

After walking into the Arab quarter for twenty minutes, he reached his goal, a copper shop open to the street and with candles set around that used the copper pots, plates, and utensils hanging here, there, and everywhere as reflective mirrors to give the shop a quiet glow. Gavin entered the shop. A merchant came forward, dressed in a blue thwab and all smiles. Gavin leaned over and whispered something in the man's ear. The merchant's smile broadened and he guided Gavin to the back of the shop, through a beaded curtain-covered doorway, to the base of a dark staircase. He gestured upward, and Gavin climbed the stairs, turned right, and opened the door into a room that was sumptuously decorated with carpets—on the floor and the walls—a line of lit candles in tall, copper candlesticks, and a divan covered in damask and silken pillows.

Slowly, methodically, Gavin took off his clothes, folded them, and placed them on a chair in the corner of the room. When he was naked, he padded over to the divan and sank on his back onto the pillows—and waited.

After several minutes, the door to the room opened and Ahmed Aziz, the Khedive's principal counselor, entered the room. He stood there momentarily, taking in the visage of the gorgeous, young, blond Englishman sprawled naked on the divan, now with a hand encasing his cock and slowly masturbating it.

The Egyptian court official pulled his thwab over his head, undid the loincloth around his pelvis, and let both garments fall to the floor. He was a large, solid man, dark of skin and of hair. His chest and arms and legs were hairy. He had a slight paunch, but he was muscular—more solid than fat. He already was in thick erection. He was of such stature that he probably could have broken Gavin in two if the young man now denied the Egyptian what he obviously wanted.

There were men that Gavin would have struggled with at this point, knowing that they wanted to take what they needed by force—that this whetted their arousal. But Gavin already knew that the Khedive's official wasn't such a man. He spread and bent his legs, raising his pelvis off the surface of the divan, inviting Aziz to take him in that position. He knew there was no preliminary with Aziz—that the difficulty of immediate entry was what whetted this man's arousal.

But Aziz had different designs this time. As he approached the divan, he gestured with a hand and, understanding, Gavin turned over onto his belly. Aziz grasped the young man's ankles and pulled Gavin's stomach down to the edge of the divan. He pulled Gavin's legs up and hooked the young man's ankles on his shoulders. Without further preliminary, he reached down with his arms, laced them under Gavin's armpits, and bowed the willowy, lithe body back, locking his fists together at the back of Gavin's neck.

"I'm told you Westerners call this a demanding variation of the wheelbarrow position," Aziz murmured. "I have wished to use demanding positions with you. You have such a supple body."

Gavin cried out in pain-pleasure and Aziz huffed and puffed as he worked his cock into the young man's slowly yielding passage. Once saddled and Gavin's experienced channel walls yielding to his extraordinary thickness, he fucked

80

Gavin to his completion in ever-quickening, long thrusts, as Gavin moaned and whimpered and half sobbed at the taking. Aziz thrust again and again, driving the young man hard and cruelly, rocking Gavin back and forth, manipulating him like the young man was a rag doll. Gavin cried out repeatedly at the pain-pleasure of the taking, voicing his ecstasy at how well, completely, and relentlessly the Egyptian was working him with the hard, thick cock. Aziz was a cruel taker, and Gavin an insatiable giver, going soft and spongy inside, begging for the full force and possession of the cock like a Sharia Wagh el Birker Street whore of one of the meanest brothels and receiving what he was begging for. Gavin tensed and cried out again when he came and then just collapsed within the Egyptian's control as Aziz fucked on, ejaculated, held, hardened again, and fucked Gavin a second time just as cruelly and possessively as the first time.

When Aziz came at last, Gavin collapsed on the bed and turned over, setting imploring eyes on Aziz as if he wanted more. Aziz slapped him across the face, the force of the blow turning Gavin back onto his belly, and stood away from him as if having come awake from some sort of trance that had taken him outside of himself and revealed wild turmoil under his surface that he didn't really wish to reveal to the world. But, like all Egyptians of his persuasion, the willowy body of a young blond European was too much to resist. Aziz was used to being completely in control on the taking of a young man, but he lost control with this nubile European. He willed himself back to a cool, detached demeanor. "Enough for now," he said in a gruff, commanding voice, even though he felt himself going hard again at the mere sight of the young blond's vulnerable nakedness.

Aziz stood away from the divan with steely determination, leaving Gavin collapsed, trembling, and mewing softly, belly to the divan, knees on the floor below the divan, arms stretched out to the side in cruciform position, and walked back to the clothes he'd let fall to the floor. He wound his loincloth back around his pelvis, folding in his now-flaccid and well-serviced cock, leaned over and searched in the bag he'd had hanging from his shoulder when he entered the room, and walked back over to the divan. He dropped a handful of piastres beside Gavin's head. The young Englishman had told the Egyptian before that payment wasn't required, even this token amount of a handful of piastres. But Aziz had said it gave him pleasure to be able to think of Gavin as his cheap British whore.

He ran his fingers into Gavin's blond curls, pulled Gavin's head up, causing the young man to wince in pleasure-pain, turned the young man's face to his, and kissed Gavin on the lips. Gavin gave him a glazed stare and a small smile. Then Aziz put his lips close to Gavin's ear and whispered to him for a few minutes, giving Gavin the token service-in-exchange that the young man asked for in these trysts. Gavin showed increasing awareness as the man spoke and nodded his head a few times—Aziz still holding it up with a fist buried in the young man's golden hair.

After he'd pulled his thwab over his head, Aziz turned and said, "Two days hence. Same time. I will teach you a different position."

"Yes, master," Gavin murmured, although, truth be told, there wasn't much about men fucking men that Aziz could teach Gavin.

And then the Egyptian court official was gone.

As Aziz was leaving the shop, walking back onto the street, a beaded curtain at the back of the shop split open and the merchant and Philippe Bey Karem emerged into the shop. Karem smiled at the merchant, handed him a fistful of piastres, indulged in one look up at the ceiling of the shop, and followed Aziz out into the busy street.

* * * *

The next morning, Gavin was sitting at his desk, two banks back, in the Agent's outer office, trembling at the knowledge of who was in his uncle's office, when the door to the inner sanctum opened, and Sir Edward accompanied the Khedive's principal counselor, Ahmed Aziz to the threshold. Sir Edward was all cheerio; Aziz was more reserved, but obviously pleased. The meeting obviously had gone well. Most of them didn't. The Khedive was known for his capricious and outrageous complaints. The eyes of the court official and the young third secretary met briefly. There was a fleeting hint of want in Gavin's pale-blue eyes, but nothing but cold steel in Aziz's hooded stare. Even this was telling, though, the young Englishmen having already taken the steely demands of the Egyptian's cock in various ways, the Khedive's counselor only giving him the shaft and a bit of court gossip, and the young man not being able to get enough of it, returning to the Egyptian's demanding cock whenever he was summoned.

Later in the afternoon, Gavin left the office, perplexed with the note he'd received. Aziz wanted to meet again. But he'd said the previous night that it wouldn't be until tomorrow. And it was in a different place—in a part of the city that it was even more dangerous for a European to go unescorted than the copper shop was. And Aziz had told him to come alone. What could be so important that Aziz needed to see him a day early and in a different location. He had invested too much in the Egyptian not to meet him, though.

Turning into a back alley in a distinctly poor section of the city, where the directions in the note were leading him, he didn't see the dark cloth coming at him, held on both sides of him. He did feel the hand-held cloth go over his face and smell the sweet, chemical smell of the chloroform as they forced him down, down, down into unconsciousness.

When Gavin came to he found that he was on his back, bound, naked, to a four-poster bed—each extremity bound to a separate post—in a well appointed Egyptian-style bedroom, other than the heavy oak European bed. Not long after he'd regained consciousness, Philippe Bey Karem entered the room. He leered down at Gavin and pulled his Thwab over his head. He was naked underneath, his body muscular, beautifully defined in swirls of curly black hair on his chest, descending down his belly into his bush. He was hung and hard.

"I found what you like, what you can't get enough of," he said with a smile. "Egyptian cock. I am told that you beg for more while you are being pounded."

"Philippe. You don't have to—"

But the Lebanese merchant was already on top of Gavin, his hands on Gavin's throat, choking off whatever the young blond intended to say, and his cock already driving up into Gavin's channel. He mercilessly pounded Gavin's ass. He was long and thick and virile and cruel. Gavin cried out for mercy and then for more and finally for everything Philippe could give him. And Philippe could give Gavin two ejaculations before he, finally, gave up his own seed and pulled away.

Leaving the bed, Philippe called in two burly Egyptians, who released Gavin's bonds and helped him over to the door into a smaller, room, with a narrow, barred window high on the wall and a slop bucket in the corner. One after the other, the two thugs fucked him too, putting Gavin on the stone floor on all fours and fucking him, in succession, like a dog, before locking him in the room.

Later, they came for him, bent him over the bed in the larger room, spread and bound his wrists to two bed pillars, and Philippe returned and fucked him from behind before he was returned to his cell.

Later—how much later, Gavin had no idea, as he was served a meal in the interim—he was brought out to the larger room and Philippe fucked him again. But this time he took him more slowly and without binding him. He made love to Gavin, and the young blond moaned and purred in ecstasy. Fully surrendering to the master's sultry and sensual master, Gavin opened fully to the cock, taking it deep and throbbing, clutching Karem's chest close to his with fingers dug into the older man's shoulder blades and wrapping his legs around Karem's thighs, rubbing Karem's undulating buttocks with the heels of his feet, moving his pelvis with the rhythm of the fuck, keeping Philippe deep inside him as he released his consuming semen once, twice, thrice in one long, mutually harmonized sigh.

The fourth time, Gavin was completely broken in to wanting Philippe's cock inside him and Philippe lay on his back and Gavin rode the cock under his own power. the palms of his hands buried in Philippe's chest hair. Gavin threw his body about wildly in gyrations of rotation on the shaft, using it to punish his channel on every surface and at great depth, while, Philippe, smiling a cruel smile of victory and complete mastery, alternated between grasping, separating, and squeezing the luscious young man's buttocks cheeks to obtain greater depth for his cock and stroking the young man off. But it was all Gavin now, frenziedly fucking himself on his master's controlling cock.

As they lay, side by side, in an embrace after this fucking, Philippe turned Gavin and kissed him on the mouth. Gavin opened his mouth to Philippe's tongue in total surrender.

Philippe whispered, "You are mine now."

"Yes," Gavin answered. "I am yours."

"You will do what I want now, or I will deny you the cock."

"I will do whatever you want," Gavin answered.

"I want you to find out a few things for me in the Agent's office and I want you to put in a word or two for me among the Agent's staff. Each time you come to me I want you to bring me a gift—responses to what I've asked you for."

"I'll come to you every night," Gavin whispered.

"No, not that often," Philippe said, with a laugh. "But often enough."

"Tell me whatever you want. I'll get it for you. Whatever you want. But fuck me. Fuck me again now."

With a laugh, Philippe rolled over on top of Gavin. The young blond, spread and bent his legs and raised his pelvis to the slide of the cock, sucking in breath and moaning as Philippe gave him the full length of the throbbing rod. As he pumped, he murmured his questions in Gavin's ear.

* * * *

"Those are just questions, though," Gavin said to the man sitting across from him at Government House. "The Khedive's counselor gives me information. Karem only gives me questions."

"The questions asked provide us valuable information as well. We will give him the answers through you that we want him to pass on," the Mamur Zapt said. The Mamur Zapt, a British Army officer, was the head of the CID—the British secret service department—in Egypt. Gavin was one of his trained agents, trained to spying before he ever left England to come here and serve as the Agent's third secretary. "Karem's questions themselves tell us what the revolutionary movement here is interested in—what it wants to learn about. That's as important to us as Aziz's gossip from inside the Khedive's court. You will continue seeing them both—and milking them for information as they milk you for their pleasure."

"Yes, sir. Do you think we should be reporting to my uncle, though?"

"Oh, I don't think that's necessary. All intelligence goes back to London. They can tell Sir Edward whatever they think he should know from what you find out. There's no reason why he needs to know about your activities."

"If you think that's the way it should be," Gavin answered, his tone dubious.

"I think that's best. And for now, it's nearly the siesta hour. I want you to come back to my house for a bit now."

"Back to your house. But why?"

"I'm sure you know why, young man," the Mamur Zapt answered as he moved his hand across the desk, grasped Gavin's forearm, and gave him a knowing smile.

Gavin, whose eyes had been downcast, lifted them to meet the Mamur Zapt's steady gaze, felt a shiver go through his body, gave a little smile of his own, and whispered, "I thought you'd never demand it of me."

Quattro Amici

"No, I think you should go ahead, take the trip, and do the article on your great-grandfather's winery, Edward. It will probably do you good to get out of New York for a few days."

Dr. Peterson and Edward Cordona had finished with the consultation and had risen from their seats to go to the door of Peterson's consulting room.

"But the hallucinations—what if—?"

"Do as we learned you are able to do. Go limp, your breath imperceptible, as in death. Let your mind float into nothingness. It's a talent you have that you can use to your advantage here. Retreat beyond the world and the hallucination will be starved for attention. The hallucinations should subside over time, Edward. You've been through a rough patch. A change of scenery and a project to work on should help you fully recover."

"You think so?" Edward didn't really want to go to California—to the Napa Valley—to do a "one hundred years later" article for the *Wine Spectator* magazine on a winery that was still going that his father and three other Italians had established there. He wanted nothing more than to crawl into bed, clutching a bottle of valium, and let the world pass him by. That he'd gone through a bad patch was an understatement. There had been Phil, with his partying and the drugs and the alcohol and then hitting bottom when Phil left him and the exchanging of dependence on Phil, drugs, and liquor for

87

dependence on Valium and a dark, isolated room, with vivid visions racing before his eyes. If only the hallucinations weren't so real and blended into reality so seamlessly.

It had, indeed, gotten better since he'd started coming to Dr. Peterson, but Edward was scared. He was scared to leave his apartment and leave New York and fly out to California, even for only a few days. The hallucinations were decreasing, certainly. But wasn't that because he had withdrawn and not taken any chances? That stood to reason. But Dr. Peterson was saying otherwise.

Peterson left him at the door between his consulting room and the waiting room. Three sets of eyes looked up at him from the waiting room. Ever so briefly what his eyes saw were three different breeds of cats—just their heads, the rest of them being in human form and human dress. It was just a fleeting vision, but it was enough to cause him to panic. He turned back to the consulting room, to plead with Dr. Peterson to put him back on Valium. But the door was closed. Dr. Peterson had given him his marching orders; he was definite about weaning Edward off the drugs.

$$* * * *$$

The man was strong, holding Edward in his embrace, both of them naked, Edward in the man's lap, facing away from him. Turned and held close as he was, Edward couldn't see the man, but he knew it was Phil. Edward's eyes went to the empty bourbon bottle on the nightstand. Had he drunk all of this? Or most of it? Or any of it? Was Phil, dark, swarthy, hirsute, and overpowering, as high as Edward was, his head swimming and bright, colored lights exploding in his brain. It had to be more than liquor. Phil would have brought drugs too. Edward squirmed around in Phil's lap, knowing Phil's dick was inside him—but Edward couldn't feel anything. He had no sense of touch at all.

A baby cried back in tourist class, and Edward returned to the reality of being on a flight from New York to San Francisco. He momentarily was panicked at the thought that he had had an hallucination, but, no, it was just that he had been sent into a reverie by the droning of the airplane engines and

88

the monotony of the cloud cover viewed from the plane's window. Sessions like that with Phil had been all too real.

It wasn't an hallucination. Those were much wilder than this had been.

As he became fully conscious of his surroundings, he almost wished he were having some sort of dream. Across the aisle from him sat a mother and small girl. For what seemed to be the eightieth time since they had taken off, the mother was reading the passage from the Sleeping Beauty fairytale in which a witch's curse had sent a princess into a hundred-year's sleep, broken only by a kiss from a prince. It wasn't the repeated reading that irritated Edward as much as a perverted version he had read once in a horror story in which the kiss woke, not a beautiful princess, but the ugly witch who had put the princess into the trance and who, awakened, sliced at the prince's face with sharp claws.

And the mention of a hundred years brought the writing assignment he was flying into to his mind each time it came up again. He was a freelance magazine article writer. He'd written essays for the *Wine Spectator* before, and the editor he worked with there had remembered him mentioning that his great-grandfather, Eduardo, had been one of the founders of the long-established Quattro Amici Winery in Napa Valley, named that because it had been started by four Italian friends. The editor had remembered the winery's founding date, 1916. She'd also remembered that there was a mystery involved with the winery. The four friends hadn't stayed together long in the winery business. Three of them had left in October of 1916. Two had returned to Italy and, she had learned from Edward, his great-grandfather, Eduardo, had left the winery and come back to New York City to open a restaurant.

The editor had thought that an article on the winery upon its hundred-year anniversary, with a hint of the winery's mystery, written by a descendent of one of the founders, would make a killer article. Edward hadn't been enthused, but he also was in a fallow work period. The ordeal with Phil had drained all of his creativity in devising subjects for articles.

So, here Edward was in a airplane, in a delicate mental state of coming out of a sexual partner breakup, and recovering not only from the threat of dependence on alcohol and drugs but also recovering from the cure of the "almost" addictions.

"Having fought his way through the brambles that had grown over the palace in the last hundred years, the handsome prince found the bier upon which the beautiful princess lay, sleeping. She was so beautiful he could not resist leaning down to kiss her. And when she did . . ." The mother across the aisle had reached the crucial passage again.

". . . the princess turned into a wicked witch, who screamed 'Murderer!' in the prince's face, slashing him cruelly with her sharp claws, gouging his eyes out." Once again, not being able to help himself, Edward had provided his own, disturbing, ending to the story. He shuddered and turned his face to the window, trying to shut the rest of the world out, welcoming a somewhat trance state for the rest of the flight.

* * * *

Edward snorted as he pulled into the front gates of the Quattro Amici Winery in his rental car and saw the scarecrow propped up on stakes behind bales of hay and pumpkins. October 31st—Halloween—was the next day, certainly, and the weather in New York, which he'd flown out of that morning, was experiencing the nippiness of the season, but the Napa Valley wasn't. He'd been surprised before he'd arrived here that grapes were still being harvested at the winery, but now that he was here he could appreciate that it was warm enough for the late harvest wine and ice wine grapes to still be on the vine. Halloween had been taken from the pagan festival of Samhain, marking the onset of winter in much of the country and of the Celtic New Year, but it was hard to believe in California's sunny climate in the Samhain concepts of this being a time when the separation of the living and dead was the thinnest it would be in the year and that it marked a time when the dead—especially those restive from unnatural death—rose and roamed the earth. The Napa Valley climate on the last day of October just didn't seem to go with all that.

Still, and he shuddered, the next day was the anniversary—the hundredth anniversary—of the breakup of the four friends who had founded this winery only to split up under uncertain circumstances. Two of them, Horace Doniletti and Bruno Abruzzi, reportedly suddenly decided to enlist to go back to Italy to fight in the wake of Italy's entering World War One on the side of the Allies, and the third, Edward's own grandfather, Eduardo Cordona, moved east, to New York, to go into the restaurant business. Only the fourth of the original friends, Alonso Morrisette, had remained with the winery. The Morrisettes still operated the business, which had become quite successful and lucrative.

Edward normally wouldn't have picked this anniversary to come here to do a *Wine Spectator* article. In truth, having reservations of ever coming to the Napa Valley that he couldn't justify other than an aversion to California that had come down through his family, he wasn't keen on doing the article at all. But the sudden breakup of those who had established a successful business that lasted for a hundred years on a day like Halloween had intrigued the magazine's editor—especially when she learned that Edward was a direct descendent of one of the four original owners. It was only the offer of extra money that had brought Edward here even now, though. There wasn't just the unaccountable aversion to coming; Edward also was in weakened health, both physically and emotionally. But he also had financial needs. Phil had paid most of the bills when they'd been together.

Despite the beauty of the rolling hills of grape vines he rode through as he approached the sprawling Tuscan-style winery complex, with its tasting room, restaurant, party venues, and attached owner's mansion, Edward couldn't shake a feeling of dread. He wanted nothing so much as to turn around and head back to San Francisco and the airport. Best take his photos, collect enough background to fill out his article, and be on his way as quickly as possible. With luck, he could be gone by tomorrow. Why, he wondered, did he feel that wasn't soon enough?

Some of it may have been the tone of the letters that came back from the winery. The owner, Antonio Morrisette, seemed hot and cold on the article. At first he had had heartily welcomed the coverage by the *Wine Spectator* and had also sorts

91

of ideas of approaches that could be made. When the editor had said she was interested in the hundred-year-anniversary aspect of the story and of the four original friends who had both started the winery and broken up that year, his letters had shown some opposition and coolness. They had turned cold when the editor had written who the author of the article would be and what his relationship to the winery was. At first, Morrisette had said that Edward couldn't be a relative of Eduardo, but then, acknowledging that he could be, he had dragged his feet on setting a visit up before eventually capitulating. Being covered by the *Wine Spectator* obviously was just too big a plum to pass up.

Edward had no idea what sort of reception he would receive. He did notice that all he saw as he rode through the vineyard and walked past the tasting room and restaurant to the owner's mansion were men—muscular men in the fields and young, handsome men working the entertainment areas. They all were dark, of Mediterranean looks, like him, possibly all of Italian heritage. He wondered if that was a feature of the winery—that it had remained totally Italian through the years.

A young houseboy, dark and more pretty than handsome, met him at the heavy, carved oak double front doors to the mansion, ushered him into a two-story, tiled floor foyer, and padded off to find his host. Antonio Morrisette entered the foyer, all smiles, and masculine virility, bare-chested and in riding britches as if he'd just come in from riding his horse on the property, as perhaps he had.

Several issues assaulted Edward's perception and senses at once, overloading his system and making him have to fight not to hyperventilate and, he was afraid, hallucinate. First, Antonio not only had all of the visual attributes that Phil had had that made Edward succumb to Phil's domination, but he also was giving Edward the possessive, knowing look that a gay dominator gives a gay submissive to establish control and access. Even if what came with the handshake later hadn't occurred, Edward would have known that he was of sexual interest to Morrisette, and that, if Morrisette demanded to have him, Edward would let him have his way. Morrisette was strong in domination and Edward was weak in submission.

As he approached and Edward tried to look away from the undressing gaze he was being given, he saw the four portraits on the wall. These obviously were the four original friends. Antonio was the spitting image of the one who had to be Alonzo Morrisette, and Edward couldn't help but recognize that he himself was a double of the one who must be Eduardo Cordona. The eyes of all four of the men seemed to be boring into him.

"Welcome home," said Antonio Morrisette, as he held out his hand, taking Edward's hand in his and folding in his middle finger to rub against Edward's palm as they shook hands, the gesture being a dominator's signal of interest in a submissive. "At first I couldn't believe that a descendent of Eduardo's existed." Other than that obvious signal, Morrisette revealed nothing of his interest openly. "The story in my family," he went on, while he was still rubbing Edward's palm disconcertingly, "was that all three of the other founders enlisted to serve in Italy and were never heard from anymore. So, you'll forgive me, but I put an investigator on your editor's claim, and, surprise, surprise, your relationship proved out."

"I hadn't known much on why my great-grandfather left here either," Edward said in a stammering voice. He was confused and off center, as Antonio continued gripping his hand and rubbing his palm with a finger. Did the man possibly not know that Edward understood the signal, Edward wondered.

"Yes, my investigator learned quite a bit about you, Edward. He even sent photographs and I saw the resemblance between you and the portrait of Eduardo on the wall here. He's a strikingly handsome man, isn't he?" If Edward was expected to answer, though, Morrisette didn't give him a chance, no doubt aware that Edward was discombobulated by a welcome far more welcoming, if covert, than he had anticipated. "Yes, I was told much about you. My home is your home. Pepe here will take your bag up to a bedroom with a marvelous view of the vineyard. But if you like," and here he pulled his mouth close to Edward's ear, "my bed can also be your bed."

There, at least, was an open declaration, no doubt fed by that research Morrisette's detective had done. Edward and Phil's life together hadn't exactly been a public secret.

"Well, umm, I'm not here long. I best get busy collecting material for the article," Edward answered.

"There's time for everything," Antonio said, cheerily, changing gears as if he hadn't made a direct sexual pass. "I'll show you up to your bedroom. Your collection can start there."

Antonio had a hand on the small of Edward's back, guiding him into a guest room on the ground floor in a section of the house that had lower ceilings and rougher-texture walls than the part of the house Edward had entered. Edward was trembling, wondering if Antonio would make a move on him immediately—and half hoping he did. But once inside the room, Antonio turned Edward to where he was facing the wall opposite the large, four-poster bed.

"Isn't it magnificent?" Antonio asked. "The mural is why I have given you this room. This is the oldest section of the house—the first building on the property after the processing sheds were put in. All four men lived in this original house. This was the only bedroom. Alonzo was an artist. He painted this. He did the labels for the wine too—they have remained the same for the past hundred years. This is the vineyard view you'd see if the wall wasn't there."

It wasn't the vineyard scape that caught Edward's eyes. What arrested his attention were the four men in the painting, recognizable from the portraits in the foyer as the four friends who founded the winery. Three of the men were kneeling in front of a vine fence, the grapes in full fruit. Alonzo Morrisette was standing behind them on the other side of the fence. The figures were finely drawn and, as Edward moved down the wall, staring at the mural, their eyes seemed to follow him. There was something about the expressions of the three kneeling figures that seemed anxious, as if they were trying to communicate something to Edward. The standing figure had more of a haughty smirk on his face, although his eyes too seemed to follow Edward around the room.

"I left some papers—background on how the men came from the same village in Italy together, each with knowledge of deferent aspects of wine making and distribution, or, in the case of your ancestor, pairing wine with food and running a restaurant. I thought this would help you with background for your article."

"Yes, thank you," Edward said, not being able to take his eyes off the mural, which fascinated him—which he felt was trying to speak to him. "I'll go through these, but perhaps now . . ."

"Yes. I know it was a long flight and drive. I'll leave you and you can shower and rest up. Dinner is at 8:00 in the restaurant. Since we have a restaurant here, I rarely eat at the house. I hope—"

"Yes, thank you, that will be fine. The restaurant will be perfect."

When Antonio left him, Edward sat on the end of the bed and gazed at the mural for several minutes. He couldn't get over the sensation that the three kneeling men were trying to convey something to him—and the standing man, as well, for that matter. The Alonzo of the wall painting was giving Edward the same knowing and possessive look that Antonio did in the foyer. Edward turned his attention to the written material Antonio had given him. It seemed to be a pretty detailed account, with anecdotes of the last hundred years of the winery's operation. There even was a summary in a glossy brochure that must be given out in the tasting room. But what was missing was any explanation for why the four men had broken up their partnership this day—Halloween, October 31st—a century ago.

Showered and dressed only in a red silk robe he'd found hanging in the room's closet, Edward drifted off into a nap.

The clinking of wine glasses against a wine bottle woke him. Antonio was standing in the doorway, wearing a silken robe identical to the one Edward wore—and as obviously naked underneath as Edward was, who was stretched out on the bed, robe open and, he realized, his hand on his erect cock. The room was dim, but through the floor-to-ceiling windows on the wall beside the bed, the rays of a glorious sunset were shining through, reaching into the room, illuminating sections of the mural on the wall in neon-like splendor.

"I thought you would like to try some of the Quattro Amici vintage Cabernet Franc before we went to dinner," Antonio said. He then put the wine bottle and glasses down on a small table beside the door and brushed open his robe, to show a magnificently muscular body and a well-hung erection. "But perhaps we can drink the wine later," he said, a knowing smile floating across his face.

Edward looked away, but he didn't try to cover up the evidence of his erection or what he'd been doing with his hand when he'd noticed Antonio standing in the doorway.

"You will submit to me, will you not?" Antonio asked, his voice calm in command.

Edward didn't answer verbally, but he turned his face back to the more powerful man and lowered his eyes.

"I thought so," Antonio said, and laughed. "My investigator was quite graphic about what you would take— what you liked, that you would be submissive to a dominate man, a man such as I am."

Antonio undid the sash of his robe and let the garment drift to the floor. His body was magnificent, his erection massive. "Open your robe," he directed. "Let me see you. Let me see if you are hard for me. Ah, yes, very nice. Very nice indeed."

Antonio fucked Edward missionary style on the bed, Edward on his back, his pelvis raised to Antonio, with Antonio's knees pressed under his buttocks. Edward's legs were spread and bent, and his feet buried into the surface of the mattress, used as leverage to rhythmically thrust his pelvis up as Antonio thrust down inside him. Antonio's hands were gripping the headboard above Edward's head, and Edward had his fingernails dug into Antonio's shoulder blades.

Edward had put up a weak semblance of resistance when Antonio had slapped his legs apart and come down on top of him and covered him. But he had spread his robe open on demand and he had an erection that negated any claim that he wouldn't let Antonio fuck him. Edward was small and

96

Antonio was large and muscular. Edward didn't have a chance against the other man even if he had wanted to resist—and Edward didn't really want to resist. It had been too long since Phil had been inside him. Once Antonio was inside him, deep and thick, Edward became docile, yielding, and was fully into the fuck. He realized that he'd gone to sleep earlier with the image of Antonio inside him and pumping, just as he was now. He had awakened hard; seeing Antonio in the doorway had just made him harder.

Antonio looked down into Edward's face with a cruel smile of domination and control—Edward had given him so little resistance when Antonio marched over to the bed and lowered himself on Edward's body that he confirmed what both had known from that first moment in the foyer—that Antonio would fuck Edward—but, though Edward was participating in the coupling, moaning and moving his pelvis in consort with Antonio's thrusts to take him deep and clutching the larger man's body to him, he was looking away. He was watching the waning rays of sunlight dance on the figures in the mural, seemingly bringing them to life.

Antonio took Edward swiftly and completely. Still weary from his cross-continent flight, Edward drifted off into sleep after he'd come, shooting up Antonio's flat belly, and while Antonio's thrusts were slowing down, his cock holding at depth for longer intervals, his breathing getting heavier. When and if Antonio ejaculated, Edward didn't know it.

When Edward woke, he wasn't even sure the encounter had happened. For the longest moment, he was afraid that he had hallucinated it. But somehow the wall lights had been turned on, and an open bottle of wine, three-quarters full, and two wine glasses, one on its side, the stem of the other overlaying the first, rested on a small table by the door.

The mural now was in shadows, the figures hard to pick out—as if they didn't want to acknowledge what they had seen.

At dinner, Antonio was chatty and full of history about the winery over the previous hundred years—and he made no mention to having fucked and possessed Edward earlier in the afternoon.

The waiters for the evening service were young, handsome, Italian men—like Edward, all slim, on the short side, and willowy. Antonio was familiar enough with them with his hands as they passed by or serviced the table that Edward had little doubt about the relationship between Antonio and his house staff. In the candle-lit room built to resemble a subterranean wine vault, Antonio took on all of the attributes of a satyr.

* * * *

Edward's eyes popped open at his usual waking time. But what was 7:30 in New York was only 4:30 a.m. where he now was. It was pitch black outside the windows of his room, one of which had the two lower sashes shoved up into the upper one, creating an open door to the stone terrace and vineyard just beyond. A lamp was on a low setting on a table beside the mural on the wall across from the foot of the bed, casting a soft glow on the painting. He propped himself up on his elbows and tried to clear the sleepiness out of his eyes as he gazed upon the mural.

The figures in the mural seemed to be moving. And they were naked. Bruno Abruzzi and Edward's own grandfather, Eduardo Cordona, appeared to be coming up from a crouch, and Horace Doniletti was still on all fours, with Alonso Morrisette saddled up behind him, covering him, and, with hands grasping his hips, fucking him. Eduardo was moving ahead of Bruno. He was stepping out the mural and into the room.

Only half conscious, Edward watched his ancestor, the spitting image of himself, cross to the bed, crawl up on it and lay down—inside Edward himself. Edward felt little different, just a tingling sensation, but when he looked down the line of his naked body there seemed to be a hazy glow above the surfaces—and his mind, in contrast to his difficulty getting his eyes into focus—was jumping around frenetically on thoughts and topics that seemed entirely out of his control and understanding. Over them all, though, was an urgency and insistence—and an atmosphere of sadness and evil.

One by one, Bruno and Horace drifted off the wall and onto the bed, Horace leaning over Edward and kissing him on the mouth—although not kissing Edward as much as he was kissing Eduardo, who, possessing Edward's body in a way Edward could not describe but could sense, was moaning—not just from Horace's kiss but also because Bruno was below him—below Eduardo-Edward—between his legs, his dick thrusting inside Eduardo-Edward's passage in a way that Eduardo, panting and bucking against the fuck he obviously could feel, but that Edward only could sense in arousal. Hands were grasping Edward's legs and spreading and raising them. They weren't Bruno's hands, though. those were spread on Eduardo's pecs, working his nipples as Eduardo thrust his chest up, outside Edward's body and into the hands.

The hands lifting and spreading Edward's legs were those of the Alonso figure in the mural, as the figure had come off the wall and was saddled up behind Bruno, fucking him while Bruno fucked Eduardo-Edward.

And then the hands no longer were Alonso's. They were Antonio's, and the four apparitions were melting away. Grasping Edward's ankles and pulling his body to the foot of the bed, Antonio hooked Edward's ankles on his shoulders, cruelly thrust his dick inside Edward's channel and was pumping him hard. The figures seemed to be pulling Edward into the wall, into the painting, and he was resisting. Antonio's hands went to Edward's throat, and he was choking him.

He was muttering in a guttural tone. Edward heard him growl, ". . .won't stay dead. Empty, but not for long. Writing an article for a wine magazine. Balls to that. You've returned to claim your share. Not in this lifetime."

Edward thrashed about, which only took Antonio's thick rod in deeper and accelerated the pumping, rubbing the throbbing cock maddeningly and meltingly on all surfaces of Edward's channel walls as Edward clawed at the choking hands on this throat without effect. He was gasping, unsuccessfully for breath in death throes at his head, while his pelvis was going wild, grinding at Antonio's crotch, pulling the dick deeper, his channel walls making love to the throbbing rod at the height of ecstasy.

He was close to blacking out when he remembered Dr. Peterson's advice on countering hallucination—as surely that's what this was, just an hallucination. It had long been remarked as being a family trait of Cordona men that they could convincingly play dead. He let his body relax and go limp, his eyes to roll up into his head, his throat to emit a low death rattle, and his breathing decrease to imperceptible.

Antonio continued pumping his channel, but slower and in a more gentle rhythm to his ejaculation, while he stroked under Edward's chin with his thumbs and purred his pleasure. When he was finished, he lifted the limp body of the smaller man, threw it over his shoulder, and went into the bathroom. He dropped the body into the shower enclosure, with Edward's head thumping against the tiled wall and dazing him. It was all Edward could do not to cry out in pain. Antonio turned the shower on, the water scalding, with Edward once again exercising maximum control at playing dead.

When Edward gathered enough strength and his wits to pull himself out of the shower and go to the bathroom door, he saw Antonio, back turned to him, humming and changing the sheets on the bed. Without fully realizing what he was doing, Edward's hand went to the closest weapon he could reach. His shaking hand closed around the neck of the wine bottle that had been left on the small table next to the door to the hallway. Stealthily he approached Antonio from behind, raised his arm, and slashed down, hitting Antonio with a loud thunking sound. Blood flowing from the back of his head, Antonio straightened up, turned, and gave Edward a surprised, quizzical look. His head snapped to the side as Edward swung again and struck him on the temple. Antonio went down, hitting his head again on the corner of a nightstand, landing on his back on the floor. He was looking up at Edward, now standing over him, still gripping the wine bottle. Antonio's eyes were fully open, but he wasn't seeing anything.

Still not understanding what had been hallucination and what reality, Edward turned his head and looked at the mural on the wall. No human figures were in the mural now. It was just a scene of a fence line draped with grape vines and the California mountains in the background. The absence of figures wasn't the only thing now different about the mural, though. Where the three kneeling figures had been before, the ground was slightly mounded.

What was it Antonio had been muttering to him as he was choking him? Something about staying dead and something not being empty for long?

Realization suddenly setting in, Edward stumbled toward the open window, now door, out onto the terrace and vineyard. Just outside the window his hand brushed up against a shovel that had been propped up on the wall. His thought went to whether Antonio had placed it there earlier, knowing what he intended to try to do in the night.

Taking the shovel up, Edward moved—gingerly because he was barefoot and naked—around the side of the building to where he stood just on the other side of the wall from his bedroom where the mural was painted. He realized that, if the wall the mural was on had been taken away, the view into the vineyard would be the same.

The sun was starting to come up and the vineyard was in shadows, but he had no trouble seeing the area in front of the fence line where the slight mounds now showed in the mural. But they weren't mounds now. Two of the rectangular areas were slightly concave. The third, the size of a grave, had been dug out.

Edward didn't have to approach this hole to know that Antonio had found that it was empty—that whoever had been buried there hadn't really been dead, and had somehow clawed his way out and escaped—clear across the continent and into oblivion as far as Alonso Morrisette—or any of his descendents—knew.

Looking at the other two rectangular depressions, Edward also had no doubt what—who—he'd find there when he dug down, as he would do as soon as he had collected his breath and his wits. He'd find the hundred-year-old bones of the other two of the Quattro Amici, the four friends—Horace Doniletti and Bruno Abruzzi.

TGIF in Lexington

I stood on the observation balcony and watched the people deplaning off the commuter jet at the Roanoke, Virginia, airport. It would take the baggage long enough to make it on the carousel in the arrivals hall that I could play my little game here and have time to get down there before this Metgev guy would be looking for me. That was the name I'd been given and that I'd have neatly printed in large, bold letters on the placard I held in my hand. Paul Metgev. That wasn't really his name, but then that was part of the game.

He'd come from London to Dulles, up near Washington, D.C., and then had to get on a commuter flight to get down to Roanoke. So he'd be bedraggled. There weren't that many on the flight, and a few of them were women—dressed in business suits, so undoubtedly on business of some sort. Of the men, only a few were likely. There were college students—a couple of tennis players. I don't know if they were from Virginia Tech or either of the two colleges in Lexington, fifty miles to the northwest, the Virginia Military Institute or Washington and Lee. They looked too casually dressed to be from VMI. That's where I was taking this guy—to Lexington. So, he had another fifty miles of road trip, with a couple of viewings scheduled on the way. He'd be too tired to be a handful.

A couple of the other men looked possible. There was a tall, beefy guy, maybe in his late twenties or early thirties, who looked interesting and somehow familiar. But he wasn't dressed for the part. The dude who had these kind of services from the real estate firm and who was looking at the type of property I was showing him today and tomorrow morning had money. The beefcake guy was wearing torn jeans, fitting his muscular legs tightly, and a loose, plaid wool shirt over a white, long-sleeved Henley. The coverage indicated he'd come from a colder climate than southern Virginia, and that tempted me to keep him in the mix for the game, but he just didn't fit. No. As usual, I was looking for someone middle aged, overweight, and expensive looking—but probably a bit hung over, out of sorts, and rumpled because of the tandem flights from London and the time change.

I picked out two, did an eeny, meeny, miny, moe between them, and decided what my reward or punishment would be on which it was. If I'd picked a loser—and as prospects, both were closer to loser than god—my punishment would be to show him a very good time. If I won, more of my fee for this job would go toward that Fiat Spyder 124 convertible I wanted than I'd settled on in my mind. And I'd be getting a pretty penny for this job.

The passengers had entered the building under the observation deck where I was standing, so I made haste to the baggage claim area. I stood on the periphery holding my sign, along with others holding signs. The passengers were more interested in retrieving their luggage from the carousel, which seemed still to be trundling baggage around the metal oval from a previous flight, than they were in meeting up with anyone. The two men I had in the bet weren't looking over where the sign holders were standing. But someone else was as he came out of the men's room and strode past the carousel, carrying a heavy leather suit bag over his shoulder with little apparent effort. I hadn't given him much of my attention when they were deplaning on the tarmac, but, yes, he was carrying a suit bag then. He must not have checked any bags.

As he walked, he was scanning the crowd, and when he saw the sign I was carrying, he nodded in recognition. I recognized him now, and a few things clicked—and my body reacted . . . in a good way. The Paul Metgev I was looking for was really Sergey Baseyev, a gold-plated striker forward for England's Liverpool Football Club. I was somewhat of a European football nut, but Baseyev was hard not to recognize, considering the number of sponsors he had who used him in their television commercials. A good reason for that, beyond his sports star status, was that he was knock-down gorgeous and was in great shape. He also was the scruffily dressed guy I'd discounted on the tarmac.

And, boy, was he big. He was at least a head taller than I was and wide-shouldered, barrel-chested, and thin waisted. But then he was a fast-moving, heavy-hitting soccer player. Of course he was in shape. And of course he could afford the services he was going to get today, Friday, and into tomorrow morning.

"Townsend Properties?" he asked, as he approached, pointing to the sign I held, not too steadily now.

"Yes. Mr. Metgev?" I asked.

"Are you the man sent to serve me?" he asked. His accent was heavily Slavic and his word choice not entirely spot on, although both were quite understandable. Under the circumstances, though, I was aroused at the word choice. Yes, I most definitely was here to serve him, in whatever way he wanted. He was a robust, handsome fellow in a god's body.

"Yes, my name is Cody," I answered, although we both knew my name wasn't really Cody any more than his name was Paul Metgev. "I have a car not far out those doors over there. And I have two properties to show you before we get to Lexington—although we can stop somewhere near here for a meal, if you are hungry."

"They fed me recently and well on the plane," he answered. "I am very much liking to see the horse farms you have listed."

He gave me a smile. It was a bit warmer smile than he'd given me as he was walking past the baggage carousel toward me. It wasn't quite as big a smile, though, as he gave the jet-black, late-model Chevy Corvette convertible I took him to. I gave a little shudder when we exited the terminal, because he'd placed a beefy hand on the small of my back. I was close to hyperventilating when we entered the shadows of the parking

104

garage, because the hand dropped to my buttocks. As easily as that he was taking possession, marking his territory. We both knew he was going to fuck me as often as he wanted and anyway he wanted for the next two days.

"I will drive. You will show me where to go, but I will drive." There was no hint of a request or question in the way he said it. He would as easily and smoothly take control of driving me as he was the Corvette.

I hesitated just a moment. I'd rented the car under instruction, but I hadn't been told that the client would be driving it. Did he have an international driving license? It didn't seem to be a good idea to ask him.

"I always drive, and I drive hard," he said, squeezing my butt cheek and giving me a pointed look. Yes, indeedy, he was going to drive me hard too.

He was laying rubber before we'd left the cover of the garage—but there was no doubting that the man could drive.

* * * *

"What is it about this town?"

"Concerning what?" I asked. We were sitting at an outdoor café on Lexington's Main Street, in a rose-covered trellised alcove. Despite what he'd said when he came off the plane, the man we were calling Paul must have been hungry, because he'd ordered nearly everything on the menu and devoured it all. On our way up the bottom of the Shenandoah Valley from Roanoke, with the Blue Ridge Mountains on our right and the Allegheny range on our left, we stopped to look at two properties. They were small horse farms, with stately mansions set in rolling hills horse country and with miles and miles of white-painted fences. Neither spread was large—less than fifty acres each—but both were mucho expensive. Just this lightning, end-of-the-workweek property inspection trip was very expensive for the client. Just my "anything goes" contract was setting him back ten grand.

"The names," he said. "All over the place. Jackson this, Jackson that. And Stonewall. What in the hell does Stonewall mean?"

I laughed. "That would be Stonewall Jackson. The Stonewall was a nickname, given him because of his stiff resistance. He was a southern general in our Civil War, a hundred and fifty years ago. He lived here. He was a professor at VMI—the Virginia Military Institute—over on that hill over there before going into the war. He died in the war. You've heard that we had a civil war here?"

"I know all about civil wars," Paul said. It was more like he almost spit it out, his face, otherwise sunny and expressive, clouding up. I thought he was going to say something else—that he both wanted to and didn't want to talk about it.

"Although your English is excellent, you don't seem to be from England." I shouldn't have gone there. It was strictly against our rules to pry into the client's background, but he seemed to be disturbed.

"Chechnya. I am originally from Chechnya. And I certainly know about civil wars." I thought he was going to continue, but he changed gears abruptly. "You have said before that this military college, VMI, is here in Lexington. Is that where you are a student? I was told that I'd be escorted by a college student."

"No," I laughed. "I go to Washington and Lee, another old college, which also is in town. The two campuses run into each other. I'm a freshman. I'll be nineteen in a couple of weeks." There, that was over with. He hadn't asked before, and they usually do ask, with me. Sometimes they are skittish enough to require my flashing the fake driver's license the office provides me—and those kinds of men were always delighted to know I was on the edge, legal but looking younger. Age almost always got laid out there on the table at some point. "The students at VMI are like soldiers. We're a lot more casual at W and L. And a lot more adventuresome." I gave him a shy smile and placed my hand on the back of his.

I wasn't really a student at Washington and Lee, or any other college. And I was older than almost nineteen. I just looked younger. I was only in Lexington for a couple of weeks myself, trying to unload some expensive properties down here for a special-services New York agency.

106

"Was there another property we were to see this afternoon?" he asked, abruptly standing up and standing close to me. I looked around to ensure that no one was looking and then I rubbed my cheek against his crotch, the bulge there leaving no question that he was hard. He'd come so close to me when he didn't have to that I knew that was what he wanted me to do. I knew where this was heading. It was an "everything goes" contract.

He briefly held my head to his crotch by palming my cheek, and he turned my face to where I was mouthing the line of his cock in his trousers. When he did that I dutifully and carefully closed my teeth over the thick cylinder inside the material. There was no doubt—I couldn't show any doubt—about what he could have from me and when and where. But then he pulled me up from my chair and kissed me. We were in the shadows in a nook, so there was little risk of being seen. I opened my mouth to his kiss, letting his tongue in, and palmed his crotch.

What he could have was established. That was fine with me. He was gorgeous and built, and whether or not we'd established it, an international sports star. He also obviously was rich. On top of that he was personable. We'd had a very pleasant time driving up to Lexington and viewing the two properties. The interest he showed in the properties indicated he was a serious buyer. I'd asked him why he was looking here for a horse farm and he'd answered that he'd always wanted to have horses, he'd been in this area before, and he was looking at someplace as far away from what he'd previously known as possible. Now that I knew that he had somehow been involved in the Chechen war with Russia, I understood where he was coming from. The verdant rolling hills of the Lexington region certainly would be as far away from Chechnya as one could get.

He'd been friendly, but, until the moment in the café, in no way aggressive or suggestive since that walk into the airport parking garage, during the drive or the viewing of the properties. Now he was signaling interest in getting all that he was paying for. I was more than ready to accommodate him.

I rose and said, "Yes. It's a great property we'll see this afternoon. I think you'll love the master bedroom."

He laughed, a low, guttural laugh, and put his hand on my butt as we left the café. As we got closer to the car, he brought the hand up to my waistband, descended this time inside my trousers and briefs, running a finger into my crack, and lodging the tip of it at the rim of my hole.

Oh, yes, he was going to have me. And soon, I was sure. The man was in heat, which was putting me in heat too. I looked around the parking lot to see whether we could be observed if he lapped me in the Corvette and fucked me. But he didn't do it. He was building up to it, though. I was afraid that when he exploded I was going to be overwhelmed. But he was a god; anything he wanted he could have.

* * * *

The cock was thick and long and I gagged on it as I knelt between Paul's spread knees and he guided my head between his long, thick-fingered hands laced in my black curls, forcing me to deep throat him. He was sitting in a chair in the window-surrounded bay of the master bedroom in the house I was showing him that afternoon. We were both naked, our clothes scattered about the center of the room, where we had come together, explosively, as we entered, pulled clothing from each other's body, and I had sunk to the floor to take his cock in my mouth. His body was all that I had imagined—muscular and hirsute, his cock full and long, his scent musky, manly from the hours of flying across the ocean. He leaned over me and ran his hands down my back and flanks and inward, grasping my butt cheeks and squeezing. The index finger of each hand searched for, found, and breached my rim. I moaned and then groaned, as he spread my hole and jittered the tips of his invading fingers. I felt my passage relaxing, loosening, giving in to whatever he wanted from me.

He lifted me and sat me in his lap, my thighs astride his spread thighs, thick and muscular, as a professional footballer's legs would be. I leaned in for a kiss and he frotted our cocks together, eventually docking them, holding the glans together, my cock cut, his uncut, and pushed the foreskin of his cock over my glans. As we kissed, he stroked our cocks together. He knew and employed sexual fetishes most of my clients didn't know about. I wondered just how sophisticated and kinky his tastes got.

I had warned him, in whispers, that I came quickly for those I'd been lusting for, but that there would be more, with a slow buildup. It was a technique I used to convince clients I found them irresistible. I didn't have to pretend that with this man.

He'd laughed and said, "I will ride you a long time before I come." He said he'd come eventually but then would quickly have a second hardening and fuck, as well—and, indeed, he later exhibited far more stamina than one would expect from a man who had flown nonstop from England that day. "And, I have to apologize in advance, but I lose control; I need to be rough at the height. I will hurt—"

"Shush," I'd interjected, laying a finger on his mouth. "Take it as you need to. Take what you want." He'd paid for the "everything goes" contract.

I groaned, pulled away from the kiss, warned that his docking of our cocks was pulling the cum out of me, gave a little lurch, and shot my first load, lathering up our joined bulbs within the sheath of his foreskin.

Laughing, he lifted me up, positioned his cock head at my hole, and pulled me down on his cock as I groaned at the thickness of his penetration despite having been prepared. When he was several inches in, he immediately started pulling me up and down, with long, deep strokes, on his shaft, taking me a bit deeper with each thrust. It was raw sex here, barebacking, nothing guarding skin from skin. It was in the contract, both of us tested yesterday, the data shared. Anything he wanted.

I cried out when I felt his cock tense and jerk and his cum blast me deep inside, and I went to pull up from him. But he laughed and held me tight, his cock tensing and jerking and releasing cum again—and then again. God the man was virile. I was bathed in his cum now.

When he had ejaculated, we held there. I leaned down for a kiss, but then leaned back, grasping his knees while his mouth went to my nipples, one after the other, and he sucked them and teased them with his teeth. When he leaned back again, I ran my hands over his torso.

I looked at him quizzically, my right hand having run over rough scars on his shoulder and on his side. "Bullet wounds?" I asked, quietly. "Chechnya?"

"I went back to Grozny too late," he answered in a low voice. "Ours was a branch family of one of the rebel leaders and thus was viciously targeted. I stayed on—to avenge in anger. At some point the bloodshed got to be too much. I became no better than—"

"Shush," I whispered, closing off what I sensed would be a flood of words that he would want to take back. But it had gone too far already. I could feel the tension in him and the trembling of his body. He was hard again. He rose abruptly from the chair, taking me with him, and holding me in front of him, started into a standing fuck. He grasped my waist between his hands, as I wound my arms and legs around his body, and lifted and slammed me down on his cock, again and again.

"Fight me for it. I need you to fight me for it," he growled, as he pulled out of me and dumped me on my back on the foot of the bed. He left me for a few seconds, but then he was hovering over me again, eyes wild with lust and anger, his belt in his hand. I barely had time to turn over, my back to him before the belt slashed down, once, twice, three times, on my back. The surprise and snapping sound of it was more ominous than the pain of the blows landing.

He flipped me over, grabbed my wrists, and deftly bound them over my head with the belt, before his weight was on me, between my spread thighs, and his dick had thrust back inside me. He had me by the throat with his hands, and I thrashed about, ineffectually fighting him, until his cock was in deep and he had begun a rhythmic stroke. He felt longer and thicker than before. He was choking me enough to control my breathing, but not enough for me to believe he was completely out of control. I was frightened, of course, of this introduction of rougher fetishes, but I understood that he was reliving something, working his anger and lust out. I also was lost to him. I wanted the fucking he was giving me. None of the usual vanilla sex I experienced with middle-aged clients. This one

110

was going to work me over well. I was going to feel and remember this fuck.

The thrusts came stronger and faster. We were bouncing up and down on the bed. He was climbing to the top, but so was I. I relaxed and opened, completely, to him, letting him fill and work the soft core of me. I came again, up his belly, but then so did he, deep inside me.

He collapsed on me and a hand went up and released my wrists. My hands immediately went to his shoulder blades and stroked him there. It had been a glorious fuck.

"Sorry," he muttered. "I just have to . . ."

"I understand. Anything. Take anything. Take anything you want," I answered in a low, purring voice. Not wanting to go any further into what was behind all of this, though, I rolled out from underneath him, sat up on the bed and said, "We can shower now and then I have one more property to show you today."

"But the mess we're leaving," he said. "This is someone's home—their bedspread, their bath towels."

"All will be cleaned up after we leave. Townsend anticipates everything." And indeed I had foreseen that this would be where we'd have our first sexual encounter. I just hadn't anticipated just how totally dominating and satisfying an encounter it would be.

* * * *

"Did you find anything today that you liked?"

"Yes, most certainly," the man not named Paul answered with a broad smile. He reached across the table and took my hand. I looked around, but no one was watching us, so I didn't take the hand away. We were on the terrace of our digs for Friday night, the House Mountain Inn, in the foothills of the Allegheny Mountains west of Lexington. I had picked the wood and glass B&B, with nine rooms, on the slopes of the mountains not only for its privacy and reputation but also because it had horses. When I booked, I'd figured that a client interested in buying a horse farm might be interested in riding one in the downtime during his visit. This man's interest in riding had gone to another direction. That was OK with me too. We were at the only table on the terrace overlooking Lexington in the distance. They didn't serve dinner here, but I'd arranged to have one catered for us.

"I mean in properties. I'm not involved in selling them myself—only in showing them to clients and providing other services. But it would be nice to know whether you were interested in any of them."

"Yes, I'm interested in the one we saw this afternoon and the one just southwest of Lexington, the one against the mountains."

"Then I suggest that you contact Townsend as soon as possible. I'm showing them to another client this weekend. I shouldn't be telling you that, but I've found that—"

"I've found you much more to my liking than I thought I would, Cody," he said, giving me a concerned look. "And this afternoon, if it was too much . . . I mean, I'm sorry . . . it's just that I have special needs. Ever since I returned to England from Chechnya—"

"You don't have to explain or be sorry about anything," I said, interrupting him and taking my hand from underneath his and reaching up and stroking his cheek. "I told you before. Anything you want."

"Are you sure?" he asked, his eyes searching out mine and holding them, boring into them, begging them. "I think you may be surprised and put off by what I really want. What I want is very kinky, but it gets me off."

"Yes," I said, "anything you want. Anything. I trust you. I know you won't give me more pain than pleasure." I couldn't imagine what could be more kinky than what he'd done already—or that he could get off any better than he already had. But I'd told him I was completely open to his demands. I didn't think I should mention the contract. By the contract he'd paid for, my answer had to be yes. But I didn't want this to hinge on the money and obligation involved. He obviously was deeply troubled in his life. He'd told me after we'd had sex that afternoon that he no longer could be fully satisfied unless he took it, unless he was rough in taking it. He hadn't come close to saying anything about atrocities he'd seen—and possibly participated in—in Chechnya. And I didn't want to know about any of them.

"Have I satisfied you so far? Have I let you have what you wanted?" I had asked, tentatively, afraid of what the answer might be—or how much rougher he would get if he hadn't been satisfied and wanted the full value of his contract.

"Yes, oh yes," he answered.

"Then there isn't any more to be said. I surrender to whatever you want from me."

We'd taken the two rooms at the B&B. They were side by side and the only rooms on the hallway. But we both knew what we'd be doing tonight—and that we'd be doing it in my room. I took the most remote of the two, to be as private as possible. It was what could be called expensive rustic contemporary—all wood walls and rough-wood furniture, but a wall of glass overlooking the valley and with a huge hot tub.

"If it maximizes your pleasure," I said in the shadows of the terrace softly lit by strings of fairy lights, "then take me as you wish. Just tell me—show me—what you want."

"Then, perhaps . . . tonight . . . you'll wear these for me." He had brought a briefcase to dinner with him and he now reached into it and took out a plastic bag, which he placed on the table. I turned the opening of the bag toward me, put my hand in, and drew out material in a snow-white shimmering silk. Looking around again to ensure we were alone, I took a closer look at the material: panties, a small-cup bra, and a sheer slip. I breathed a sigh of relief. It wasn't nearly as taxing as I thought it would be. The man had already strapped me with his belt. I was imaging something far worse than role playing a woman for him.

"Will you wear these to bed, let me steal into your room, and struggle with me as I take you by force?"

"Yes, if that's what would pleasure you," I answer.

"I would take you roughly and totally."

"You can have what you want."

* * * *

I didn't even hear him come into the room—not until he was on top of me and overpowered me—I did try to struggle, but there was nothing doing with that—and had flipped me on my stomach, straddled me, tied my wrists and ankles together with leather strips, and put a pillow over my head to muffle my cries. He'd come in with a pistol—a toy one, I hoped and prayed—and dug the barrel of it up under my chin when he first landed on top of me. He held it there until I realized I was defeated and went docile for him. Then he'd bound me to erase all hope of escape, and I didn't see the gun again.

I could hear his heavy breathing and smell his enticing musky scent. The room was dark, but moonlight was coming in through the wall of glass, mostly through the panel where the drapes had been pulled aside and were billowing in the breeze. So, he had come in from the balcony. That was part of his fantasy. We had adjoining rooms with a door between them. And I hadn't locked the door to the corridor. But he'd wanted to come in using stealth.

He was straddling my hips and I could tell that he was naked—and in erection—as his cock was slapping against the small of my back, as he grabbed and pinched me here and there with his hands. I cried out as he grasped the sheer silk of the back panel of the slip, but he pressed my head down on the pillow with one hand, smashing my face into the mattress. I bucked and he rode my hips, emitting a low laugh. He worked fingers into the leg hole of the panties and then, roughly, into my hole. One, two, three fingers, up to the knuckles, as he pressed down on the pillow with the other hand and rode my bucking hips. After a minute of knuckle fucking me, with me opening to him shamelessly despite the forcing, I heard and felt the panties rip. He readjusted his position on my hips and worked his cock inside me.

I settled immediately into the rhythm of the fuck, going with him, even though he was dry humping me and it wasn't all pleasure. This apparently didn't satisfy him. The sting of leather on my now-bare back was more of a shock at first than painful, but he put more muscle into it, flogging and fucking me. I collapsed under him in sobs. The belt was laid aside, he ran his hands around my sides and under the cups of the bra, palming my pecs, and went into jockey at the races mode, hugging me close and pistoning me hard and deep. I came in the panties and he fucked on, interminably long considering how long a day he'd had and how far he'd traveled.

He eventually ejaculated deep inside me as well—the expected one, two, three blasts—and held here for several minutes, breathing heavily, a low growl coming up from deep inside him. I was whimpering and moaning.

He held there, going flaccid—but only half flaccid—inside me, his breath slowly calming. I had no illusions, though, that he was done. I remembered that he said he did doubles. And, sure enough, I felt him rouse himself and finish the job of ripping the slip, panties, and bra off me. He left the wrist and ankle restraints in place. His weight lifted off my body and I felt him pulling me up. He threw me over his shoulder and marched over to the hot tub, which was filled and bubbling. I whimpered I know not what to him, but he just muttered, "Shut up, bitch," and when he got to the hot tub, he dropped me in.

I went under the water in surprise, sputtering to find my head under the hot water. He climbed into the hot tub himself, grabbed a hank of hair on the back of my head, and pulled my face out of the water. I gasped for air, but while I was still taking it in, he dunked my head again. He did this twice more, laughing at my sputtering and gasping. Then he draped me half in and half out of the tub, with my bound wrists, which he'd switched from my back to in front of me, scraping the floor next to the hot tub. My knees were on the seat rimming the inside of the hot tub. He mounted me from behind and fucked me again.

After a few minutes of slow fuck, I felt a noose made out of his belt slip over my head and down to my throat. He tightened the noose and used the other end of the belt as reins to pull my head back and release it in the quickening rhythm of the fuck, while I sputtered and gagged.

I never remember coming before as massively as I did then.

After he'd ejaculated, he exited the tub and gently pulled me out as well. He unbound my wrists and ankles, and, using two towels, he patted my body dry, all the time kissing me and murmuring that he was sorry. He had completely changed demeanor.

"Did it satisfy you?" I asked.

Somewhat sheepishly he admitted that it had fully satisfied him—the first time he'd been that satiated since he had left Chechnya.

"Then there's nothing else to say—other than it was the fuck of my life." I gave him a grin, and he visibly relaxed.

"What now?" I asked.

"I'm exhausted. Let's just get some sleep," he asked.

"I can't imagine why you'd be tired," I said. But then I gave him a look to assure him that I was just teasing, took his hand, guided him over to the bed, spooned my buttocks into his crotch, and we were both asleep within minutes.

* * * *

We were both standing on the observation balcony of the Roanoke airport late the next morning, waiting for him to be called to his commuter flight back to Dulles and then on to Heathrow.

"I'm sorry I couldn't stay longer," he said. "We just had the one day—Friday. But I have a game Sunday night. I have to drop these trips into short periods of opportunity."

"It was worthwhile as long as you saw something you wanted to acquire," I answered.

"I most certainly saw something I'd like to acquire," he said, giving me a meaningful look. He placed a hand on my arm, but took it away almost immediately as we weren't the only ones on the observation deck. "I'd like to throw you to the deck out here and fuck the stuffing out of you," he said in a low voice.

"And we both know you can do that," I responded.

"Look, I *am* sorry for—"

"They were the best fucks I've had for some time," I interjected, but letting him finish with yet another apology.

"You know I'm not really Paul Metgev," he said. "I'd like to be honest about—"

"I know you're not. I knew who you were as soon as I saw you in the arrivals hall here yesterday. I follow European football. But we have to leave it there."

"And I'll bet you're not named Cody, either," he said.

"No, of course I'm not."

"Or a student at college here."

"Oh, fuck no."

"Or nineteen in a couple of weeks."

"I'm older."

"Well, that's a relief. You know, no one has let me . . . has taken me so high. I'd like to see you again."

"You know that's not allowed," I answered. "Sorry." And I was. "I think that's your plane I hear being called."

"Is it? Well, unfortunately it's too public up here to—"

"A handshake will have to do."

"Yes, I suppose you're right."

We each put our hand out. Each of us had something we were palming. We shook hands, he winked at me, and he turned and walked off. I looked at what he'd passed to me—a wad of fifty-dollar bills. Well, that was probably as it should be, I thought. Him emphasizing the reality that I was just a rent-boy, paid to give him a good time.

He walked a couple of steps and then turned, gave me a big smile and a salute, and then walked off to board his plane. I'd given him a slip of paper with my real name on it, address in New York, and cell phone number. The execs at Townsend would go ballistic if they found out I'd given my contact numbers to a client. But fuck 'em.

I stood there, watching him board his plane. As the plane taxied out to the runway, another plane was landing. My client for the weekend previews of the horse farms should be on the plane. I opened my briefcase and took out the sign with "Larkin" printed on it in bold letters.

I watched the passengers deplane, falling into my "who is it to be this time?" game. The contract on this one didn't call for "everything he wants," but it did include sex. There were only two possibilities this time, both dumpy-looking, but expensively dressed middle-aged men. All of the other passengers obviously were members of a college girls' lacrosse team from the evidence of their apparent age and perkiness and the lacrosse sticks they were pulling out of the plane.

One of two dumpy old men. It was hardly worth playing the game for, but I'd make a choice. Well, you can't win them all. Thank god for the Friday I had.

Political Biography

The relief I felt when he repositioned himself on top of me was short lived, as I gasped and grabbed onto the log bar of the double bed's headboard in the cabin when he thrust inside me again, hard, thick, deep, and resumed the slow, rhythmic mining of my channel. I'd never been done in reverse like this before, me stretched out on my belly, raised slightly on my knees, my hands curled under the log above my head, while, his buttocks to mine, grasping my ankles in his fists, and leveraging his feet off the same log headboard, he did pushups on my ass. I took him deep, gasping at each thrust. Most men would have had trouble achieving depth in this position. Not this cowboy.

The man had to be twice my age, but he was tall, muscular, and solidly built in keeping with what must be a taxing life as a rancher fifty miles west into the tumbleweed from Cheyenne, Wyoming. Once he'd changed to this position, coming after we'd sucked each other erect, I'd ridden his cock the first time as he sat in a chair, and he'd missionary fucked me on his bed, he made quick work of coming. I'd already shot my wad earlier, but I managed to come weakly with him at his initial climax.

How had he known that I could so easily lay down for him?

Cameron Olson climbed off me, rolling the spent condom off his dick and pivoting slightly to make a three-point toss of it into a trash can on the other side of the nightstand,

119

patted me on the buttocks with a "Good job" comment, and sauntered off to the bathroom attached to the single bedroom of the log cabin he called the ranch house.

"Stay there. I'm gonna spike you again," he tossed over his shoulder. Just like he knew I was so submissive that I'd just lie here and wait for him to mount me again. I turned over onto my back on the bed and opened and spread my legs, ready for him when he came back.

Panting slightly and looking down the full length of my naked body, I watched him go, 240 pounds of six-foot-four hard muscle, veins popping out on sinewy arms, torso, and legs, as there was no layer of fat in which they could hide. The nut brown tan of his torso stood out in stark contrast to the whiteness of his pelvis and legs and accentuated that he was hung. He obviously worked outside shirtless a lot. By my calculations, he had to be in his early fifties, but one would not have known that from how well he was built. Maybe there was gray to be seen salting his reddish chest hair, but the buzz cut on his head made it hard to discern there. His bush and pits showed the reddish-auburn of his earlier life, when he was a jet pilot. Cattle ranching had obviously been good for his body, though. It had favored his libido too. The thrust had been strong, the stamina that of a much younger man. He still was half hard as I watched him move to the bathroom.

I moaned and reached for my cock, shaking it, the mere thought of his domination and self-confidence, of him inside me, making it go hard again.

The mystery was how he'd gotten my legs open and his cock inside me as easily as he had. I wasn't exactly promiscuous—at least that I showed to the world. I didn't dress gay or anything or have that mincing walk. I didn't have piercings or wear any signaling jewelry or anything. I hid my preferences well—or so I thought. But he had come on to me from the beginning. Now that I thought about it, he was playing me even when I called him, first from Washington, D.C., and more recently from Cheyenne, to set up this interview. It was as if he'd known I could be had. I'd had to send him my photo so he knew it was me when I arrived. He must have liked what he saw.

I was here because I had sensed some reticence in General Stowell's willingness to talk about the Air Force Academy years of his life, and I thought this man, Cameron Olson, could provide some background and color. Before I knew it, though, it wasn't him revealing much to me, but, rather, me revealing to him that I would take cock.

It had come out of the blue when I wasn't expecting it. "You look like you want it bad. You're gonna love my cock," he had said. He had put his coffee cup down, risen from his chair, and brought me up from mine. He then immediately went to town on me. And he'd been right. I loved his cock. I lay there on the bed, listening to the sounds from the bathroom, impatient for him to return to me.

I was working at calming my breathing as he came out of the bathroom, still naked, now standing full frontal to me and causing me to moan at the mature beauty of his powerful body. Just a few minutes earlier, I'd had that cock inside me. How had I managed it? With great pleasure-pain, I had to admit. It had been some time since I'd been covered by a man as strong, filling, self-confident, inventive, and experienced as he was. With no small amount of guilt, I wondered if he had been putting me on for his own amusement—to make clear how much he dominated me. I wondered if he really would come back to bed and do me again. He was still half erect.

"Coffee will be ready in ten," he said, showing a gleaming white-toothed smile in a craggy, but ruggedly handsome tanned and wind-etched face. "Black or ruined?"

"Black will be fine," I answered with a groan, still sore from the workout he'd given me, not wanting to show my disappointment that he wasn't climbing back onto the bed and on top of me.

"I'll be in the kitchen." He laughed. I got the joke. Other than this bedroom and a bathroom, the entire cabin was one large living-dining-kitchen area. "Bring your notebook and recorder with you," he said, as he shoved off from where he'd been leaning against the bathroom doorframe. "I'll dish the dirt on Bobbie there." He sauntered out of the bedroom, fully in command—certainly fully in control of me. He still was naked.

I groaned as I sat up on the side of the bed. I reached over to the nightstand for support as I stood up. My hand brushed the small pile of condom packets there. I felt the chill of the thrill of thinking he'd do me again. I wanted him to do me again. But then I shook the thought out of my head. I was here to interview him—to pull background information out of him that would help me in my writing, that would help me in understanding the man, General Robert Stowell, secretary of Homeland Security, and maybe a candidate in the next presidential election, that would help me write his political biography in time for that campaign.

This interview wasn't about me. My instincts had told me that there would be something significant in the general's years at the Air Force Academy that would give me a hook in writing about his character and the influences on his life. Stowell hadn't asked me to come here. I'd decided myself that I needed to make this trip. The general had only mentioned Olson in passing. I hadn't had any idea what to expect. Finding a Zeus-like hunk who was sexy as hell, randy, and sure of himself with me wasn't what I imagined I'd find at this ranch outside Cheyenne.

But, fuck, I wanted Olson to do me again. I pulled my trousers on and stumbled for the bathroom. God, my channel was sore—but in a good way. A highly memorable way. And gaping open; I didn't remember having ever been this opened—and still throbbing—before.

"Are you sure?" He said, standing at the kitchen counter, with a coffee pot in his hand—and looking oh so sexy and capable.

"Sure of what?" That I want you to fuck me again? Fuck, yes. But I didn't say that last part out loud. I sat in a chair at his kitchen table, turning it sideways to the table top so that I could face him directly where he stood leaning his butt into the kitchen counter. My hand went down beside where I'd put my notebook, recorder, and pen, and I felt a small stack of condom packets. God, did he salt them around everywhere in the cabin for convenience sake? I felt myself going hard again.

"That you take it black?"

Take it black? I thought. Why did the image of Robert Stowell rear up in my head? Because the general was black and appeared to be as built at this rancher? And they knew each other? I was going giddy. But there was reason in the back of that—why I here, the rumors I'd heard about these two at the Air Force Academy.

"Your coffee. You're sure you take it black?" Olson repeated. He was giving me a little grin. He knew he had me off center. He'd known, for some reason, that he had me as soon as I had entered his cabin—probably as soon as I talked to him on the phone and was all pleading and such to get him to agree to the interview. Everything he'd done and said from that point had been focused on getting me into his bed and his dick inside me. And I'd given in to him, passively, submissively. And I wanted him to spike me again.

"Yes, that's fine," I answered. I cleared my throat as he poured the coffee, coming close enough to me, in his nakedness, for me to tremble. "I understand that you knew General Stowell at the Air Force Academy—that you were on the football team there with him. That the team did well in those years." I reached over to turn on my recorder, but his hand covered mine and moved it to beside the recorder—to lay on top of the condom packets. He was standing close to me, his half-hard dick touching my cheek.

"Yes, we were on the same football team. We also were roommates for the last two years. I've got a lot to tell you, if you want to hear it. But you don't want to turn on the recorder yet."

"I don't?" I asked dumbly.

"No, you want me to fuck you again first." He put the coffee pot down on a pad on the table, took his cock in his hand, and rubbed the shaft against my cheek, I instinctively turned my head and took his cock into my mouth.

He made me slit the condom packet open and roll the rubber on his shaft. He crouched down in front of me, sliding his thighs under mine so that he was sitting on the chair too, facing me, and I was in his lap. The chair legs did a staccato beat on the bare wooden floor as we ground our bodies together in the fuck. His arms went around me, his fists clasping at the back of the chair, and he buried his face in my neck and sucked on my throbbing vein there as he humped me.

Eventually, he pulled me up, pushed me belly to kitchen table top and grasped my wrists, forcing my arms over my head, my palms pressed to the table, while he pounded my ass into glorious submission. I lifted my head and focused my eyes across the room to the fire he already had going in the fireplace. My jaw was slack, my panting heavy, my head bobbing up and down in consort with his deep thrusts up into my channel. I was in ninth heaven, every nerve in my body concentrated on the friction of the hard, latex-sheathed rod sliding in and out of my ass.

He let loose of my wrists, and I grasped the far edge of the table top to hold myself in place, while his hands went everywhere on my torso and ended up grasping my waist and pulling my hips hard toward him with each strong thrust inside me. From his repeated mutterings of "Fuck, yes," "Give it to me," and "Tight and sweat; just how I like it," I knew that he was dancing on the clouds too. That made it all the more pleasurable for me—made the hugeness and cruelty of his cock all the easier to take, more the center of worship.

I took up the cry of "Give it to me! Punish me! Shaft me! Put me to the sword!" He laughed and complied.

I had to take a wide stance to handle the thickness of him; my eyes were watering and I was babbling from the length of him. My legs felt like rubber and I would have sunk to the floor, if I hadn't been held in place by the solid bulk of him, my chest rubbing on the rough kitchen table top from the relentless powerful thrusts of him. I was sobbing from his strength, stamina, and expert swordsmanship.

"This is what you want," he growled. It was a statement. "This is what you came for."

"Yes, this is what I want," I whimpered. I'd had no idea that this was what I'd come for, but I would not complain that this was what I got. He had worked me into position expertly and was taking skillful care of all the wants I hadn't admitted to myself that I had. "Yes . . . this is . . . what I want," I repeated, stuttering it out in rhythm to his thrusts.

When I left the cabin the next morning to fly back to Washington, I was hobbling and humming. I also was filled to the brim with "color" for my biography, although there was very little that I could use in the book. I also understood why General Stowell had played down the Air Force Academy part of his life.

× * * *

"You weren't answering your phone last week, Kevin," the general said, turning to me in the backseat of the black Escalade and giving me a piercing look from underneath his bushy eyebrows. It was as if he could look right into me and know everything I knew.

I didn't want him to know everything I now knew about him.

We were gliding down a dirt track, the trees meeting over our heads, a black Escalade in front of us and another one in back of us. The men in both of those SUVs were armed, submachine guns butted into their thighs, the barrels pointing to the ceilings of the vehicles, their eyes darting everywhere, ready for anything. Two men were in the front seat of this vehicle. A driver and Jacks, Stowell's burly personal bodyguard, the most macho of all of them—built like a tank; a Marine buzz cut; young, not much older than I was; Army recruiting film handsome; and clearly devoted to the general. He too had a submachine gun at the ready.

We had entered the Marine training base at Parris Island, South Carolina, and were still driving through the thick forest, toward, I assumed, the seafront. Stowell had told me to bring a swim suit—"and bring all of your notes thus far," he had added. "You only have the one set of notes, don't you, as I instructed," he tacked on.

"Yes sir, just the one set of notes," I squeaked back at him.

He'd also told me not to tell anyone else where I was going—not that I knew where I was going—or that I would be with him. That was something long drilled into me. The biography was to be a surprise. That Stowell would be running for office at all was to be a surprise. My part in this was to be totally nonexistent. I understood that from the beginning.

"I can make you disappear altogether," he said, "without a trace left behind." I believed him. He was the head of Homeland Security.

"I was doing some research on the book," I said. "Just getting a feel for the Air Force Academy in Colorado Springs—nothing too deep." I didn't want to straight out lie to him. He could check on my airplane tickets. He was the fuckin' head of Homeland Security, for God's sake. I didn't think he'd check as far as the rental car I drove up into Wyoming from there.

I saw the armored Escalade in front of us veer off into a turnoff and come to a standstill. The men had bailed out of it before we'd gotten past it. The men already were deploying into the surrounding forest. I turned and looked behind us. The other Escalade had stopped too and the men were getting out of it. The vehicle we were in kept moving forward. It was just the four of us in the one vehicle now. The trees weren't as dense. I was getting glimpses of the water edge of the base, open water beyond.

"Did you enjoy the attentions of Cam?" the general asked. I turned my head toward him. The thin smile on his lips was more of a sneer than a smile.

"Excuse me?" I said, a chill going up my spine.

"Cameron Olson. I assume he fucked you good."

He knew where I'd gone.

"I'm sorry I didn't tell you, General," I said, trying not to have it come out as a squeak. "I was just trying to fill in some information from your years at the Air Force Academy. I didn't want to bother you with details down in the weeds like that. Just background. Nothing need be—"

"So he told you how we hazed the new cadets— between us. How we fucked them like he fucked you. And how they begged for it and lay there and took it from us. The two of us doing them together. And never spoke of it after that. Because we told them not to. Because we were football stars. Because nobody with believe them over us."

"As I said, nothing needs be—" I was sweating. How did he know? Did he have eyes everywhere, even in Wyoming? Yes, of course he did. He and Olson had coordinated on this before I went to Wyoming. That's why Olson was ready for me.

"No matter. I don't mind that you found out. I hope you enjoyed him. Cam told me he enjoyed you. I picked you out for him, you know. I knew you'd go there. I knew you'd easily submit to him. It's lonely on that ranch of his. I send him a gift of young tail now and then. It keeps him happy and quiet. Ah, here we are at the guest house."

He knew about me. I wondered before how he'd picked me to write his biography. I'd been at the Barnes and Noble in Tyson's Corner, signing books on my biography of Senator Paxton after a book talk and everything had gone quiet. I looked up and there he was—with his squad of goons around him. His smile had been more friendly then. He'd invited me for a drink after the signing, saying he had a proposition for me.

I was to write a political biography on him. He was thinking of taking a run for the White House and he needed a biography. He'd liked what I'd done for Senator Paxton. Would I be interested? Of course I was interested. If so, I'd have to do it in secret. I'd have to devote my time to him for a couple of months. I couldn't let anyone know what I was doing, who I was doing it for. Was I still interested?

Yes, God help me, I still was interested. And now, after seven weeks, he was telling me that he'd picked me because I'd let Senator Paxton fuck me? Not just fuck me, but dominate me. I'd worn a slip and lace panties for him. I'd let him bind me and whip me. And I'd let him plow me again and again. And I was stupid enough not to realize that the head of Homeland Security wouldn't have known that—not because of me certainly. I was a nobody. But he'd have been keeping tabs on Paxton.

The surprise was that he'd want something like that too.

I looked around in panic. I was isolated, on a Marine base, just me the general, his devoted bodyguard, and a driver.

Jacks and the driver knew the general fucked men. He'd just openly talked about it with them sitting right there in the SUV, and they hadn't flinched. I'd get no help from either of them.

Up ahead of us was a wood farmhouse, sitting close to the water line. White with dark green shutters. Benign and inviting. The land jutted out into the cove, with water on three sides. There was land across the water in all directions, but it wasn't close. Buoys bobbed in a semicircle a couple of hundred yards out in the water. I was sure they were connected with nets that would signal any breach. There were ten men from the other two SUVs spread out, on watch, somewhere behind us in the forest. And we were on a closed fuckin' Marine base.

"Listen, general. If what you want . . . if you want me to—"

"I know I can. Whenever I want, and what I want." It was said with a low growl, but then his voice turned friendly. "Come, we have time for a swim before dinner," he said, as he and Jacks opened their doors and climbed out the Escalade. The driver stayed put. I hesitated as well.

"Come on up to the house, Kevin," Stowell said in a voice not to be ignored.

With a shudder and a sigh, I opened my door and climbed out. As soon as I was out of the vehicle, it moved off, back in the direction we came from. Now it was just me, the general, and the devoted bodyguard.

Stowell beckoned to me and I moved to beside him. A beefy hand went to my butt cheek, and he guided me forward, toward the house, with it. Jacks was carrying all of the luggage—three suitcases and my computer case and the briefcase with all of my book notes—and he was hefting it all without effort.

I knew that Stowell was going to fuck me, and he obviously knew that as well. Olson had told me in no uncertain terms how the two of them had shared new cadets—how they'd fucked them silly and reamed them big, left them sobbing. I just didn't know when, how much, and what kink it might take.

I was panting and moaning inwardly as Stowell guided me to the house. And my feelings were mixed. Yes, I was

128

scared. But I wanted it, and Stowell knew I did. He'd be a cruel lover. Olson had made that clear. As we walked, I was trembling, but I licked my lips in anticipation.

* * * *

So, where did the bodyguard, Jacks, fit into this I wondered. Was he just pledged to protect the boss or was he farther into it than that. I found out.

We had come up from the water, Stowell and I, and plopped down on two lounge beds at the edge of the Bermuda grass as it filtered into the sand of the small beach. Jacks had stood under a couple of trees on the edge of the beach, in combat boots and khakis, although his shirt was open, showing a muscular chest and dog tags. He looked the part of a poster-boy Marine, and, for all I knew that's what he was. He was holding a machine gum cradled in one of his arms and his eyes were looking everywhere at once.

They didn't stray to Stowell or me much of the time, though. That wasn't where any threat was coming from. All I was wearing was a Speedo. There wasn't anywhere I could have hidden a weapon. Stowell was naked. He was big—tall and meaty, with a slight paunch, but a muscular chest and biceps, and he was horse hung, as I knew he would be. He was a veritable black bull, a bit past his prime at his age, but still obviously capable of snapping someone like me in two if he had half a mind too.

He eyed me as we both toweled off. He was half erect. I knew that it wouldn't be long before he was fucking me. I knew that's why he brought me to Parris Island. Maybe he wanted to work on the book too, but before we'd come out of the house to swim, he'd made me give him a blow-by-blow description of what Cameron Olson had done to me, and there was no question that he intended to do the same.

He pointed to one of the lounge beds and I lay down on that, as he went down on his back on the other one. He motioned to Jacks to come over and at least part of Jacks's function here became revealed. At a gesture from Stowell, Jacks went down on his knees by the lounge bed, placed the machine gun under the bed, took the general's cock in one hand, and lowered his mouth over it. As Jacks gave the general head, Stowell ran a hand over the bodyguard's head. Turning slitted eyes to me, Stowell growled. "Watch this. Lose the Speedo and jack yourself off as you watch this. Fingerfuck yourself with the other hand. I'll tell you when you can come."

Panting and moaning, I stroked my cock and opened myself up with my fingers, searching for and finding my prostate, as I watched the hunky bodyguard giving Stowell head. I came when he told me I could come, which was at the same time he did. He pushed Jacks off him, and the bodyguard stood and wiped off his mouth with the back of his hand.

"Help me up," Stowell said, and Jacks helped pull the general off the lounge bed. "I'll be in the house," the general said. "You can use him and then bring him up to the house to me."

This took me by surprise, and I turned my head toward the retreating figure of the general and started to come off the lounge bed. But Jacks was immediately on me. He had taken his trousers and briefs off at some point during the blow job and worked his cock up. Straddling the lounge bed, with both of his feet on the ground on either side of the bed, he swiftly had my ankles on his shoulders and was forcing himself into me.

I grunted and groaned, but I took him. He was a handsome devil and thick, if not overly long. I didn't resist. I'd worked myself open and hard. I was ready for a cock. I just hadn't figured it would be the bodyguard's first. He, of course, was athletic and in top shape, so he worked me hard and long. I dug my fingernails into his shoulders beside my ankles and took his dog tags into my mouth and sucked them as he plowed me—raw, barebacking me like neither of us had to worry about the future. And just now, just for these twenty minutes that he fucked me, I didn't let anything else worry me.

He exhausted me. So that, when he was done seeding me and rose from me, I gave no opposition as he lifted me up, threw me over his shoulder, and marched me into the house. I did no more than moan and murmur a quiet, ineffectual opposition, as he laid me down on the bed in the master bedroom and tied my wrists and ankles to the posts at the four corners of the bed.

My eyes were glued to Stowell, who was standing across the room, a multithonged leather hand whip in his fist. He was smiling cruelly and swishing the whip against his leg.

* * * *

I lay there, on my stomach on the bed, an arm dangling down the side of the bed to the floor. I had no energy left to raise the arm. The welts didn't sting too badly. He'd only raised a bit of blood. There were some smears of it on the sheets. Someone would wonder about that when they cleaned up the guest house. Or maybe not. In any case, it wasn't my worry. I was beginning to calm my breathing.

He'd been cruel, yes—and methodical, giving my back and legs as much attention with the whip as my chest and arms. But he'd more played with me than put power into it. His power had gone for the fucking. He'd done everything to me that Cameron Olson had done—and more. And I'd given it all to him. I'd opened my core to him, let it go spongy, and had yielded everything to him, denied him nothing, made love to his cock with the undulating walls of my channel even while he was cruelly conquering all.

He'd had me bound just at the beginning, while he whipped me on the chest, belly, thighs, cock, and balls. Breaking me down; loosening me up. He covered me close, penetrated me, pounded me cruelly, came inside me. I then was totally his. I told him so; he knew it was true. He unbound me then and turned me and whipped my back, mounted me, and fucked me again. I denied him nothing.

All the time Jacks stood at the door, leaning into the doorframe. Still in his open shirt but trouserless, magnificently hard, watching everything.

Afterward, standing cross the room, by the window, the general was going through my written notes, reading everything, shaking his head, scowling here, laughing softly there. Occasionally he looked up and gave me a hard look. I hadn't held back in my research. I'd found out a lot—a lot that

131

he didn't know I'd find. I wasn't going to write it, of course. I knew what a political biography was to contain. But I wanted to know the whole man.

Now, I think I did.

"They are just notes," I called out softly. "Much of that wasn't going to go into the book."

"Shut up," he growled and went back to reading. After he'd been through it all, I watched him take a book of matches off the desk next to him, strike one of the matches, and light the corner of the ream of notes. When the flame was going good, he dropped it all into a metal trash can under the edge of the desk.

I knew then. In my heart then, I knew they were going to kill me. They'd fuck me again, of course—probably even rougher this time. They'd had their sport with me, but then they'd kill me. And there'd be so many ways to hide my body out here in the depth of the Marine base without it ever being found again.

What was that that Stowell had said when telling me we were going on this trip—that he could make me disappear altogether—leaving not a trace behind? There was no doubt that he could.

"Kevin." The voice was commanding, with a touch of irritation. He'd said something and I hadn't heard him.

"Yes? What?" I said.

"Your notes were useful. They told me what could be found out about me by a good researcher. I'll have to cover some tracks."

Here it comes, I thought. Would they at least let me live through another fuck? It was idiotic that I could think of being fucked at this time, but they were so good at it—both of them. And I was so submissive and needy. Stowell, of course knew that. That's why he had picked me.

He was opening a drawer in the desk beside him and taking out a thick manuscript.

"You don't have to write the biography," he said. "I've written what I want the biography to say. But you're a professional writer. I liked what you did with Paxton's biography. You'll rewrite this, in your own words. You'll just keep to the facts as I give them."

They weren't going to kill me. My emotions soared. He just wanted me to polish up what he had written. I could do that. I almost didn't catch what Stowell said next. He was speaking to Jacks.

"You take the bottom. I'll take the top."

I barely had time to turn on my back, before Jacks was up on the bed and under me. He put me in a full Nelson, his strong arms laced under my pits, pulling my arms helplessly over my head. I was too spent and exhausted to have struggled with him anyway. He moved his legs inside my thighs and spread and raised them. His thick, hard cock found my hole, which was still wide open from the general's attentions, and with a thrust and a yelp from me he was inside me.

My eyes went to Stowell, moving toward me, his erection massive and hard. He came up onto the bed between Jacks's and my spread legs, moved his cock head to my hole, and, as I cried out in pain and passion, pressed his cock inside me on top of Jacks's buried shaft.

Giving me no mercy, he began to pound me hard. Jacks was holding his thick cock steady inside.

"You. You too. Fuck him hard. You too," Stowell cried.

"But we're both big."

"Do him. Do him hard, like I am," Stowell growled. "Anything short of tearing him up. Whatever you want short of that. I want him completely cowed and malleable to the demands of either of us."

Huffing and puffing, trying as hard as I could to accommodate them, one thought raced through my mind, over and over again. They aren't going to kill me. He needs me to rewrite the biography. They aren't going to kill me. He needs me . . .

Gorilla

It all started with the illustrated article from a nature magazine on primate intercourse that I received at home in a manila envelope in the mail—no return address. There wasn't any explanation for why I received it either. An article, with photos of monkeys, baboons, and gorillas doing it. It showed that they did it pretty much like we did it, so we haven't evolved all that much. The larger the apes the more into it they seemed to be, though, and the more control they established over their partner. I held the article for a couple of days, thinking I'd get some sort of explanation for it or I'd find it had been misdelivered, but there was no follow up, so I just tossed it.

That was a Monday. Thursday was my evening at the gym near the Charlotte Motor Speedway, where I spent a good deal of my time. That was my home base. I traveled a circuit from Atlanta in the south to Dover, Delaware, in the north, but I trained in Charlotte and had my house here. I owned a log cabin near enough to Lake Norman southeast of town for me to get to the speedboat I had moored there in under a half hour but not close enough to the water that I'd have to have a million-dollar house. I was a modified stockcar race driver. I was built for it—small, lithe body. That was the easy part. I had to remain flexible too to fit in the cars and to be able to enter and exit them quickly. That's where the gym came in. I was continuing working out to remain slim and limber.

Jason Hall was slim and limber too. He was a college kid on a sports scholarship to the University of North Carolina in Charlotte and had qualified for the U.S. Olympic fencing team. Fencing was his ticket to a college education, so, like I did, he spent a lot of time at The Stable, a serious men's gym not far from the speedway and owned by a sponsor of the Charlotte Colts semipro football team. Most of the guys on the football team worked out here too, as the team sponsor gave them free access to the gym. Thus guys like me—and Jason—had the added benefit of being around a lot of randy beef cake while we fought to keep our bodies flexible for our jobs. I liked the landscape of that, and I was pretty sure that Jason Hall liked the landscape of that too.

That's why I was not in the best frame of mind on Thursday when I thought I was seeing Vince Turner, a running back for the Colts who I lusted after, putting the moves on Jason while he was spotting the college kid. Jason certainly thought that's what was happening and wasn't doing anything to fend him off.

I'd been cultivating Vince myself for several weeks, trying to let him know I was available. He was a hunk and a half—a blond Nordic type with strong legs, a great body, a Samson mane of curly hair, and a fine smile. He was a star on the team, rumored to be heading for the Miami Dolphins next year, and, to put it bluntly, I wanted to be laid by him before he left. It'd seen him in the showers and he had everything I wanted to have and hadn't gotten since the pit stop boss I'd been laying under had split and gone to work at the Richmond track. And here he was sniffing around Jason while spotting him on the bench press.

But first impressions were sometimes misleading. He looked over to me and smiled and called out something. I didn't hear what he said, so he repeated, louder, "Get a load of Enzo over there, Matt."

I looked across the gym floor to see that the Colts defensive tackle, Enzo Fava, was entertaining some of the guys by doing his ape routine. He was Italian, olive skinned, but one of the hairiest men I'd ever seen. He also was massive, solidly built, bowlegged, and his muscular arms seemed long for his torso. When he hunched over and hopped around on his feet, as he was doing just now, he was downright apian. He was making monkey noises to go with the act. My mind immediately went to the article on the apes breeding that had mysteriously appeared in my mailbox two days earlier.

Vince kept the image in my mind at that point because he suddenly was beside me, an arm going around my shoulders, and was commenting between laughs, "How'd you like to be fucked by something like that, Ben?"

I turned my face to him, appreciating that he had come over to me and left Jason, and aroused to hear him talking about sex when I'd had many a pleasant moment thinking of having sex with Vince. He'd even hinted at that before, telling me now and again that he'd like to take me home, without getting explicit about what we'd do there. But the look he'd give me when he said it gave me ideas of what he was suggesting and sent shivers up my spine.

He was giving me that look now.

"What you say to knocking off early this evening and coming over to my place for a beer?" he said.

I looked him straight back in the eyes and said, "Yeah, I'd like that."

"You sure?" he asked, his hand going to one of my butt cheeks.

"Yeah, I'm quite sure," I answered.

* * * *

I'd never done it this way before and it was sending me over the moon. Vince was standing, crouched, in the center of his bedroom, taking both his weight and mine on his strong thigh and calve muscles as he held me, fists gripping my wrists, my torso cantilevered out from his pelvis, my legs streaming back over his hips, my ankles crossed, and the palms of my hands gripping the back of a straight chair. He was inside me, thick and long, and making short thrusts, rubbing his shaft against my channel walls, punishing my prostate. Mouth slack in a grimace of pain-pleasure, completely overwhelmed with the demanding position and the novelty of it, I panted and groaned. He was grunting happily, complimenting me on my flexibility, on the perfect proportions and size of my body that fit his indulgence in unique, demanding fuck positions.

He tensed, stopped the thrusts momentarily, panting heavily. I heard a muttered, "Here it comes." Another couple of jabs up inside me, and he released his cum with a snort and a long sigh. I was gently lowered to the floor and lay there, turning onto a side and watching, as he stripped off the condom, tossed it into a waste basket, and went over to his bureau. He patted a cigarette out of a pack, lit up, took a drag, and then looked down at me.

"Your workouts have done you well. You've got great flexibility. A good lay. Charlie was right."

Charlie, the pit boss who had wandered off to Richmond after revving me up and letting me loose. In some ways Charlotte was a small town. Everyone must know everyone else's business, especially in a small, tight community of sportsmen fucking sportsmen. When a guy good at subbing came along, did all of the power tops in town just pass him around, I wondered. Vince didn't now make me stop wondering that.

"You do it with a lot of the guys at the gym yet?" he asked. "Do they know what a good lay you are? The guys on the football team who are into guys have talked about wanting to get into you, but I haven't heard any of them crowing about having scored yet."

"No, not guys from the gym," I answered, looking up at him from the floor. He had the body of a god, standing there like he was, nonchalantly leaning on the bureau and taking drags from his cigarette. He was solid and muscular, as a football running back would be expected to be. Thick everywhere. Everywhere. Hung like a horse. "Just you. And you're enough. I'm satisfied."

"Not yet, you're not," he answered with something between a grin and a sneer. "Not nearly enough yet. I know Enzo hasn't had you yet. Because he whines over how much he wants to fuck you."

"Enzo? The hairy Italian."

"Yeah, Enzo. You got a thing against hairy men?"

"No, I like hairy men. And certainly ones built like Enzo," I answered.

"You have trouble with having casual sex with a hung football player—a one-night stand with a guy just for the fuck of it?"

He was telling me that this wasn't anything serious. That we were just fooling around with no strings attached. But that was OK with me, and I told him so. "The guy is built and hung and gets me off—that's all I need," I answered.

Vince seemed relieved. "You caught Enzo's gorilla act at the gym this evening, didn't you?"

"Yeah, sure. You pointed it out to me."

"You ever thought about a gorilla fuck before? A ripsnortin' primeval down and dirty rutting around with a hairy gorilla type?"

"I'm thinking about another Vincent Turner fuck now," I answered. I wasn't the only one thinking of it too, I could see. He was erect again. And then, with a sly smile he was on me again, after stubbing out his cigarette in a dish on his bureau top.

I went on my back and elbows on the floor, spreading and bending my legs, and lifting my buttocks and rolling up my pelvis to receive him going on his knees between my thighs. But he didn't want anything as basic as a missionary fuck. Instead of going on his knees, he, first, grasped my ankles and pulled me up to where only my elbows were on the carpet. Then he pulled around to where my knees faced his torso. "Put your legs into the splits," he growled, as his hands moved down to grasp my buttocks. I did as he commanded and felt his bulb at my hole. Squeezing my buttocks, he lift me up and pressed down with his cock at the same time, penetrating me again, going deep, and, once again, going into the rhythm of the athletic fuck.

I didn't think again about what Vince had said about a gorilla fuck or of Enzo Fava, the Colts's dark, hunky, and hairy defensive tackle. Vince had fucked me royally, and he'd said he wanted me again. He said that I'd be his victory lap after that Saturday's football game. All weekend all I could think of was Vince and what exotic fuck position he'd put me in next.

The Colts lost their Saturday game, though, and the coach had laid on extra practices. Vince had dropped a couple of passes, so I knew he was sweating bricks in practice and probably wouldn't be interested in me again until Thursday in the gym. Enzo had had a few great plays in the loss, but all I could think of was Vince's dick and the next time he had an inventive way of fucking me with it.

Thus, I was taken completely surprise by the manila envelope—again with no return address—that arrived in my mail on Monday. Photos this time. Not an article, but glossy copies of photos. I immediately saw the resemblance to a gorilla. The photos were of Enzo—naked, hairy, muscular and in gigantic erection and primitive fuck positions. He had the college fencer, Jason Hall, in various Godzilla complete control positions and obviously was fucking the stuffing out of the little guy. Jason looked totally wiped out, but he also had the expression on his face of having been completely dominated and taken to heaven.

If this was a signal to me. It worked. I moaned, went hard, and went straight to the bedroom to masturbate myself to release.

* * * *

Of course this was a signal to me, I decided. Enzo Fava wanted to be a gorilla for me. He'd had Jason Hall and he still wanted me. So, I could stop being jealous of Jason. And Vince Turner wasn't a consideration. Vince obviously was in on Enzo having me, as he'd brought having sex with his hairy teammate to my attention. He obviously didn't care if I let Enzo lay me—that wouldn't mean he'd be less interested in laying me too. I'd said I didn't mind casual, no commitment sex. All I had to consider now was whether I wanted Enzo manhandling me—or "gorillaing" me, I guess.

What a question. Enzo was a hunk and a half. And I liked hairy men. He took that a bit too extreme but his body otherwise and his great cock made for a perfect package.

The question was whether I could wait for Thursday, which was the next night I was going to the gym. And what if he wasn't there on Thursday? And what if both of them were there—Enzo and Vince—and both wanted to screw me? Would it be one after the other or could I take two hung hunks at the same time? Would they want to share me? I'd done doubles before but not with two guys who both were hung. I decided I'd just have to cool it until then and when I got to the gym take it from there.

I climbed off my bed, pulled on a pair of athletic shorts, and padded downstairs. Saturday's Colts game had been run on the local TV station. I hadn't been home to watch it—and I didn't go to the game itself—as we had a full day of races at the track. But I had recorded it. I got a beer from the refrigerator and settled down on the couch to watch the game. It was a disappointment that they lost, but since I knew some of the players, it would still be entertaining to watch—and to think of how some of them looked without those football jerseys on. Or maybe how they'd look with just the tight pants on and watching them peel them off to reveal giant erections.

I picked out Vincent and Enzo whenever I could, pulled out my dick, and played with it while I watched them on the field. I didn't have any trouble imagining either one of them manhandling me. Their satiny pants were tight over their muscular legs and glutes and across their jock cups. I could see that Enzo wasn't having the best of days in terms of missed tackles and a few penalties—but he made up for those with a couple of brilliant moves and he still looked sexy as hell doing what he did. The material was tight, tight, tight, across his butt. The cheeks were big and rounded. I wondered if there was extra padding there.

The grunting of the men on the field, as conveyed by the TV, started to come at me in stereo. I muted the sound on the TV out of curiosity and I still heard grunting sounds—apelike sounds. I turned my face toward the French doors out into the garden and then laughed.

He was there. Enzo Fava, naked, hulky and hunky and hairy—and, no, his butt didn't have extra padding at Saturday's game—was crouched over outside my window, dragging his knuckles on the flagstones of the patio, and giving me a gorilla impression. His big dick, sticking out of the black, curly

140

matting of his pubes, was hard in erection. I laughed and got up from the sofa and turned toward the window. He was gone, but I knew he just wanted to lure me outside. I wanted him to lure me outside.

When I went out onto the patio, there he was, in the dense foliage of the back corner of my garden, which was fenced with bamboo stalks, carpeted with ivy, and with the spiked leaves of semitropical plantings. He had peeled a banana and was eating it—making the impression that he was eating a cock. He gave me a grin, and as I turned and started walking away from him, he gave a high-pitched gorilla-like cry, threw the banana aside, and started loping toward me. I loped around the house myself, passing Vincent at the edge of the driveway as I rounded the front of the house. He too was grinning. He too was naked and erect.

I let Enzo catch and cover me when I'd gotten around to the garden again. He enveloped me in his arms and gathered me into his hairy chest. My athletic shorts slid off my legs. I fought him, as I knew he wanted me to, struggling within his powerful grasp and covering body. Both of us knew there really wasn't any use my struggling, but we both knew it was a game. He'd gone to great lengths to role play the gorilla with me, and I let the game play out of him manipulating my body at will and having his way with me.

I was basically on all fours in the ferns, with him all over and on top of me, pulling me back into his body whenever I tried to break away and hugging me and giving me sloppy kisses in the hollow of my neck. When I felt him go into position and enter me and plow his dick up my channel and hold, with it throbbing there, I went docile for him. When I was quiet, buried within his grasp, he started to slow pump me. He only continued this long enough for the acceptance of the fuck to be established, though, when he started playing with me—putting my body into all of the controlling, flexible, submissive positions I'd seen in the photos I'd received that he'd put Jason into. It was a lesson not only in how flexible I was but in how many exotic positions a gorilla like Enzo could put me in while still being in the saddle with his dick up my ass.

It was also a lesson that I was to be completely submissive for him—submissive to the point that, during the fuck, he held still and told me that if I want it bad to fuck myself on his shaft, and, wanting him bad, I did so. For nearly an hour there in the ferns in my backyard, he put me through all the positions I'd seen in the photos of Jason and him that had been sent to me—and more.

I wasn't quite Jason. I had my ways too. When Enzo came, he was on his back in the ferns, his arms and legs spread, his knees bent, and me on top of him, riding his cock. When Vince at last got into the act himself, pulling me off Enzo and standing there, over Enzo's panting body, and bully fucking me in a standing position, with me draped in front of his body, my arms trapped in a full Nelson, my legs hooked on his hips, the tops of my feet rubbing his meaty calves, and his pelvis thrusting his cock up inside my ass again and again, Enzo just looked up at us with slitted eyes. I knew now what Vince had meant by a down and dirty primeval rutting.

We lay there, side by side, on our backs in the foliage, panting and moaning low.

"You know you don't have to play these games to have me," I said. "Either one of you. You can have me anytime you want. You can do me together if you want."

There was silence other than the heavy breathing and Enzo making low grunting sounds as though he was still taken with the role as a gorilla.

"In fact if you want to take me upstairs now and—"

"Yeah, I'd like that," they said together in stereo, as they both sat up and turned and reached for me.

I made sounds like a monkey in heat as Enzo climbed the stairs to my bedroom, with me slung over his shoulder and Vince followed close behind.

And, yeah, they were willing to share me, and, yeah, even as hung as they both were I could take both of them working their shafts inside me at the same time.

Prince's Choice

Sam Winterberry, who had been sitting beyond the fence at the side of the court with the entourages from the palace and embassy, plucked at my arm as we passed each other and hissed, "Get to the showers ahead of him, Jack. Give him a show. I've been watching; he's interested." I didn't look around to the man who'd spoken. I'd been told not to acknowledge his presence. But, at his instruction, I pushed on ahead to get into the locker room.

We were at the courts of the military school in the Asian capital and had just played a complex set—complex because the chief of station at the embassy, Ted Shackleford, and I were faced off against Ambassador Zimmerman and the prince. Although the COS and I were much the better players, it, of course, was a foregone conclusion that we were to lose the match. We won the first set, but it was all downhill from there, as it was programmed to be—at least by the embassy. The kicker is that we had to make it look like they weren't just the better team but that we all, especially the prince, were near pro. Well, I was near pro. That was one reason I'd been brought over from the States on temporary assignment at the embassy. Who would have known that a CIA officer would be sent on an expensive TDY overseas just to play a tennis match and be dangled in front of a potentate the United States wanted to manipulate?

It wasn't that hard to beat the prince to the showers. He was posing with the ambassador for a photo op. The country's press was all there. The prince wasn't in the country very much of the time, even though it was his country and everyone assumed he'd be inheriting it soon. He was a military nut, and a coalition of the Americans, the British, and the French had done what they could to move him around the various elite military schools. They didn't want him here much of the time. The king doted on him, but the prince's idea of a good time was going to war with the country's neighbors, and he was reputed to be as crazy as a loon. As the United States, Britain, and France were all entangled in mutual assistance treaties with his country, it was in our interests that his country not go to war with its neighbors.

Shackleford had gone off to call in the ambassador's limo. They wouldn't be showering and dressing at the military school. That decision wasn't by accident. Not that the ambassador had any idea what was going on.

During the game I had made sure of getting the prince's attention whenever possible. That wasn't hard to do. He had zeroed in on me the minute he'd entered the court. Winterberry had been confident that the prince would be interested, and Winterberry had been right.

In the communal shower, I stood under the water at one side of the tiled room, got wet, and was soaping myself up when the prince, a towel around his hips, arrived at the entrance. He was accompanied by a beefy young soldier, who moved to enter the chamber, no doubt to tell me to vacate while the prince showered. I could see out of the corner of my eye, though, that the prince grabbed the soldier's arm and hissed at him. The soldier took a step back, although not without sticking his head in the room to assure himself that I was the only one there and not so far back that he couldn't see the two far corners of the shower room at all times. The prince slipped the towel off his hips, handed it to the soldier, and came into the shower to stand under a head at the other end of the room from me.

I decided this might not be so bad. From a glimpse of him, I thought he was in magnificent shape. I'd been briefed that he would be—that he spent considerable time working out and that his love of everything military extended to being very hands on, including with personal training. From the first indication, I wouldn't have much trouble going hard for him. With me, being a Marine type was enough for that—any indication that the fuck would be rough and raw.

In rinsing myself off, I managed a slow, full turn, holding at a full frontal pose, facing him. He was rinsing himself off under his showerhead, but he wasn't making any effort to hide that he was watching me. He did the same turn for me, and I made a point of going full frontal toward him again and soaping my body up while watching him turn and soap his. My first impression of his body had been correct. His obsession with everything military had paid off. He was solidly built, taller than most men in his country and Marine muscular and hard. There were a few scars on his torso and thighs that indicated he wasn't afraid of hand-to-hand combat. He wasn't the most handsome man I'd ever seen, but he had the rugged, almost thuggish strong, chisel-chinned face of a young army general, which he was along with several other titles.

At first his equipment was a bit of a disappointment. He was stubby, albeit thick as the proverbial beer can, but as we posed for each other, he filled out toward a respectable length. He wasn't the least bit embarrassed about fisting and working his cock. Taking his lead, neither was I. His balls were big and hung low in the sac between rock-hard muscular thighs. His pubes were shaved, and he was tattooed in a spider web pattern across his groin, complete with a long-legged black spider, poised to attack his balls. I'd been told he was the commander of the country's Spider Special Forces regiment, which engaged in nefarious activities, all of which protected the palace from plots, and I wondered if all in his unit were tattooed this way. I let my eyes stray to the soldier at the entrance of the shower, who was as hunky as the prince and better looking in the face, and speculated if he might have such a tattoo too and, not incidentally, how he'd look naked. But he just stood at half rest, but full observance—an observance that didn't reveal that he was looking at two men posing for each other in the nude, though, and who were observing each other playing with their cocks.

The prince and I were both soaped up. We also both were hard. As he rinsed off under his showerhead, the prince grasped his erection in his hand—now having enough to get a good grip on, showed me a three-quarters profile, started stroking his cock, and gave me a half-amused, half-aroused look of expectation. I did as he was doing, and we both stood under the cascading water of our individual showerheads, turned three-quarters to each other, crouched slightly with bent knees, and beat ourselves off.

There was nothing coy here. I'd been briefed that the prince was simple, primitive, and straightforward in his pleasures and, being a prince, did just as he damn well pleased. He clearly wanted for both of us to pose and for me to beat off while he watched me and beat his own meat, so that's what we did. During the introductions, he had been told that I was here to serve his needs, and he'd obviously taken that literally. Yes, I'd been told, the power of the monarchy in this country was such that those in service gave whatever service was demanded, without question or hesitation.

He came first, splashing an admirable arc of cum against the tiled wall. He took two steps toward me and reached down and brushed my hand off my shaft. He fisted my cock—his grip was strong—and slowly finished beating me off, teasing me by bringing me to the brink and then backing off until I'd recovered some control—edging me. I remained in position, not touching him, our eyes locked together. I'd been told to give him whatever he wanted—occupying his time and attention was the point. He wasn't shy about taking what he wanted.

He placed his other hand on my right bicep and ran it up over my shoulder. He grasped my throat with it in a strong grip, and I saw a flare in his eyes of cruelty and lust. I fought not to show fear, to hold his eyes with mine in a level stare. I maybe could have taken him in a fair fight, but a fight with the prince would not have been fair. Even if I weren't under instruction to let him win—to let him have whatever he wanted—there was the other man, the bodyguard, nearby to assist him. There was no question that the bodyguard would assist in whatever the prince wanted.

I briefly panicked, wondering if there had been encounters like this before in which the prince wanted it all, including his prey's life. I knew of the scandals, of the rumors of orgies and missing young men. Had I enflamed him too much by playing this game with him in the shower? I'd had the Agency courses on hand-to-hand combat. So had he. Where he had his thumb and fingers positioned on my throat, he could easily either black me out or snap my neck. He clearly wanted me to know that too.

Releasing me, he slid his hand slowly down my chest and belly and then down onto my right flank. All the time he continued stroking me off with the other hand. He came in close, touching his forehead to mine, and his hand went around to my buttocks. There was pleasure in his eyes. I had been told that he admired commando-hard bodies, and I knew mine would meet muster. I flinched as a finger penetrated my ass, but still I held steady. He hadn't been quite able to reach my hole as he squeezed one of my butt cheeks, but it was evident where he was headed, and I submissively jutted my pelvis forward to give his finger access. He was looking for my reaction to penetration—testing how far I would go with him. My signal was of complete surrender to his desire and need. Causing my sphincter muscle to grasp the finger and pull it in clearly told him I was willing and able.

Beyond a slight smile, he went no further, though, pulling away from me, touching me only with the hand stroking my cock and with his eyes locked on mine. He was going to the edge again, and I sensed he'd go over the edge now. He was watching for the moment of climax, and I gave him a grimace and a look of lust, awe, and total surrender I knew he'd like as I shot my load.

When I had ejaculated, he gave me a little smile and a nod of his head, and exited the shower. He took the towel from the soldier, and they padded off. Trembling a bit, I placed my cheek to the cool tiles of the shower's back wall and let the water continue to flow over me. I spread my arms and pressed my palms to the tiles in a cruciform sacrificial form of total submission. Jutting my buttocks out from the wall, I half expected the prince to return, mount my ass, and fuck me. I more than half wanted him to. The exotic nature of this encounter had brought me more arousal and been more pleasurable than I had thought the first intimate meeting with him would be—I hadn't even been sure that he would find me desirable, that there would be an intimate encounter. I had been focused on seducing him—not considering that he might seduce me. God help me, I wanted him to return and complete the coupling.

But he didn't, and when I finally turned the shower off, toweled myself dry, and walked out into the locker room, he was gone. Two soldiers were standing on either side of the door to the corridor, but they were impassive. If they watched me dress, they gave no hint of doing so.

I hoped that wouldn't be it. I would have failed if that was all there was to it. Winterberry certainly wouldn't be pleased if that was the full extent of the prince's interest in me that I could generate.

An army car was waiting for me outside the military academy administration building. Winterberry and the COS had driven me over, but they'd told me to make my own way back to the embassy to report to them—the embassy was just down the street from the military academy compound.

Two soldiers were in the front seat of the car and a Spider Regiment major was in the backseat. I recognized the insignia on his shoulder. When he asked me where I wanted to go, I told him my hotel. It might be suspicious if I went directly back to the embassy from here.

He said nothing else to me and sat ramrod straight beside me in the car. If he knew what the prince and I had been doing in the shower—which he undoubtedly did—he said nothing to indicate it, nor did he signal to me in any way that I was the submissive male whore that I just had been. When we got to the hotel and the doorman had opened my door, the major leaned over and handed me an envelope with the seal of the palace on it.

"I'll be here at 9:00 tonight to escort you," he said as I exited the vehicle. I turned to ask him what he meant, but the doorman had already shut the car door and the vehicle was moving off.

I opened the envelope and pulled out a thick card. The writing was fancy and in ink. I marveled that it had been prepared in such a short time. I was being summoned by the prince for a late supper at the palace that night.

So, Winterberry had been right. That this was the right approach to the prince. Now it was up to me to reel him in.

× * * *

A week earlier I was in the last days of the Agency's Deep Cover Commando course at Camp Perry in Williamsburg, Virginia. I was on my back on my bed in my Spartan cinderblock walled room, my arms over my head, my hands gripping the brass headboard rail, my knuckles bruised by the banging of the headboard against the wall, my pelvis elevated, with my knees bent and my feet pressed to the mattress, giving me leverage to counterpiston Denzel's wicked thrusts.

A black bull, Denzel Jackson, my commando course instructor, was crouched over my body, between my spread thighs. His fists gripped my wrists, his forehead was plastered to mine, he was grunting deeply in harmony with my tortured moans, his toes digging into the mattress as he did pushups on my body. The bull's horn was throbbing, stretching, punishing my channel brutally. He was close to either giving me his load or killing me with his monster dick. I was beyond caring which.

I had gone completely docile and submissive to him. The belt he'd used to beat me with when I was still struggling with him—wanting him but knowing that being caught with a man here was a career killer—was curled on the floor beside the bed. The slashing strikes of the leather on my back, thighs, buttocks, and chest had only aroused me and made me want him inside me more. It was a fetish I wasn't proud of but that had helped pull me into the rough military life.

The door to the corridor banged open and a man in a suit, tall and gangly, pushing middle age, hard but wiry, came in, pulled a chair up to the bed, and sat down.

Surprised and shocked, I tried to twist to the other side of the bed and roll out from underneath Jackson, but the black brute held me in place. His dick was still inside me, deep, throbbing and stretching, but he was in a holding pattern.

"No, don't let me bother you," the man said, in a mocking baritone. "Finish him sergeant."

Three more thrusts and Jackson's body jerked and I knew he'd filled the bulb of the rubber. Once again, I made to move out from underneath him, totally nonplused with embarrassment—and fear too. Men got drummed out of the Agency for behavior like this, and I'd fought like hell—and covered up so much—to get in the Agency.

"No, stay like that, please," the man said. "It obviates any denying and excusing you might try to do before our little talk is over. I don't have much time." Jackson remained hovering over me, his dick going flaccid but still inside me, his fists still gripping my wrists at the headboard.

"We have need in the short term for a young man with the looks and skills and the proclivities you obviously have, Jack," the man continued. "Taking the belt was a nice—and useful—touch. Jackson wasn't sure you would. My name is Winterberry, and I run a special unit that works in special ways. Are you with me so far? No, don't bother to look embarrassed. We're beyond that point. Are you with me so far?"

"Yes," I squeaked. "Get him off me, though."

"I like to talk to my recruits in this position, Jack. It makes it so much easier for them to say yes. We don't have to have any pretense about what they will do—what they want to do. Tell me, have you ever heard of Prince ___, and he reeled off a name that seemed to go on and on—from the country of ___, and he named a country."

"I've heard of the country, of course." I answered. I didn't have to admit I'd never heard of Prince Whathisname.

"The prince is a military man, Jack. He likes all things military and he likes military men. He likes to fuck hard-bodied military men. He also is partial to the lash, which I think you will appreciate."

He gave me an amused look and I shuddered for him.

"He's rather a nuisance to us and to other Western countries as well, however," Winterberry continued. "He's more than a little bit crazy and he likes to go to war. We'd prefer not having any active wars in his region of the world, Jack. Therefore we—the Americans and the British and the French—do what we can to keep him distracted so that we can keep him entertained and out of his country. Do you follow me so far?"

"Yes, but where do I come in?"

"Well, you've done very well in our course here. You are presentable and hard bodied. And, of course"—and here he paused to smile wanly at me—"you obviously have no trouble letting men fuck you—and to give you a bit of the taste of the whip. Have you enjoyed this course, Jack?"

"Yes, but what—?"

"Would you recommend it to another rugged Ranger type?"

"Certainly."

"Good. We want you to sell this course to the prince. I understand you are a semipro tennis player too."

"I do well enough, yes, but—"

"A week from Saturday, you, as a TDYer at our embassy in ___," and here he named an Asian capital city, "have a celebrity tennis game date with our errant prince. We will set up a close encounter with him, and we want you to sell him on a long-form of this course here at Camp Perry. Now, that's the broad-brush operation plan here. I don't think you need to know more. But I suppose you should know the risk. The prince sometimes becomes overenthusiastic. There have been loses, but, as he's the prince, he suffers no consequences for his excesses. He has no concept of limitations. You'll have to do enough to win him over but not too much."

"So, my life will be in danger."

"Your life will always be in danger in this work, Jack. You knew this before you sought to join the Agency—and you did apply. We didn't coerce you."

"At least not to this point," I said.

He didn't respond directly; he pointed to the corner of the room, where the wall met the ceiling. "Perhaps what you'd want to know is what those little devices are in the upper corners of your room here. Didn't notice that they just appeared, did you?"

I looked more closely to where he was pointing. Two video cameras, not too well camouflaged. I'd been is such high heat when Jackson pulled me into the room that I hadn't seen them before.

"Now, you have two choices, Jack. We can use the film footage of your little exercise session with the sergeant here or you can start boning up on the Asian assignment. Which is it?"

"And then get kicked out of the Agency?" I asked.

"If you do this assignment well, you not only won't be kicked out, but you will come to work for me in a special Agency unit that uses the skills and proclivities you've already exhibited. Otherwise, yes, you'll be outed and ousted."

"If you put it that way . . ." I didn't have to complete the sentence.

"OK, you can go now, Sergeant. Thank you for your help. No, Jack, stay where you are, please." He had stood up and he was stripping off his clothes. He was hard bodied for his age, lean but hard. He had a dong that wasn't thick but it might have drooped to his knees if it wasn't hard and sticking out in a slight, cruel upcurve.

"I control my agents the old fashioned way, Jack. Your boning up on this assignment is going to start with me boning you, taking you for a test drive. We've established that you have agreed to the assignment. I need to know that you have what it takes to do the assignment."

Jackson was out of me, off of me, and out of the room. Winterberry climbed on top of me in the position Jackson had vacated, thrust inside me, deep, and started banging me hard. He was good. Despite the embarrassment and fear, I lifted my pelvis to him and went with the rhythm of the fuck. After a few minutes he pulled out of me and rose from the bed. I looked up and into his eyes, which flashed a cruel intensity. He had picked the belt up from the floor and was snapping it against his leg. I moaned and turned onto my belly.

I jerked up my head and cried out, "Yes, yes!" as the stinging lashes rained on my back. I made an effort to rise again and he hit me with the belt again. Harder. With a deep moan, I sank to the bed on my belly, throwing my arms out to the side in submission. His arm went under my belly and he coaxed me up to my knees, my chest still flat on the bed, me panting heavily. When he remounted me and began to pump again, I was whimpering and begging him for the fuck, reaching new heights of pain-pleasure.

What he proceeded to do was to give a clinic on fucking a man, not only taking me in a variety of positions but testing my flexibility and endurance. He fucked and beat me until he broke me—until I was a whimpering puddle of pain, sexual satiation, and exhaustion. But when he left me, he declared me fit for duty in his unit, which I was to learn was high praise from the man.

* * * *

I was told it was the game room that I was ushered into and I didn't have any trouble figuring out what kind of games were played here. A large bed, covered in silken pillows of many vibrant colors, dominated one wall. Two French provincial arm chairs, with cigarette tables next to them, were set facing each other about four feet from the foot of the bed. Other than that, the room was dominated by BDSM equipment. I readily recognized a set of chains ending in wrist restraints hanging from a hook in the ceiling beside something that looked like a sawhorse, covered in black padded vinyl. A black leather sling was hung from the ceiling in one corner. To my left was a table with restraints on it, and a long table against the wall with an assortment of sex torture tools on it. And, intriguingly, there was what looked like a kneeling bench with the yoke of stocks on its rail.

The men who escorted me into the room were hard-bodied soldiers in physique and bearing and were in dress whites—white gloves and white tunics over black trousers. The prince himself, who rose and met me half way to the door I'd entered, was wearing camouflage fatigues, with heavy black combat boots. Two gold stars gleamed on either shoulder. The top two buttons of his tunic were unbuttoned. His hard chest was smooth, the pecs bulging. A Buddha image on a heavy gold chain nestled between his pecs.

"I wasn't sure you would come," he said in greeting. He spoke in a low, hoarse tone, but his English, as I had found on the tennis court was impeccable, with a British bent. He'd said nothing in the shower. He'd let his actions speak for him, and they had spoken volumes.

"You knew after our last meeting that I wouldn't be able to stay away," I answered, giving him a direct stare. He smiled at this flattery, this acknowledgment of his charisma, seductive in its own exotic—and scary—way, as I had already discovered.

"You are a connoisseur of physical pleasure . . . and pain . . . then, I am thinking."

"More a student," I responded. "I believe that you are the connoisseur. I am more a servant in these matters." This obviously pleased him as well.

"You are at my service then?"

"As you wish . . . what you wish."

"As long as I wish?"

I gave him a slight bow, lowering my head in submission.

He lifted an eyebrow and smiled again. "This is my game room," he said, letting both of his arms make a sweeping gesture toward the room.

"Apparently," I answered.

"Are you afraid or put off? I would be disappointed, but I don't force men. I use them hard, but only with their submission. You can leave now if you wish." He ran the back of a hand down my cheek, ending with a thumb pressed under my chin, where I knew that, if enough pressure was applied, I'd be put out of commission.

"No, I'm not disappointed. Yes, I'm afraid. But I assume that's what you want."

"That's what pleasures me, yes. Men with magnificent bodies. Military men. Reduced to submission. Conquered. Vanquished. Completely open to me. Are you willing to submit all or do you wish to leave?"

"No, I'll stay," I said. Winterberry had not really given me an option. I wasn't sure the prince was giving me an option either. I strongly suspected I'd been given to him to do as he pleased.

"Your Mr. Shackleford tells me you are military. The Marines? An officer?"

"Yes. I'm a captain. But I am not in a regular unit." I had been given a military cover. It was important, I was told, for the prince's men to be military—and in special units.

"Tell me, have you seen hand-to-hand combat. Killed men in battle?"

"I probably shouldn't answer that."

"Have you endured pain on the battlefield?"

"Yes, certainly," I replied.

"And how did that make you feel, Jack? Did it scare you? Did it start your adrenaline pumping? Did it make you go hard? For some men, the fear and pain heighten the pleasure. It takes men to new sexual heights. I am such a man. Are you?" He was standing close to me now. He had one hand on one of my upper arms, but the other one was on my crotch. He knew that I was hard.

"Yes it makes me hard," I answered. "The pain and fear heighten the pleasure for me." I let my breath out in admitting that. It's what I would have to say, what I'd been sent here to endure. But I had to admit that it was true nonetheless. But the fallacy here was that I was quite sure that the prince wasn't saying that *his* pain would heighten his sexual pleasure. I was sure that it was *my* pain that would do that for him.

"We normally would have supper first," he said. "But I haven't been able to think of anything but you since this afternoon. I want you to strip down for me, Jack. I want for you to give me pleasure and I want to use you in a way that will make you feel alive. Take off your clothes for me—all of them. I am going to use you hard."

He backed off but just a few steps so that he could watch me as I undressed. Two hulky attendants stepped forward and took my items of clothing as I took them off. The attendants neatly folded them and placed them on an ottoman.

I knew that later they would be returned without a crease in them. I would be the one to show the creases. The prince hadn't said he'd disrobe too, and he didn't. But he did unbutton the fly of his fatigue pants, worked his cock out, and was stroking it as I undressed.

While two of the attendants folded and took away my clothes another two stepped forward with objects in their hands. When I was naked, the prince stepped in close again, encased both of our cocks in one hand and began to frot them—stroking them together. His other hand went over my shoulder to the back of my head, where he dug his fingers into my scalp and pulled my head back painfully. Obviously it was the pain that was important to him, so I grimaced for him. Normally, I would fight that, but I decided he want to see it.

The attendants got busy. My arms were pulled behind my back and my wrists were bound together. Another attendant was at my feet, attaching a leg extender that bound my ankles and held my legs in a wide stance. Yet another attendant attached weights to my balls that pulled them downward and then, as I gave a little yelp, attached nipple clamps to my nubs. The clamps were joined with a metal chain, which, taking his hand from our cocks, the prince jerked down, causing me to yelp louder.

"Are you enjoying the pain?" he asked. "Can you feel the pleasure of it?"

"Yes," I whispered. And then I groaned as his fist closed over my balls and he squeezed them hard. I moaned and almost cried out, doubling up and going toward the floor with my knees. He let me go down on my knees, which put my face at the level of his cock, which he thumped against my cheeks until I opened my mouth to it and gave him head.

They put me on the kneeling rail, with my neck and wrists in the stocks and my knees on the pad. The prince was in front of me, feeding me his cock, and one of the attendants was behind me working my ass open with a lubricated dildo. There would be no condoms. One of the glories of the Agency's technical research was in inventing a pill to protect men from the known diseases of unprotected six. Winterberry had first used it with me, saying he abhorred rubbers. A

156

package of the pills had come with me as a gift to the prince, and he had seemed to be delighted with them. For one thing, he said that such a gift dispensed with any pretense or preparation for why I was here.

When he felt prepared sufficiently, the prince came back around to behind me. He beat me, on the back and legs, mostly lightly, but with a few strokes of enthusiasm, with a wide leather belt. Tiring of this and as my cries of surprise and violation subsided into low moans and whimpering, he mounted my ass and fucked me to an ejaculation, edging me with his cock as he had done with his hand in the showers. The pain involved, of course, was all mine, and the dick work was the least of it. I had been opened up well, and, though he was thick, he wasn't long, and his rhythm was very military—a steady beat without invention that would surprise and make me gasp at being off cadence or more cruel than anything else he had done to me.

I couldn't say it was the best fuck I'd ever had—strangely enough Winterberry gave the best fuck I'd ever had. He not only was cruel and demanding but he also was inventive and could make me gasp with a change in cadence. But I couldn't deny that the domination and control of it—and the fear of what was to come—with the prince aroused me to unusual heights. He entered me strong and thick, and he understood how to punish the prostate with his bulb. I came before him—and then again with him.

His attendants, in their pristine white tunics and gloves, and well-pressed black trousers stood at attention around the room, seemingly not watching what the prince was doing to me, but ever ready to respond to his every whim. I wondered how many other young men he'd brought here and done the same with. And I wondered how many of those young men had walked out of here alive.

One thing I did know was that if they didn't, the prince's attendants would clean up and paper over everything—and that my handlers would just walk away. That knowledge alone should have frightened the shit out of me, but I was learning something about myself in this sexual torture chamber, something that frightened me even more—that this, all of this, aroused me more, made me harder and more sexually charged, than I'd ever been before.

* * * *

I might have thought the supper was downright civilized if I wasn't sitting in one of the French Provincial chairs with a folding table in front of me and still in the nude. It also would have been less worrisome if the prince hadn't said, "We'll resume after we've eaten." When I was freed from the stocks, one of the attendants had rubbed salve on my back and legs—although they didn't hurt as much as they stung after the salve was applied—and I was helped to the chair—which had been covered in a cloth that I hoped wasn't absorbent enough for the prince not to remember my visit with a bit of regret. No doubt the pillow they added to make me more comfortable did soak it all up, though.

He was without tunic now too, as were his attendants, his having been discarded when he got overheated in using my body. They all had good bodies. I must admit that I did some dreaming of more than one of the attendants fucking me too. But that didn't happen. I guess that would be some form of lese majesty here—taking sloppy seconds from their prince in his presence—unless, of course, that was one of the many kinks that turned him on.

The food was delicate and delectable. The drink was good Scotch. The conversation was a bit strange. He'd worked my body over and fucked me and, during supper, he was like a little kid with his toys in wanting to talk military hardware. He was totally oblivious to how he had degraded and used and abused me. What had been as intimate as it could have been for me to the point that the rest of the world had disappeared and it had become just the two of us working together as one grasping fucking machine striving for the highest arousal and release and balance of pain and pleasure possible appeared to be impersonal exercise to him. He prattled on as if we were sitting together at a seminar waiting for it to begin. He'd just had his dick inside me, pumping me with cum that I could still feel squishing around deep in my intestines, and had been licking blood off the welts on my back that he had put there, for fuck's sake.

He knew all of the guns used in the armies of the major countries as well as their comparable advantages and disadvantages. I couldn't keep up with him, but there was little indication he needed me to.

"I've inspected an M1A3 Abrams tank," he said enthusiastically. "I suppose you have seen it as well."

"No, I haven't," I answered. "I have specialized in commando operations and we don't see many tanks in that form of battle." I had a mission here. I needed to bring the conversation around to the Camp Perry special commando warfare course.

"My favorite attack helicopter is the Apache. I'm sure you've been in those in commando operations."

"Yes, of course," I said.

"I have flown those. I have qualified on those. Did you know that?" He was gushing now, his eyes flashing. He was attractive this way. I wouldn't mind going with him for a straight fuck. I wondered how he was in covering a true lover in a missionary position marked by heavy kissing and long, deep strokes inside a channel that had gone soft and spongy for him, caressing every inch of the most he could fill out to.

I suspect he'd never tried that. I momentarily considered trying to seduce him to that, but then I remembered I was here for a specific, short-term purpose. I couldn't become involved with this crazy man. I'd best concentrate on surviving him.

"No, I didn't know that," I said. But, of course, I did. I'd been told he'd inspected and been trained in every system that kept him out of his country and occupied with his toys. "Then you would be a double threat if you also had the commando training. You would be qualified to fly in and also to perform the mission."

"Would I?" he asked, clearly intrigued by this thought. It was time to strike.

"I've just been on an Agency training course on special commando operations. It was a terrific course. You have done that one?"

159

"No, I don't think so. A good course, you say?"

"First rate. Terrific. I think it would be just the thing for you. I could mention the possibility of you're being invited to do the course. I think one will be starting soon."

"Would you?"

"Of course, I'd be happy to." If you let me live, I might have added. Mission accomplished. I started thinking of a successful exit strategy. It had been fun, but . . .

The prince had other ideas. After supper, as two of his attendants were suspending me from the ceiling hook with the wrist restraints, another attendant was handing the prince a hand whip. He was fully naked now, and in erection. With a gleam in his eye, he was telling me how much fun we were going to have—new heights of pain-pleasure.

I was able to take this session more calmly, as there was every indication I would survive it. I had him hooked on the Agency course, and he thought that I would have to propose him for it for him to be invited to take the course. I couldn't do that if I was dead.

* * * *

I was taken directly from the palace to a private clinic that probably specialized in recovering the prince's pain-pleasure subjects and knew how to keep its treatment private. I, of course, wasn't charged for anything. There were no broken bones and the welts and cuts weren't even that serious. It was more a matter of keeping them from becoming infected. Either the station at the embassy wasn't told where I was, they didn't think it wise to let the palace know I was close to them, or they just didn't give a shit. No one visited me in hospital. I'd done my work. That was more important than whether I would survive the operation.

Four days later when one of the local country's military cars returned me to the hotel, Sam Winterberry was waiting for me with the news that the prince was delighted to accept the invitation to take the special commando course at Camp Perry.

"The Agency is busy building a course that will take three times as long as the normal one and finding the right students to take the course with the prince," Winterberry said. He was sitting in a chair by my bed, which I was lying on on my belly, as it would be a while before I wanted to lie on my back—or my buttocks, for that matter.

"Your next assignment, in case you wondered, will be as an assistant teacher of that course. The prince, of course, will stay at one of the camp's guest houses rather than at the student dormitory. He'll naturally bring attendants, but he was pleased when he was told you'd be involved in the course and could bunk in his quarters to help him acclimate to the camp."

"He was pleased, was he?" I said, accompanied by the semblance of a moan. "And I have an ongoing assignment, do I? You're not going to follow regs and drum me out of the Agency for having homosexual relations?"

"No, of course not," Winterberry said with a smile. "The regs are the regs, of course, and if need be at any time to separate you from the Firm, we can fall back on them. But, in fact, you did a bang up job of this operation and I head up a unit that uses talent such as yours. Some say that espionage is the oldest profession, while others say it's prostitution. We at the Agency are quite happy to marry the two. We've found the blend to be quite successful."

"What now?" I asked.

"Now I'd like to do an inspection of where we stand on your fitness for maybe an interim assignment before you return to Camp Perry." He stood up, came around to the foot of the bed, reached up and around my waist, and undid my belt buckle. He was pulling my trousers and briefs off, when I asked him what he was doing.

"As I said, I need to take a look at these welts to see how long they might put you out of commission." He had his hands on my bare buttocks and was separating the globes and blowing on my hole.

"Most of the damage is on my back," I said.

"We'll see to that eventually," he said cheerfully. "I also want to remind you who is in charge—who you work for and must please."

I groaned as he buried his face in my crack and went for my hole with his tongue.

161

As he came up on the bed, positioned himself over me, placed the bulb of his cock at my entrance and penetrated me and started to pump, I groaned in the knowledge of who owned me now.

Avril's Ploy

Troy was staring into the Cross Keys Winery shelf of the dimly lit wine cellar in the basement of Professor Hammond's house, his arms extended and his hands grasping the edge of the shelf, as Brad Baylor, Hammond's "significant other" rose up from behind him where he'd been knelt, working Troy's hole with his tongue. The strong hands of the James Madison University assistant football coach grasped Troy by the hips as he came in close behind Troy. Instinctively, feeling Brad's erection between his bare thighs, Troy widened his stance and moaned. The coach dry fucked the young student between his squeezed thighs.

"We have to be quick about it," Troy murmured. "Can't be gone for long." Dry fucking like this was a frequent "getting it off" technique in the dorms at JMU, and Troy briefly wondered if there would be more than this.

"No problem," Brad whispered into Troy's ear as he nuzzled the English Department sophomore's neck with his scratchy chin. "I've been hard for you for the last hour."

In anticipation of Troy's reaction, Brad covered the young man's mouth with one hand to muffle Troy's cry. Troy struggled a bit when he heard the snap of the condom being put in place and realized that this was going to be more that the anticipated between-the-thighs dry fuck. The coach moved his cock into position with his free hand and gave a little upward thrust with his hips, penetrating Troy's channel from behind.

He moved up into the soft, yielding channel deep before starting to pump him.

No, this wasn't going to be the typical safe dry fuck of the dormitories, Troy realized. The coach *had* told him he wanted to fuck him for real, and Troy now believed he hadn't just been teasing.

Troy looked around wildly at the shelving stretching along in front of him until his eyes focused on a Cross Keys Meritage label and he left it there, his mind going to Aaron, the Staunton men's clothes store owner who had hired Troy as a clerk and then a model, bedded him, paid for him to start college here at JMU, and who had recently died in an automobile wreck, leaving a wife and two children to inherit— and Troy all alone and penniless. Troy was still devastated. Aaron had taken him like this, like Brad was doing, although he wasn't as rough about it as Brad was—or as long or thick.

Troy had struggled a bit against Brad's roughness as first, but when Brad had established a rhythm of the fuck, Troy, ever the submissive, settled down, memories of Aaron and Aaron's lovemaking sufficing and the very fact that Troy had a man inside him again, giving him a sense of comfort and satisfaction—even though it was while he was supposedly selecting wine for the Thanksgiving dinner party going on over their heads.

Brad was quick about it: in, finished, and out within seven minutes of invasion. He stepped back from Troy to strip off the spent condom with the sound of a snap, and Troy, his knees having gone to rubber and Brad no longer holding him up with a strong arm around his waist, sank to the floor in front of the wine shelf. He turned his head and dully watched as the muscular football coach expertly tossed the spent rubber into a waste basket. Everything was done with efficiency and fluid movement. The coach obviously had done this many times before—just not with Troy. Was Troy just a notch on his belt or would they do it again when there was more time? Brad had played him like he was aching for him.

For a brief minute Troy wondered who would empty that waste basket—Brad or Professor Hammond?—and he felt the sting of guilt. Avril Hammond was one of his professors, the chairman of the English department. Hammond had been good and attentive to him—great to him in his grief over the loss of Aaron, who Hammond had known as he had known about Troy's relationship to Aaron. So few others knew or cared that Troy was grieving. Brad was living with Hammond, no doubt sleeping with him as well, and this . . . this would be seen as a betrayal, wouldn't it, if Avril found out about it?

"Give me five minutes to get back into play upstairs before you come up," Brad said, as he zipped up his trousers.

"Yes," Troy answered dully. "But the condom . . . the waste basket."

Brad laughed. "Avril won't know. I'll empty the can. You're a sweet lay. Nice ass and tight gut. We'll do this again sometime soon. Avril won't know unless you tell him."

"Yes," Troy murmured, not clear himself on what he was saying "yes" to. Yes he was glad his professor needn't know that his partner was screwing his star student on the side. Was he glad Brad said he wanted to lay him again? Yes, Troy hadn't gotten any full-out sex since Aaron had died.

When Troy got upstairs, he took his time opening the bottles of wine he'd brought up and then went into the large dining room of the old plantation house that Harrisonburg, Virginia, had swallowed into its outskirts near the campus of James Madison University and poured the wine at the dozen place settings around the table. Brad was in the other room boisterously passing around hors d'oeuvres to the other ten male guests Professor Hammond had gathered for a Thanksgiving Day dinner party.

Brad poked his head into the dining room to see that Troy was back and then returned to the living room to ring a "dinner is served" bell.

As the men moved into the dining room, still chatting among themselves, Avril Hammond stopped beside Troy and said, "And what do we have here?"

For the briefest second, Troy was afraid that there was something revealed in his demeanor or dishevelment of dress that told Hammond that his companion had just been in the basement fucking Troy. He didn't respond immediately and knew that he looked confused—and, probably, guilty.

"The wine, Troy, my boy. What wine did you choose for us?" Troy lifted the bottle and turned the label toward Hammond. "Ah Cross Keys Meritage. Very discerning selection." Laughing, he helped his guests find their seats. Troy and Brad exchanged a furtive look and then Troy went to his seat. There were a few other students at the table, but there were some important men there as well. Troy was fortunate to have been invited here for Thanksgiving. Hammond had been so good and understanding to Troy in ways that had gone beyond Hammond being one of Troy's professors. Troy was sitting near Hammond's end and Brad was at the other end of the very long table from Hammond. Troy thought that was just as well. He didn't know if he could do fluffy chit chat with a man who had just ejaculated inside him.

* * * *

With one exception, the dozen men at Avril Hammond's Thanksgiving dinner were an understandable group. There was no gender—or basic lifestyle interest—separation here that Troy could figure. This was a gay male gathering—Hammond had told Troy it would be when he invited him here—although some men here seemed more comfortable and active with it than others. There was a near-even divide across them in age group, four being successful men in their fifties, three being in their late twenties or early thirties, four being JMU students, and that one exception who didn't appear to fit in at the party.

There was a racial divide. Two of the men were black. This included the host himself, Avril Hammond, who was in his fifties and every inch in appearance and demeanor the university English department chairman that he was in life. He was tall, handsome, in a Jamaican mixed-raced background way, slim, and in control. The other black, in his early fifties, was Lawrence Shelton, an art professor at JMU, specializing in photography. Lawrence was neither as distinguished looking nor as handsome as Avril was, but he was formidable enough. He was tall but had a bit of meat on his bones. He wasn't ugly, but he commanded his environment with penetrating eyes that saw and observed everyone.

One of the men was of Chinese ancestry and it was fairly obvious why he was there—he had brought the food, and quite a spread it was. Chan Tang, another of the men of fifty, was nearly as distinguished as Avril Hammond and was twice as imperial. He was the executive chef for the ritzy Homestead Resort in the mountains southeast of Harrisonburg, in Hot Springs, Virginia. He did a lot of catering and he had become friends with Hammond because of their shared interests in younger men. Chan was of normal height but more than normal girth, as befitted his life preparing rich food. Hammond had warned Troy to beware of the man, that he could be a cruel man and his sexual appetite was as insatiable as his appetite for food. He exuded that image this evening.

Three of the older men were attached for the evening to others there, although Shelton and Chan weren't as attached as Hammond was trying to be. One of the older men wasn't, the man sitting between him and Hammond, a quiet novelist, Gideon Grimes, who Hammond had told Troy should be of interest to Troy.

Troy knew that there were strains in Hammond's relationship with the man living with him, Brad Baylor, who had hooked up with Hammond when he was an undergraduate student at JMU. Baylor had been a football star at the school who Hammond had helped secure an assistant football coach position here to keep him in Harrisonburg and in Hammond's bed, topping the professor. As Troy well knew, though, Baylor had a roving eye and a hungry dick. Troy just hoped Hammond didn't know that and that Baylor's interest would move on from Troy before Hammond found that out. Troy couldn't resist Baylor. He was grieving and in need and Baylor was a hunk and a half—and he was a dominator, like Aaron had been. Troy went completely submissive for a man who commanded him.

Baylor also was attached to Hammond, and while that had complications, it also had advantages for Troy. Troy wasn't up for a committed relationship this soon after Aaron's death—if forever. He had sexual needs, but they were best served for now in casual, uncommitted lays.

Chan Tang's relationship with the late twenties' History department instructor, Cory Kavanagh, and Lawrence Shelton's relationship with early thirties music department instructor, Marcus Taylor were more loose than Hammond's fixation on Baylor. Both Chan and Shelton fucked other young men when they had the opportunity. Their "others," though, were more interested in permanent, monogamous relationships. Chan and Shelton, of course, were dominant and topped in their relationships.

The fourth older man, Gideon Grimes, was someone Troy recognized, as he was a mid-market novelist who Troy had heard in readings and was an instructor in creative writing at JMU. Grimes was a tall, well-muscled man, who was handsome in a graying sandy-haired way but who seemed sad, a bit detached, and withdrawn this evening. Troy wondered if he too were grieving a loss, and Troy found that possibility was attracting. Grimes gave the impression that perhaps he was ever constructing phrases and weaving plots in his mind and thus wasn't fully "there" in the present circumstance.

Four of the guests were undergraduate English department students, invited to the party, Troy surmised, to provide eye candy—and maybe more—for the older tops there. It hadn't taken Troy long to catch on to this party being as much a hook-up activity as a traditional Thanksgiving meal.

The group of students included Troy himself, relatively small of stature, dark and sultry looking, and somehow always quickly picked out for attention by dominant men. His relationship with Aaron had brought stability to his life—and a bit of protection from being hit on by other men. This Thanksgiving dinner party was really the first public gathering he'd attended, feeling bereft and unprotected, since the funeral, and indeed, he hadn't been here longer than an hour before the host's boyfriend was humping him in the wine cellar.

One of the students, star running back of the football team Dale Hunter, knew exactly what he was doing here. He was the campus gay male stud. He was there because he was a pet project on the gridiron of Brad Baylor, who had gotten

Hammond to invite him and who had come because he knew that fresh meat had been invited to charge the juices of Hammond's senior guests.

Troy certainly was one of the eye candy invitees, and he knew enough of Dale Hunter to do what he could to avoid him. Dale wasn't really hitting on him this evening, though, probably, Troy thought and was afraid, because Brad Baylor had told the football star that Troy was off limits.

Not off limits, clearly, were the other three guests. Jacob Bernstein, every inch the good-looking, dark-haired, hirsute Jew, and Tim MacDonald, a somewhat effeminate, androgynous, and beautiful and delicate-looking blond, had both been brought in from the English department. Although if either was cut out of the herd and pinned to the floor by one of the preying tops tonight, it wouldn't be their first experience, it would be close enough to the first to be a traumatic and memorable experience for them. In recognition of this, the two were almost clinging to each other, at least thus far in the dinner, which, as this was basically a university gathering, was moving along nicely with glib and lively conversation up and down the table.

The odd one out—that one exception to how the rest fit in with each other—was noticeable because he wasn't engaging in the conversation and wasn't dressed as nattily as the rest. That one exception was Peter Lambert, a young man who, as good looking as any of the narcissistic men present, had no relation to JMU. He was a clerk at one of the local supermarkets, Kroger. He was there, everyone had been told over drinks in the living room before dinner, because he went to the same gym as Brad Baylor. In mentioning him to Troy, Brad had given a fuller explanation: Lambert had been fucked by Brad and was vetted as of interest for the evening to a few of Hammond's guests. He was cleanly attired, but his T-shirt, worn jeans, and open-toed sandals were not in keeping with the meticulously preppy and expensive party clothes of the rest. He also was as self-conscious as the undergraduate English majors present, but more aware that he had nothing to contribute to the sophisticated conversation of this gathering and filled in his time with drinking the wine—on top of the beer he'd had during the social hour.

Dinner went on for nearly two hours, with the quality and quantity of food vying with the high-level conversation for accolades. Hammond had seated everyone with a purpose, Troy suspected as the dinner went on. The first clue of this was when Hammond gave a series of toasts at the beginning of the meal. One of them caught Troy in the solar plexus. Hammond actually referred to Troy's recent loss of his significant other and benefactor, Aaron, who was well known in the region; noted that this was Troy's first outing since the funeral; hoped that Troy now could find the means to continue his studies; and urged everyone to wish him well. Immediately thereafter, Hammond had launched into a similar toast to Gideon Grimes, noting that the novelist had recently lost his wife, Penny, and was, Hammond had heard, working his feelings about that out in the novel he currently was working on. This, also for him, was the first social outing since his wife's funeral.

Troy had only a moment to wonder why a heterosexual man had been brought into what clearly was a gay male gathering—and that this possibly might explain why Grimes had been somewhat withdrawn during the social hour, when Hammond added, "Gideon has been of two minds, and I'm looking forward to the possibility that he will come back to us. He and I were very special friends before he found his sainted Penny. Would you say that was fairly stated, Gideon?" Grimes had simply nodded his head in acquiescence.

And that's when Troy began to observe the possible method behind the seating chart. Grimes had been seated to Hammond's right, in the guest of honor spot, and Troy had been seated on the other side of Grimes. Perhaps Hammond was trying to rekindle something with the novelist, Troy first thought. But that didn't meld with his obvious devotion to Brad Baylor, sitting at the other end of the table.

The longer the dinner progressed, though, the more it became apparent that Hammond was trying to get Grimes and Troy to converse with each other—which they did, in fact, do, getting into deeper areas of their separate griefs than went with the general level of conviviality across the table. On top of this, the Kroger clerk, Peter Lambert, had been seated to the left of Troy. Although Troy exchanged a few civilities with Lambert, it was obvious that the clerk was out of his element and didn't want to try to talk much. He wanted to drink more. This seating seemed to be contrived by Hammond to throw Troy and the novelist together, Troy thought. And then when he saw Brad seated at the other end of the table from him, too far away to exchange any conversation in private, Troy began to worry about what Hammond might be trying to do. Did Hammond have an inkling after all that Brad had been hitting on Troy? Did he have any idea how successful that had been and how far the two had progressed?

All of this speculating was wiped away, though, eventually, when Hammond rose from the table, raised his empty glass, and declared, "I think we need to check out the drinks cart in the living room. Could you do the honors behind the bar, Brad, at least until everyone has been set up with a drink? After that they can refresh as they please on their own. And as for the rest of us, I think we need to move on to the dancing?"

Dancing? Troy thought. He'd never before been to one of these, but . . .

Hammond obviously was serious, though, Brad had preceded them into the large living room and slow, dreamy dance music already was coming out of the living room. Troy had wondered how an evening like this—purposely gay—would go. Slow dancing. Of course. And later, maybe . . .

It was dawning on Troy that this was a sex party. Of course he and Brad were well ahead of everyone else in that department.

* * * *

The living room was large, running the full depth of the original house, and, with a couple of sofas pulled back, there was plenty of room for dancing. Couples could even drift out into the even larger, all-glass, stone-floored conservatory, stuffed with large plants, that opened off the rear of the living room through an open double-door French door. The lights

171

had been turned down low in the living room. Hammond obviously wanted the atmosphere to be romantic. He also wanted to maximize the possibilities. He continuously urged couples to mix and match—and to dance close together. He told them there were bedrooms available upstairs.

Yes, this was a sex party.

The dancing started at an overall level of comfort, established couples dancing together. Lawrence Shelton, the art professor, was dancing with his live-in, Marcus Taylor, the music department instructor. Chan Tang, the chef, was dancing with Cory Kavanagh, the history department instructor. The two English department undergraduates were huddled together. Troy was sitting with them and the three were chatting, ever conscious that someone might ask them to dance, thereby expressing a sexual interest that would have to be considered. Brad, in fact, had headed for Troy to ask him to dance, but had been intercepted and taken onto the floor by Hammond. The novelist, Grimes, was sitting across the room from Troy, nursing a brandy and gazing into the distance, beyond the walls. The overly confident football player, Dale Hunter, had latched onto the Kroger clerk, Peter Lambert, and was squeezing the life out of the poor young man while they danced. They were kissing as much as dancing.

After a couple of dances, the couplings changed. Lawrence Shelton pulled Troy up to the floor, Brad was dancing with the Kroger clerk, Chan Tang had Tim MacDonald in his clutches, Dale Hunter was mauling Jacob Bernstein, and the rest were standing around, talking university affairs, and ogling and, no doubt, rating the younger guests obviously brought there to interest—and, Troy now realized, to service—the older guests.

Lawrence Shelton wasted no time at all expressing an interest in Troy while he held him close, just swaying in place, and squeezed one of Troy's butt cheeks with his hand.

"You modeled clothes for Aaron Bainbridge, didn't you?" he asked.

"Yes. For his catalog."

"So, you have experience as a photographer's model."

"A bit. There wasn't much catalog work involved."

172

"You have a very nice body. And you have the looks of a movie star."

"Umm, thanks," Troy said. He looked around the room to see if there might be rescue in sight. Shelton was not his type at all. And he had the hands of an octopus. The room had thinned out a bit. He saw Hammond pry Brad away from Peter Lambert and send him on an errand. Dale Hunter immediately took up Lambert and moved their dancing out into the conservatory. Chan wasn't anywhere to be seen, and Cory Kavanagh didn't look too pleased about that. The delicate blond student, Tim MacDonald, also was missing. Hammond was pulling Jacob Bernstein around the room, but they weren't dancing. Gideon Grimes was sitting where he'd been before.

"I do photography," Shelton whispered into Troy's ear.

"And teach a class in it too, I understand," Troy responded.

"I do some special photography, for special clients. Hammond said at the table that you may have trouble coming up with tuition money. Maybe I can help. Do you have any tattoos? Any birthmarks or other blemishes on your body?"

Troy didn't answer and after a moment, Shelton went on. "Have you done any all-male porn films? There's good money in that."

"Time to mix and match again," Hammond said, cheerily as he gently pried Shelton off of Troy. Troy wasn't sure if Hammond had heard the proposition and intervened because of that or not, but Troy was relieved he'd shown up.

"It's time to get Gideon out on the floor, and you're the one to do it, Troy," Hammond said.

Troy wasn't as relieved anymore. He'd enjoyed the table conversation with the novelist—if one can enjoy exchanging griefs about missing partners—but he'd gotten the clear impression that the man didn't want to be here. And he didn't see it as his, Troy's, responsibility to jolly the man up. Of everyone here, Troy was the one who could understand why Grimes wouldn't be in a party mood.

It took Hammond to get the two dancing, but Grimes was polite enough about it. "I have clumsy feet," Grimes said.

173

"Maybe it would be best if we went out in the conservatory for more space to have a go at it."

They did and Troy found that Grimes didn't have clumsy feet at all—that he was a great dancer. Troy fit comfortably in his arms. There was a nice scent about the man—something pine and clean—and they resumed their conversation of how difficult life was for them now and how hard it was to fight loneliness. "And to make up for what the other did all of those years," Grimes said. "I'm a klutz at anything technical. I haven't bothered to look for the thermostat in my house since my wife died, and it's getting colder. I wouldn't know what to do with it if I did find it."

"I know what you mean," Troy responded. "Aaron was always saying the same thing—that he'd be lost without me. I took care of all of the technical and mechanical issues in the place. But I found that it's I who am lost now. My apartment is spick and span from top to bottom but I miss what he brought to the relationship. I wish he was there, making his little messes that he didn't clean up and screwing up his home maintenance projects."

"I wouldn't know where to start on a home maintenance project," Grimes said. "I'm impressed that you are so capable in that department. You smell nice too," he added.

They were dancing closer together, swaying with the music. Troy felt the heat coming off the man—the sexual heat. And were they close enough together that he could feel arousal in Gideon as well? Yes he thought so. But then, Grimes suddenly stopped and his hold loosened on Troy. He lowered his hand hold, although he didn't let go of Troy's hand. Rather he was squeezing it tighter. Troy looked up into Gideon's face, to see that the man was looking beyond him, and his eyes were big. Then Troy saw it too.

There was a space amid the tall tropical plants where a chaise lounge had been placed. The lighting was dim, but Troy was able to pick out three figures—all naked. He immediately knew why the Kroger clerk, Peter Lambert, had been invited to the party. He was the invited rent-boy entertainment. He was stretched out on his back on the lounge bed, his legs raised and spread. Dale Hunter was crouched between his legs and over his body and was fucking him. Brad, naked, was standing beside them, stroking his cock and watching them fuck. Lambert was grabbing Dale's shoulders in his hands and was moving his pelvis in counter thrust to Dale's cock, fully participating in the fuck and taking Dale deep and hard. Brad moved closer to Lambert's face and the clerk opened his mouth to take in Brad's shaft.

Troy felt Gideon suck in breath, but he didn't move. He had his eyes glued to the sex scene. He was squeezing Troy's hand hard, but Troy couldn't feel the pain. He was equally glued to the spot at the surprise and shock of what he saw. As they watched, Hunter ejaculated and pulled himself off Lambert. As he pulled away, Brad was turning Lambert and raising the young man on his knees. He was holding Lambert from behind just as he had held Troy earlier in the wine cellar. Lambert was allowing himself to be manipulated into any position Brad wanted him in. Brad covered the young man's mouth with one hand, used the other to position his cock, and then snaked his arm around Lambert's belly. The clutching and release of his bulbous butt cheeks and movement of his pelvis were evidence that he was fucking the grocery store clerk with deep strokes. He was fucking Lambert just like he had fucked Troy earlier. Hunter stood by, working his cock.

Troy heard the rumbling in Grimes's throat and turned his face up to the novelist's face, only, surprisingly, to feel Grimes's lips on his. Troy instinctively opened his mouth to Grimes, and they kissed, hungrily, as Grimes pulled Troy close into his body. There was no mistaking feeling the urgency of the need of the novelist's body this time. Troy melted in the older man's grasp.

But then Grimes released him, growled a "Sorry, so sorry. I didn't mean to . . . sorry," and he fled the conservatory. Troy stayed on for a few more minutes, watching Brad fucking the young man who obviously had been invited here to provide just this service for Hammond's guests. But he wasn't really seeing the sex scene. He was fixated on the urgency and neediness of Grimes's kiss.

When Troy entered the living room, he sought out Hammond and mumbled, still feeling numb. "Sorry, Avril, I need to leave. It's late and I have studying to do."

"Oh, what a shame." He made no effort to dissuade Troy. "Did you drive over?" Avril asked.

"Yes, yes I did."

"Then can you do a favor? Gideon says he has to go home now too, but I brought him over from his house. His car is in the shop. Would you be a dear and give him a ride home? He's upstairs retrieving his coat."

"Sure, I'd be happy to," Troy said. His insides were doing flip-flops. Did Avril set all of this up? Was Gideon Grimes in on this? Was this just something the two of them hatched up to get Troy hooked up with Grimes? No, that couldn't be. At least he couldn't imagine the novelist being in on the planning. He'd opened up so slowly and then he'd have to have been a great actor to have feigned the surprise at seeing Brad and Dale fucking the Kroger clerk.

Would taking Grimes home and ending up in his bed be a bad thing, though? Troy couldn't think of a single reason why it would be. But then he could. He couldn't see Grimes in a casual lay situation. There was a vulnerability about him—about them both. Troy had to be careful about attachments that could go beyond the casual satiation of sexual need.

Grimes was coming down the stairs with his coat as Troy was going up the stairs to retrieve his. The man still looked like he was in shock and moved like a zombie.

"Avril has asked me to drive you home, Mr. Grimes," Troy said. "I'll just be a minute. I'll get my coat."

"Gideon. Call me Gideon. No mister." His tone was a monotone and the words came out stilted. But then he stopped and put a hand on Troy's forearm and whispered, "Sorry" again.

Troy said "Sure thing," as he went past Grimes on the stairs. He was embarrassed that Grimes repeated the apology. The kiss had aroused him. It wasn't anything to be sorry for as far as he was concerned. Was Grimes sorry he'd kissed Troy? He'd found the kiss wanting? Should Troy be insulted? Damned if he knew.

When he got to the top of the stairs, he saw why the man still seemed to be in shock. One of the bedroom doors was open to the hall—not the bedroom the coats were in but another one—and he could see Chan Tang, naked, straddling Tim MacDonald, also naked, on the bed. Tim was on his belly on the bed, his pelvis elevated on pillows, and his arms were stretched above his head, his hands clutching the rungs of the headboard overhead. The bed was rocking against the wall and Chan was riding Tim's ass hard. There was a wide-eyed expression on Tim's face and tears in his eyes. The man Chan had brought to the party, the history instructor, Cory Kavanagh, was sitting, knees folded into his chest, against the wall beside the bed, rocking back and forth and watching his partner hard fuck the young student.

* * * *

"Can you come in?" It came out as almost a plea. Troy had pulled up to the front of a substantial-looking old, wooden house, although one that needed attention. None of the leaves had been raked in the yard yet and a shutter was hanging askew on a window on the second story. He hesitated in answering. He felt he'd been in a marathon as he drove across town, into the countryside, and to the Civil War battle town of Port Republic, where two branches of the Shenandoah River met. Grimes had spoken the entire time about his wife, Penny, about what a saint she was and how much of a loss she was to him. The man was throwing out conflicting—and, it seemed, conflicted—vibes. The kiss at Hammond's house had been genuine—needy—and Hammond had good as said that he and Grimes had been fuck buddies before Grimes met his wife.

But he'd repeatedly said he was sorry he'd kissed Troy. Was all of this talk about his perfect wife a barrier he was raising against Troy thinking he would now be interested in another man sexually? Troy wasn't sure himself if he was ready to move on, but it certainly seemed like this guy wasn't.

"Please," Grimes repeated, "do come in. It was good for me to talk about this. I've had it bottled up inside. And it's good that you listened. I'd like to return the favor, if you want

177

to talk about Aaron." He touched Troy's arm as Troy gripped the wheel of the car with both hands but immediately drew his fingers away as if Troy's arm was hot or he thought better of the gesture.

There was a pause in which each man focused on the breathing of the other. "OK, for a few minutes," Troy answered. Who was he kidding? He'd stay long enough for Grimes to fuck him, if the guy could decide he was up to it. He knew that. He just didn't know if Grimes realized that yet. Something had happened between them. A surge of electric want had gone through them both in that kiss and in the shared observance of three men fucking that neither had pulled themselves away from immediately. A fuck was what they both needed—a casual fuck in which both decided the other wasn't for them in the longer term. It would be a sexual release for both but would also let each return to his safe place, knowing that anything further wouldn't work out. Troy wouldn't have said yes to coming in if he wasn't hoping for a fuck, though. There was something about this guy—he was special—if he could just decide what he wanted.

If Troy could decide that Gideon wasn't what he wanted for anything longer term.

They walked up onto the front porch, close to each other, but not touching—purposely, Troy wondered, confused by the mixed signals. Grimes had trouble opening the front door—first because he seemed to be trembling too much to get the key in the slot and then because the door stuck a bit and he had to apply force to open it.

"It's been sticking like this for a couple of weeks," Grimes said. "It must be the weather."

"I think it's more a loose hinge," Troy said, reaching up to touch the upper hinge. "I could fix that for you, I'm sure."

"You could?" Grimes asked, moving his hand up to cover Troy's, and looking down into the young man's face. They exchanged looks of raw need, but then Grimes looked and moved away and swung the door open. Once inside, though, and the door shut, Troy pulled Grimes around and close, reached up and cupped the back of the head of the older man, and pulled his face down to where their eyes met again. "Kiss me," he murmured. "I know you want to."

Without seeking agreement, Troy pulled Gideon's face down to his and took his lips in a tentative kiss. The kiss went hungry for both men.

Coming out of it, Troy spoke in a strangled voice. "Fuck me. You know you want to. I think we both need laid bad."

A growl came up from deep in Gideon's chest and he grabbed Troy by the waist and lifted and slammed the back of the smaller man against the wall by the door. He took over the kiss, hungrily pushing Troy's lips open with his and giving him tongue. Troy moaned.

When they came out of the kiss, Gideon's body relaxed and he set Troy's feet back down on the floor. He started to say something, a look in his eyes that Troy didn't want to see, but the student raised the fingers of a hand to Gideon's lips, and said, "Don't. Don't say you're sorry. Don't say it again. Don't be sorry for something we both want—that we both need. Fuck me."

Gideon gave him a wan smile and took a step away from him. "I'll go put the coffee on and then I want to listen to you talk of your life and circumstance. I've said enough tonight."

Troy struggled hard to regain his dignity. Better to pretend he hadn't just begged the man for something the man wasn't ready to give him. "Better that you turn the heat up," he said. "It's colder than a witch's tit in here."

"If I only knew where the thermostat was," Gideon said, showing that wan smile again. "It was something that Penny—"

"Shhh," Troy countered. "It's right here, on the wall beside my head. But I don't think that's the problem. Have you turned the system on yet for the season?"

"Turned the system on? That would have been something Penny would have done. And she—"

"Where's your heater?"

"In the basement . . . I think."

"You think? Jesus, you seriously need a handyman here."

They both tensed and their eyes met. Troy seriously needed to be fucked. He thought Gideon did too, but the man was fighting it hard. It was Troy who broke the awkwardness. He stripped off his coat and said, "I'll go exploring, starting with the basement. If the system's working at all, I'll get it turned on for you."

It took a while. The basement of the old house, which Gideon said had been standing here while a Civil War battle was being fought around it, was a rat's warren. No one had been down here and tidied up for some time. He eventually found the heating system, turned it on, and waited until it kicked in, which it did. When he came upstairs into the kitchen, the first thing he saw was a sink full of dirty dishes. The second thing was Gideon, standing over by a perking coffee pot. He had changed—stripped down. He was wearing a knee-length silk robe. And nothing else. His sash was loosely bound around his waist. It was open down to his navel, showing good muscle tone—excellent for a man his age—and a matting of salt-and-pepper hair that curled around his nipples and descended in a thin line to the sash. The lower part of the robe flared enough for Troy to see a trimmed bush and a jutting cock. The man was hung and was aroused.

Confused again by the mixed signals, Troy mumbled, "I got the heater started," and walked straight to the sink, searched in the cabinet beneath and found dish detergent, and started filling the sink with soapy water.

"I heard," Gideon said in a low, hoarse voice. "But I don't think we need any extra heat for a while. You probably think I didn't hear you, but I did. I just don't want to hurt you."

"But you stripped down anyway, didn't you?"

"Yes."

"Even in spite of your reservations, you're going to fuck me, aren't you?"

"Yes, I'm going to fuck you. You can stay the night, can't you? We can save any regrets for the morning."

He came in close behind Troy, who turned the water off and braced himself on arms stretched out to the side, hands gripping the edges of the counter. He moaned and turned his head to Gideon's possessing kiss. As they kissed, Gideon stripped Troy all the way down, unbuttoning his shirt and pulling it off the young man's back, unbuckling and unzipping his trousers and slipping those and Troy's briefs to the floor. Troy stepped out of them as Gideon's hand cupped and weighed and measured Troy's balls and engorging cock with a hand.

"Nice," he murmured. "You have a beautiful body. So smooth, like marble."

Gideon took Troy's lips into another kiss. When he released them, he buried his face in the hollow of Troy's throat and repeated the compliment. "You're so nice, so young and beautiful. It's been so long. Can I? Will you let me? I need this so bad."

"Yes, oh yes," Troy murmured. He felt the insistence of the man at the small of his back and then lower, between his thighs. He squeezed his thighs on the long, thick shaft, and Gideon was dry humping him, similarly to, but more arousingly than Brad had done earlier, the side of the cock rubbing back and forth on Troy's hole. Troy felt himself blossoming open.

"Can I here . . . now? . . . or . . ."

"Here . . . now . . . on the counter."

Heavy breathing took over anything they might have said. There was nothing to be said, really, and Gideon required no instruction or further permission. He was dominating Troy now—just as Aaron had dominated Troy. In matters of sex, Aaron had always dominated. That's how Troy had wanted it then. That's how Troy wanted it now. And the best sex had been spontaneous—and anywhere the mood had hit them.

He didn't want Gideon to ask for permission for anything again. He wanted Gideon to take whatever he wanted.

Gideon knelt behind him and grasped his hips, digging his thumbs into Troy's butt cheeks and spreading them open. With a moan, Troy widened his stance and Gideon buried his face in Troy's crack and ate out his ass. It was all smooth, deliberate . . . effective.

181

Gideon came back up close behind Troy and Troy saw, out of the corner of his eye, the split condom packet—Trojan Magnum Ribbed—flutter to the countertop. Grasping Troy's hips again, Gideon lifted the young man's feet off the floor. He was being lowered on the cock, which penetrated, penetrated, penetrated him, as Gideon wrapped an arm around his waist, Troy arched his torso back and grasped the back of Gideon's head in both his hands. He opened his mouth in a big O and blew bubbles, shuddered, panted hard, and came close to hyperventilating as the thick cock relentlessly invaded up his channel into the soft, vulnerable core of him, stretching him in its progress. The muscles of his passage walls began to ripple over the corkscrew effect of the ribbed condom sheathing a throbbing, steel-hard conquering weapon.

The cock in deep, and Troy fully vanquished, quivering and moaning, Gideon snaked his free hand around, grasped Troy's cock and balls, and began to stroke him off in the same slow, slightly off-beat rhythm of the deep fuck.

After a few minutes, Gideon pulled Troy away from the sink, laid him down on his side on the kitchen table, and slung Troy's right leg up his torso. Troy's left leg was hung over the back of a chair pulled up to the table. His left hand was clutching the edge of the table, holding him steady under the hard, long, quickening thrusts of Gideon's cock. He was squeezing Gideon's right bicep with his right hand. Gideon was stroking him off with his left hand. Gideon was taking him hard, deep, and vigorously, the rapidity of the thrusts increasing, becoming more frenzied, more demanding. It was all Gideon now, taking the younger man fully, mercilessly, and Troy loved it this way. No mixed signals or indecision now.

"Come for me," Gideon growled as he felt Troy tense up, and Troy responded as demanded. Then it was Gideon's turn to ejaculate, which he did in the condom deep inside Troy's ass.

Afterward, they sat next to each other on a leather sofa in the living room, coffee finally served. Gideon was in his silk robe, flared open, hiding nothing, half hard. Troy was just in his briefs. Gideon put his coffee cup down—Troy hadn't lifted his from the coffee table yet—and leaned over into Troy for a kiss, during which he ran his hand over Troy's chest, paying attention to the young man's taut nipples.

"I am sorry, if—" Gideon said, coming out of the kiss.

Once more Troy put his fingers to the man's mouth, and said, "No more 'sorry,' I told you. All sorrow and guilt are banished here. Neither one of us is sorry. There is no guilt in seizing what we want, no loved ones to betray." Then, "Are you going to fuck me again now?" he asked, "because you certainly can. I want you to."

"Eventually, I hope . . . if you want," Gideon answered. "It will take time, though. I'm an old man."

"You don't fuck like an old man. You don't feel like an old man." He had his hand encasing Gideon's long cock. The man was half hard and hardening more at Troy's touch. But Gideon pulled away and settled back in the sofa. Troy continued slow-stroking his shaft.

"I spilled my gut to you about my departed wife. Tell me about your Aaron."

"What is there to tell?" Troy said. "He was good to me—in all ways. He was good to me sexually like you just were."

"Your relationship. Were you yin and yang like I said Penny and I were. Were you different people, with different interests, but fit together perfectly when joined?"

"When you fucked me in the kitchen, I felt like we were one, synchronized machine, yes. And that's the way it was with Aaron and me too."

"Yes, but in other aspects of your relationship. I'm a drone. There's one thing I do well. I write well—and profitably. And I think I teach well—about writing, about nothing else. I'm technically clueless, and I don't keep schedules. That was all Penny. But she enjoyed it and she was content with me the way I am. Did you and Aaron fit like that—yin and yang, completing a perfect circle?"

"Yes," Troy answered after a bit of thought, "that was Aaron and me too, except we were reversed. Aaron was great with clothes and with clothes buying, but he was messy as hell about everything else and all thumbs with anything involving handyman work. I did that for him. I even came to his house and did it for him and his family without his wife knowing he was fucking me—until he unexpectedly died and tried to leave stuff to me."

"It's rare for couples to meld like that," Gideon said.

"Yes, I think you're right. And what about you and Avril Hammond? Was he right—that you two were a couple before you married your wife? Did you and Hammond fit together like that?"

"Alas, no. Yes, we were lovers, but it was volatile, and we switched back and forth on what we wanted and needed, never being on the same page at once. I think that's why I escaped so radically—why I went with a woman, with Penny. I wanted stability and monogamy and Avril was sleeping around. And then when I married Penny and was initially interested in going with them both, Avril demanded sole possession. By the time he came around to sharing me with Penny, I no longer wanted to be shared—by then it was just Penny. And has been until just now. I can't tell you how happy you've made me tonight. I struggled with it but I'm so happy I gave in. I hope you are too."

"Yes, I am. I think I wanted it before you did. That worries me. You keep trying to say you're sorry. Are you sorry you've done it with me? Not quite sure still, or what?"

Gideon laughed, which hit Troy wrong. The young man took his hand off Gideon's now-rock hard cock, and leaned away from him into the corner of the sofa, turning his back slightly to the sofa arm.

"No, don't mistake the laugh," Gideon said. "It wasn't that I didn't want you. I wanted you when we were talking at dinner. It's because of Hammond. He gave me the impression that he was throwing the two of us together, and I didn't want it to be that easy for him. I didn't want to fall into something just because he had pity on me and was throwing me a bone. It was the sort of thing he'd done when we were together to show his dominance when I wanted to dominate in a relationship. But maybe you didn't get the impression from the Thanksgiving dinner—that it was all set up to get us together."

It was Troy's turn to laugh. "No, that's exactly what I thought he was doing—that he was pitying me and trying to set me up with another sugar daddy."

"Cheeky of him, but I still worry about Avril," Gideon said. "I think he's chosen wrong this time. I think he now wants permanence and a life mate. I don't think that Brad Baylor is going to give that to him. You saw what Brad was doing at the party—fucking that rent-boy Hammond had brought in. I don't see Baylor being faithful to Avril. Do you?"

"No, I don't," Troy agreed, looking away so that Gideon didn't see Troy's own contribution to Brad's betrayal of Hammond in his face. His hand went back to Gideon's cock, finding it in full erection. "I think we've talked enough for now, though," he murmured. "You seem to be ready again."

"Yes, I'm ready again," Gideon answered in a low, hoarse voice. "I'm ready for more even. I sense that this isn't going to be just a one-night stand. Could you possibly—?"

"I sense the same thing," Troy answered.

Gideon twisted toward Troy in the sofa, turning Troy too so that his back was fully pressed to the sofa arm. He grasped Troy's legs after stripping off his briefs, and bent them and pressed them up into Troy's chest, Troy's knees going into his armpits. At the same time, he spread Troy's thighs and lowered his face to Troy's crotch. Troy grasped the wavy hair at the back of Gideon's head, arched his back, and moaned, as Gideon prepared the young man for mounting again with his mouth working Troy's cock, balls, and hole.

He rose up and crouched over Troy, teasing the young man's hole with his cock head and deep kissing Troy on the mouth. He was taking his time preparing Troy, just as he had in the kitchen, and he was putting the young man into high heat. Troy broke away from the kiss and cried out, "Fuck me. Fuck me now. Put it in me. Pound me!"

The cock head was pressing at his hole, and Troy was willing his muscles down there to grasp it and pull it inside. He didn't care that it was unsheathed. He didn't care if Gideon barebacked him. He wanted the cock inside him, and he wanted it now.

Once again, out of the corner of his eye, he saw the slit Trojan Magnum packet hit the coffee table top, and he gave a great sigh as the cock bulb positioned itself at his entrance. Gideon was holding him close from above, completely controlling and dominating him, rocking him back and forth against the arm of the sofa, teasing his entrance by rubbing the bulb head over it again and again. Troy grasped the man's shoulder blades with his hands, dug his nails into the flesh, and cried out, "Yes, yes. Stick it in. Fuck me to heaven!"

Gideon moved a strong hand around to the V where Troy's tailbone descended to between his butt cheeks and gave Troy's lower back a strong pull, impaling the young man's passage in one swift movement on the cock to the soft core of his gut. Troy cried out in pain-passion-pleasure and Gideon commenced pumping him deep.

* * * *

Avril stood at the door, watching what he assumed were the last of the Thanksgiving dinner guests, the art professor, Lawrence Shelton, and music instructor, Cory Kavanagh, off. He turned and looked around the living room. Brad certainly had his work cut out for him getting this straightened up tomorrow, he thought. Good thing Brad was neat. It was always important that one of a couple be good that way.

He looked up in surprise as he saw the rent-boy, Peter Lambert, nearly stumble into the living room from the conservatory. He was wearing his jeans, but his T-shirt was hanging on his bare shoulder—and were those his briefs tucked under his arm? He was looking good—very sexy. He looked dazed and sleepy, but it made Avril think of bed and fucking. If Avril had any interest in topping . . . but he didn't. Avril had forgotten the young man, although he had his fee for the evening in his pocket. His hand went to his pocket to ensure the wad of money was still there. He wondered if the young man had earned his keep. It had been Brad's idea to bring him in for the party.

"Peter," he said. "You're still here."

186

"Yes, but I'm leaving now," Lambert answered. Over the course of the evening, he'd taken four of the five tops who had attended the party, only missing out on the novelist, who Peter had been most interested in shagging. He'd even been given an address card by that big photographer guy, There was a possibly to be paid bigger bucks for it—to appear in a movie or two. "I just needed . . . I wondered . . ."

"Yes, I can pay you now, while you're here." Avril took the bills out of his pocket and handed them over. "Have you seen Brad? I haven't seen him in a while."

"No, I've been busy," Lambert said, resisting the urge to turn and look back into the conservatory where Brad had just finished fucking him for the second time that night. "It's been interesting. If you ever need me again—"

"Yes, yes, thank you. Brad will know how to get in touch with you, I'm sure."

He walked the young man to the front door.

In the conservatory, crouched between the spread thighs of the Jewish student in the English department, Jacob Bernstein, who was on his back on the chaise lounge, moaning softly, Brad Baylor stopped in mid thrust to listen to the conversation between Avril and Peter in the living room. As Avril was walking the rent-boy to the front door, Brad finished Bernstein, his hand held over the young man's mouth to muffle his reaction to being stroked off hard and deep.

Pulling off Bernstein's body and reaching down for his trousers, Brad hissed, "Leave quietly by the door out into the garden. When I want you again, I'll find you."

"Yes, please," Bernstein whimpered, his eyes full of worship.

There was an entrance from the conservatory into the kitchen, and Brad, fully dressed, was there, working over a sink of pots and pans, when Avril found him.

"Well, I think that went well, don't you?" Hammond asked, coming up behind Brad and kissing him on the back of the neck. He wrapped his hands around Brad, one hand descending to the man's crotch.

"Yes, very well indeed," Baylor answered.

"I'm tired, but not too tired," Hammond whispered. "Leave this for tomorrow and I'll meet you in bed."

When Hammond was finished in the bathroom and padded out into the bedroom, naked, he found that Brad was already in bed, turned to the wall on his side, and snoring up a storm.

Oh, well, Avril thought, he enjoyed morning sex as much as nighttime sex. He lay there, feeling very smug with himself. As far as he could see, his ploy was working. He'd seen Brad with Troy. He could tell that Brad wanted to stick it to Troy. It had been hell trying to keep Brad in line, but Avril would do everything he could do accomplish that. He wanted to settle down in a monogamous relationship at this time of his life—and he knew that Brad was the one he wanted to settle down with. Troy was vulnerable, just coming out of a grieving situation. Avril had thought hard about how to shunt Brad off from going after Troy. Avril's old friend, Gideon, also had needed a new relationship. All in all, Avril thought that putting Troy and Gideon together would settle Brad down. He went to sleep masturbating himself and thinking of what Gideon and Troy might be doing at the moment. It was a godsend that Gideon had needed a ride home.

* * * *

It was still in the dark of the night when Gideon woke in his bed to arousal. It took him a moment to realize that he wasn't in bed alone, as he had been for the past couple of months. Someone—Troy he quickly realized—was below him, sucking his cock and balls and running his hands up and down on Gideon's inner thighs. Gideon contentedly sighed and folded his arms behind his head. He would give Troy free rein for a few moments, but he remembered what the young man had said—that what he wanted was a partner who dominated him.

When Troy had moved up Gideon's body, straddled his pelvis, positioned his hole on Gideon's cock head, and descended on the shaft, Gideon gave Troy a few moments of control. But then he grasped Troy's hips in his hands and took over control, slamming Troy up and down on his buried cock while he counterthrust up with his hips. Troy cried out in ecstasy as he flopped around under Gideon's full control, riding the cock like he was riding a bull—which, to Troy's delight, was exactly what he felt he was doing.

Hours later, in daylight now, Gideon woke again to the sound of a hammer hitting a nail head into wood just outside his bedroom window. Once again he initially was disoriented. He reached out with both hands, searching for another body— at first thinking Penny, but quickly changing to an image of Troy. But he was alone in the bed. He felt the sting of loss.

As he became fully conscious, though, he figured out that someone was outside his window, repairing the broken shutter. With surging hope, he connected Troy's absence with the repairing of the shutter—and he hoped to hell that that meant what he wished for it to mean. To hell with resenting Avril's sure satisfaction that his ploy had worked. Happy Thanksgiving after all.

Tantric Teng

"I miss you too. But I'm glad the children are having fun at the beach."

I looked at Richard where he was leaning against the kitchen counter, turned away from me. He was still naked, trim and muscular for a man of thirty-five who indulged himself in everything—and could afford to do so. That everything included a gym and a good personal trainer, though. He'd come from the shower with a towel around his waist, but that had dropped to the kitchen floor while he was talking with his wife. He didn't seem the least bit embarrassed that had happened, nor should he have been, I guess, other than he was talking to his wife on the telephone—in front of his boy toy. We'd both been naked on my bed, me writhing under him as he tried hard to fuck me, before he'd taken his shower.

But there was embarrassment there. He wouldn't look at me while he talked to his wife, who had taken their children to her parent's house in the Hamptons for the month of July.

His eggs were getting cold, but I'd be damned if I'd cook up another batch for him because he was on his cell phone, talking to his wife. Clarissa hadn't called him. He'd called her, no doubt just to be sure she was still in the Hamptons and so that she wouldn't call him on their home phone before he left for work and wonder why he didn't answer there.

When he rang off, he came over and sat at the table in the bow window overlooking the Baltimore Inner Harbor from my apartment at the Promenade at Harbor East. He left the towel on the carpet back by the kitchen counter. This was a choice one-bedroom apartment and I couldn't afford the rent, but Richard paid half of it. He sat, without embarrassment, with his thighs spread and his manhood tipping over the front of the chair—just like Richard Hineman owned the place. And just like he owned me as well. I guess both were true, even though the arrangement wasn't working smoothly yet. I had to give him credit for trying to make it work, though.

He still wouldn't look at me while he ate, although, just wearing sleeping shorts, I knew I looked good to him—ten years his junior and with the look of a model, which I'd first been when I came to work for his men's clothing firm. I had a desk job there now, but I still modeled for his catalog—and laid on my back and opened my legs to him—not yet as successfully as either of us wished, though.

We'd tried again last night, taking advantage of the absence of Clarissa and his children, with him staying the whole night and fucking me three times. He'd managed to get off all three times, but it had been an effort and I know he wasn't fully satisfied. I know he'd been looking forward to an all-nighter without worrying about where his wife and kids were and not being available for Clarissa's possessive beck and call. I know he also was looking forward to me being comfortable enough to open entirely to him, to let him sink all the way into me and pump me deep. He wasn't that big that I shouldn't be able to take more than four inches of him.

All of our encounters before that had been furtive and rushed. I know he had thought that I wasn't melting to him because of that, and I had thought that too, but last night I had frozen in the act as much as ever before, and he'd had to take his pleasure with me tensed up and gripped with pain and him not being able to get it in to the hilt. He was hung but not overly so. But he was the first man I'd let screw me, and I just wasn't loosening up, even though I wanted to.

God knows I wanted to enjoy it. He was my boss and I was his toy. And he was good looking and in good shape. He was going to fuck me if he wanted to and I wanted to keep my cushy job and lifestyle, but I wanted him to enjoy it and I wanted to enjoy it too. And it seemed so important to him to put it all in me.

I didn't want to think it was his fault—there was no question that he didn't want to think it was his fault—but it wasn't like I was an expert in this. I just felt that, maybe if he spent more time preparing me rather than forcing it in and starting to pump as soon as I'd sucked it hard, with him going hard quickly . . .

He finished his eggs, mumbling something that passed as thanks for fixing him breakfast, and went back into the bedroom to dress. I'd shower after he left. He didn't want us to arrive at the office at the same time. He didn't want there to be any talk of the two of us. In fact, he went overboard in flirting with the office women to avoid any suspicion that he was spiking—or trying to—one of his male employees. That must be working, because every time I'd seen him with his wife, she was watching him like a hawk when he was interacting with another woman. She didn't show such suspicion when he and I were talking.

I heard him on the cell phone again in the bedroom, and when he came out, elegantly dressed as the CEO of a men's clothing empire would need to be, he looked at me for the first time since I'd gone rigid when he'd forced himself in me the previous night and just lay there, groaning as he worked his way to an ejaculation without much response from me—and without getting more than maybe three inches in me before I started closing down. Each time I'd taken considerable time jacking myself off after he'd come and withdrawn from me, stretched out beside me, smoking a cigarette, and staring at the ceiling. Sometimes watching me jack off heated him up again and he made another run at me—never with enough success to fully satisfy him, though.

"I want to meet you for lunch at a Chinese restaurant near the corner of South Broadway on Eastern Avenue, Marco," he said. "The Jade Garden. It's just a hole in the wall. Meet me at 1:00 and check out of the office for the rest of the afternoon. I have you booked for a photo shoot over at Fort

McHenry, but there isn't really one. I'll supposedly be at a meeting in Washington. I want you to be there, at the restaurant, though. That'll give us the time to do what we need to do."

The time to do what, I wondered. But Richard wasn't a man you quizzed about anything he didn't freely tell you. God knows he was keeping secrets even from his wife.

He was giving me a piercing look of command, just as he'd done that night we'd both worked late and I gave him a blow job that he said was memorable. He clearly enjoyed dominating and I didn't think I'd mind being submissive. I just hadn't been able to get comfortable with it yet. And I needed to. I enjoyed the lifestyle this apartment gave me and the free clothes I got from working for Richard—and I even found Richard sexy. It just wasn't clicking with him yet.

It was the first time I'd been with a man all the way and it was the first time that he had tried a relationship with a man. All of his lays before that had been casual, with rent-boys, and he was clear about wanting something deeper, more mutually satisfying, with me. I was grateful that he was trying with me. I didn't know what the problem was—whether it was me, him, or us. It wasn't our bodies. We were both in superb shape and we both went hard just from seeing the other one naked. He was of solid Nordic stock and my family on both sides had been Brazilian. We fit together in theory like Yin and Yang, both in size, him being large boned and light skinned, and me being smaller, delicate-boned, and darker.

Another surprise for me was that I had had no idea that Richard liked Chinese food. He seemed much more the straightforward steak and fries man. I wasn't much for Chinese either, sticking pretty close to citric salads to keep in trim. The camera put on weight; it didn't take it off.

* * * *

Richard was just pushing his food around on his plate. I was doing about the same, although I did take a bite or two from time to time. It was OK—I mean the food was OK. Richard was stewing about something, I could tell. But he hadn't spoken much. He certainly hadn't told me why we were having lunch here.

"Anyone show any suspicion why you were leaving early?" he asked.

"No, not that I saw. I wasn't looking for it, though. You provided a perfectly plausible explanation for both of us," I said. "Why are we here, Rich?" I added.

"It'll be OK, baby," was the only cryptic response to that. I hadn't really expected an answer. I just wanted some said to pop the bubble of tension in the booth. "Excuse me a few minutes. I'll be back," he said, and then he slid out of the booth, spoke briefly to a waitress, and then went through a doorway at the back of the restaurant that was covered by a beaded curtain. Off to the can, I thought, and took a few more bites of food. He was gone a good ten minutes, more like fifteen, and when he returned, he was followed by a Chinese man of about forty who was quite handsome and hard bodied. He wore a tight T-shirt that showed him to be muscular and well-developed, particularly for his age. My eyes, as they tended to do ever since I knew I was interested in men, went to the bulge at his crotch. The material there was stretched tight over something quite impressive.

Richard slid back into the booth across from me, and the Chinese man slid in next to me, causing me to move more toward the wall. His thigh was against mine and his bicep pressed into mine. He felt hard as a rock, and I found him arousing. Getting aroused by a man wasn't a problem I had— not even imagining myself lying under a man. My brain was certainly filled with thoughts of lying under this man.

"Your friend here says you two are having difficulty in your sexual relationship," the man said, turning a concerned smile to me. His voice was soft, a rich baritone. My forearm was on the table and he took my hand in his and wove our fingers together. My thoughts of him inside me had been so real that I made no effort to pull my hand away from this intimacy. Still the first thing that had come out of his mouth was so baldly sexual that I was off balance.

"Excuse me? I'm not sure—" I'm sure my voice sounded strained. What was going on here? Still, I found the man disturbingly arousing.

"This is Eddie Teng, baby," Richard said, breaking into my expression of confusion and concern. "He owns this restaurant, but he also is a counselor in tantric sex—gay tantric sex. I called him this morning about your discomfort and tensing up when I fuck you—and not letting me in. He was recommended to me at the gym."

"You've been talking about my sexual problems at the gym?" I asked, nearly swallowing my words. Teng's hand gripped mine strongly as if to tell me that he understood and to remain calm. Richard certainly didn't seem to understand. And what he said next didn't make it any better.

"Mr. Teng uses massage—he calls it tantric massage— and he's a surrogate sex partner. I understand he can calm you down for sex and help you to open to it."

"Can he now?" I said, looking down at the table top, thoroughly embarrassed and angry, but not wanting to show it. I had too much riding on a relationship with Richard to fly off the handle. But, shit, I didn't think this was all my problem. The Chinese hunk was rubbing his thigh against mine, and I was warming to him more than I'd done with Richard yet and we were just sitting next to each other. "Do you mean he's going to fuck me?"

"If you and your partner wish, I'm going to work you through the stages of becoming one with the cosmos in a mutually fulfilling Yin and Yang relationship," Teng answered for Richard in a soothing voice and with a reassuring smile. "I understand that you, Marco, are the Yin of the pair—the female essence—and Richard here is the Yang, the male dominator. If you wish me to I will guide you two—both of you"—and here he moved his hand under the table and grasped the top of my thigh. I understood that he was conveying to me the understanding that this wasn't just my problem, that the instruction would be for both of us, and I melted to the man—"through the phases of getting the most pleasure you can—both of you—from Karezza."

"Karezza?" I asked.

"Yes, that is the tantric term for prolonged arousal and fulfillment. I will teach you both how to master Karezza to embrace the natural energies of your bodies—you, Marco, being prepared in your Kundalini, your receiving channel, to take and give pleasure to Richard's Lingam—his staff of the Yang. It is the path for you to become one with the other."

"The problem is that I can't get it all in. He won't open completely to me. I want him to take it all, not to clinch on me," Richard interjected, with an edge of exasperation.

"Yes, yes, we will work on that," Teng said, the tone of his voice soothing.

"You will fuck me?" I asked, looking only at Teng.

"Yes, he will fuck you if it will help you open up and let me get the fuck from you that I want," Richard said, breaking in again, obviously impatient.

Teng responded as if Richard hadn't said anything. "I will take you on a long path before that, but yes, I will be Yang to your Yin as a surrogate for your lover. I will fully possess your Kundalini with my Lingam, helping you to take the full length and thickness of it, as your partner wishes you to be able to do with his Lingam, and I will do so while ensuring your pleasure. And if you are receptive—open to the experience—I will help both of you marshal your mutual sexual energy to maximize your ability to reach spiritual growth and healing together through the merging of your bodies. We will strive for Karezza—you with me first before you with your partner, if that is necessary. And I can see that you both have very fine bodies. I am confident that I can bring you to tantric Nirvana—to the plateau of sexual paradise—and that you can achieve it with each other."

I was close to coming just from his explanation of the services he was offering and from his lack of embarrassment in graphically, if flowery, talking of the most intimate act. But he was taking it beyond talk.

He took my hand and moved it to his crotch. He was huge. More important, he was hard. He was signaling to me that I aroused him and that he would go through this tantric business with me with pleasure. I already was panting. I didn't know if I swallowed any of this tantric gobbledygook that he was selling, but just hearing him talk about it aroused me. Having him touch me aroused me. What he was doing now—moving my hand, with his, to my own crotch, revealing to him that I was hard too—was bringing me close to hyperventilating. Richard hadn't brought me to this stage. Still, it was Richard I wanted to have the relationship with, not this Chinese guy.

Or so I was telling myself. I had to admit that my interests were tipping in that direction, though.

Teng leaned in and whispered in my ear, "I will teach your partner to seduce you as I am doing with you now. I *am* seducing you, aren't I?"

"Yes," I whispered. I wondered whether Richard had any inkling how much farther we'd gone beyond talk, with each of us getting the measure of the other with our hands below the surface of the table. Teng obviously was conveying to me that he understood that I needed attention that I wasn't getting from Richard.

"You would be ready for me to cover and fully possess you now, wouldn't you, if you had walked into my restaurant alone and sat with me here? You would be open to me—to all of me—as your lover wishes your Kundalini to be fully open to his Lingam, don't you believe?"

"Yes," I murmured.

"Good. You must believe it for it to transpire. You aren't nearly as open to it yet as you could be under my instruction. I will teach Richard to bring you to this point too—and beyond. To heaven—to tantric sexual Nirvana. Is that what you want?"

"Yes." I looked up at Richard. I could tell from his expression that he very much wanted to try this out. But I also knew that he still thought it was all my problem.

"When would we do this?" I asked.

"Now. My tantric method studio is here, at the back of the restaurant. Your partner has already engaged me for a full release session. All that awaits is your acquiescence. I believe you are ready. Tell me that you are ready."

"Yes, I am ready."

* * * *

The room Teng took us to behind the restaurant was like it was in another world. It was all stucco walls and arches and a pool with a burbling fountain and the ripple of its waters reflecting off the ceiling, silken pillows and wall hangings. He had us recline on a divan covered with pillows and look through a portfolio of beautiful men fucking younger men. Somehow he'd managed to pull together photos where the similarities between the men and Richard and me were striking. There were a couple of photos that included a Chinese man and the sexual positions and evident size of the man's cock aroused me in particular—and chills went up my spine when I realized that the man was Teng. He told us to arouse each other as he prepared the massage table, and Richard and I kissed and fondled each other as we'd never taken time to do before. I must admit that some of my thoughts went to Teng. They weren't all about Richard.

Already I was learning what had been missing in our lovemaking and I could only hope that Richard was learning it too. The foreplay was all important.

Teng had me strip—or rather had Richard strip me, taking as much time as he could to do so and, at Teng's instruction, to run his hands over my body as he did so. Then I was bid to do the same to Richard and Richard was told to stand by and watch as Teng gave me a massage with warm oil.

OK, I thought, this was just going to be like any massage. But, of course, it wasn't. Teng had sensual hands and he worked every muscle of my body—except the essential one, although I ached for him to stroke that and I got hard and throbbing before he was finished.

But he wasn't finished.

"Now for the Lingam," he said, by which I knew I now was going to get the attention for the cock that I was aching for. I looked over to Richard to make sure he was taking this in. He needed this, I realized, more than I did, but neither I nor Teng could directly tell him so. I sensed that Teng knew what the real problem here was. He was trying to teach Richard the importance of the foreplay, the preparation.

198

"You have a very nice Lingam. Do you ever give as well as receive?"

"I have never . . . given . . . no," I mumbled.

"Pity. I both give and receive." He let that possibility sear through my mind before moving on. "I will concentrate on the center now," Teng said. "I will open the Kundalini, although you may not realize it is happening until I could possess you with my whole fist if I wished or you begged for it."

That certainly brought a moan out of me. I heard Richard moan as well.

"You are to work with me in lingering just short of the release for as long as possible, but when it, at last, cannot be denied, release without embarrassment. We will continue until you have. And there will be more releases."

That latter comment was as arousing to me as anything else he was saying. The thought of achieving multiple ejaculations in this session . . .

With that, he positioned me on my back, a pillow under my neck and another one, covered with a towel, under the small of my back. "I will set you in the position you are to remain in," he said. He spread my thighs slightly apart, with my knees bent and my feet flat on the surface of the massage table. Then he dribbled me with oil and resumed massaging my body with a sensual touch, working his way up my body, starting with my feet, then my calf muscles, thighs, abdomen, chest, shoulders, and moving to behind me and working my neck muscles and my temples. He was naked now, and he let his long, thick cock nestle within the crook of my neck as he worked my temples.

"If you have the urge to take my Lingam into your mouth, do so," he murmured. He had told me that, as a surrogate sex partner and an illustration for Richard, I would be taking his cock in my mouth, he would be taking mine, and, ultimately, he would be fucking me—although even now he referred to it as fully possessing my Kundalini with his Lingam—"to the root," he added, for Richard's benefit and looking reassuringly at him. "But you are not to be concerned with any sexual urge you have in this session," he said.

"Nothing is beyond acceptability here if it brings pleasure. Even if you should wish to sheath both your partner and me together. That would be the height of sexual Nirvana. We could achieve that."

I almost hyperventilated on that suggestion.

The whole purpose of the session, he assured me was for me to be prepared for sexual relations and to be fulfilled and satisfied by them. "You are having trouble opening to the Lingam," he said. "When you have lost your anxiety over that, I could even service you with this, my fist, and you would open to it and take pleasure from it." He showed me his fist, and I shuddered. I realized he would be taking me far beyond my current comfort zone.

Even so, it took me by surprise when he pulled my body to where my head arched back at the head of the massage table, and he moved to massaging my cheeks and opening my mouth so that his cock could slide inside. I heard Richard's intake of breath as he stood off to the side, and it pleased me that he was paying attention. Even though he was longer and thicker than Richard was, I took Teng's cock into my throat with greater ease than I had experienced with Richard, and I felt confident that we'd already learned enough, the two of us, of what we needed to do to satisfy each other.

But we weren't anywhere close to the end of teaching.

I instinctively reached for my throbbing cock with my hands as Teng massaged my pectorals and slid his cock in and out of my mouth, but he commanded, "No. You may not touch it," and gently took my hands away, moving them to the sides of the massage table where I discovered there were restraints for the wrists, which Teng employed to hold them there. "Your Lingam belongs to your partner in this coupling just as your Kundalini does. You are the Yin, the submissive receiver. Your Yang partner will possess what of you he—or I, when I am your partner—wishes. Every part of you in your Yin mode is there for your lover's Yang pleasure and, in giving him supreme pleasure, you will receive supreme pleasure as well."

He withdrew his cock from my throat and asked permission to pay honor to my Lingam, saying that it was

200

tradition not to proceed from this point if I wasn't fully vested in the tantric ceremony. I croaked my acceptance. He could have mounted me and fucked me then, I'm sure, and I would have taken him with pleasure—all of him, just as was Richard's goal.

Teng came back around to the foot of the massage table and pulled me back into position so that my head rested on the surface of the table. He placed a few drops of massage oil on his hands and moved his hands to the top of my thighs, where they met the crease of the pelvis. He held them there, his fingers pressed into the creases for nearly a full minute. I trembled under his touch. And my dick—my Lingam—went straight-up, throbbing erect.

"It is important to pause occasionally to heighten the anticipation," Teng whispered. He was talking over my body to Richard, though, and I hoped the lesson was sinking in. The arousal of anticipation certainly was rising. My cock must be hard as stone, and I could feel—and was fighting—the rise of precum. I could also feel my passage throbbing, the muscles of the channel walls rippling—hungry for a cock and, no doubt, more open to receiving one than I ever had been for Richard.

Then, working on the muscles of my thighs and belly, alternating between stroking and kneading, he massaged me until I was sighing and groaning. His hands worked their way to the lower part of my pelvic bone with his fingertips pressing into the flesh and making small circular motions. His fingertips went to my perineum, which he stroked, alternating glides with the circular motions.

"Oh, god, I think I'm going to—"

"Not yet. Not nearly yet," he murmured, and the pressure of a finger went to a spot on my perineum that suppressed the urge to blow. When he felt me relax and gain control, his fingers went to my ball sac, and I jerked and moaned, as he hunted out the testicles and rolled them between his fingers. When he felt I was about to come again, he let go of the sac, which he also was distending, and applied pressure to that spot on my perineum again.

Richard wasn't as successful at holding off as I was. I heard his heavy panting and then his little cry of ecstasy and

201

the wetness of his ejaculation on my arm. I hadn't realized he had been standing that close. I had had my eyes closed, sure that if I looked down the line of my body to the magnificent muscular body of Teng, I could not hold my release.

Teng moved his hand to the bulb of my cock, rubbing the bulb with oil and cupping it with his fingers and lightly massaging it. One hand went back to my ball sac and the other one moved down my cock, stroking lightly and then continuing down onto my perineum. Stroking back up to the tip of my cock and then down again, this time going lower on my perineum. Up and down and his fingers were at my anal opening.

I ached for him to be inside me. On the next stroke down, he was, but just inside the entrance, holding there for nearly a minute. He withdrew the finger and commanded me, "Look at me," and I opened my eyes. He was showing me, over my belly, his hand, palm up, and all but the middle finger, which was curved up, folded back. "Imagine this as my Lingam," he said in a low voice. "I will possess your Kundalini with it now. And because your need is to be open to a master, imagine this as my Lingam in erection." He then opened the other three fingers, and bunched them together with the middle finger. "But do not worry. Your Kundalini is open sufficiently already and is hungry for the Lingam."

He certainly had that right.

I moaned as I watched him extend just the middle finger, make it descend to below the curve of my belly, and invaded me with it, moving it up to my prostate. I closed my eyes and felt myself open to it, as I groaned at the possession.

"Look at me," he commanded again. This time his four fingers were bunched together. I panted as they descended below the curve of my belly. As he pressed them inside my entrance, my sphincter muscle grabbed at the fingers, trying to draw them in—something they'd never done for Richard's cock. I whimpered my need. He pulled them back and stroked the rim of my hole—and then pressed them in again, with my sphincter grabbing at them again. He pulled them back.

"You are the Yin, the female, to my Yang," Teng murmured. "Your Kundalini—your passage, your channel, will

202

yawn open to me. It is hungry for me. It will uncoil and make straight for the entry and progress of the Lingam. It will open as it never has before and take a Lingam more possessive than it has ever known before. Your Kundalini will become one with the Lingam. Yin and Yang. The natural energies of the two bodies will become one with the other and connect with the cosmic energy into an orgasm the likes of which you have never known before."

"Yes," I whispered, my voice rising to a cry, "make me come; let me release. Fuck me!" Wanting it, even when knowing how big he was, how much bigger than Richard was—and Richard wasn't small.

On the next stroke down, the fingers entered me, and I arched my back and moaned deeply. They found my prostate and pressed there, again for nearly a full minute, as I panted and moaned. Richard, beside me was panting heavily, and he had his hands on my chest, rubbing my nipples. Teng didn't stop him.

His hand moved deeper inside me, and I felt his bunched knuckles at my rim. Still my passage was blossoming open. I was panting heavily, but my gates continued to roll open for him. The knuckles were past the rim, past even the sphincter. I felt completely filled by him and stretched to the limit, but he kept murmuring to me in reassuring and encouraging phrases, and I felt the tension flowing out and away from me. He had much of his fist inside me, as he had hinted earlier he would do, and I was accommodating him. I even was taking pleasure from him—both from the physical sensation itself and from the knowledge that, yes, I could take all of Richard's cock.

"Shit, he's almost in to his wrist," Richard exclaimed, and I closed down and worked to expel the hand. Teng shushed Richard, who moved around to my head.

Teng restarted the process but didn't go as far this time, having already made his point. He worked me with just the middle finger, rubbing my prostate, methodically, mercilessly, as Richard massaged my nipples, and my pelvis went into a motion of its own volition. The urge to ejaculate became excruciating. Teng pulled his fingers out until I relaxed

203

and then inserted them again. Build up and relax. Build up and relax. And then he told me to open my eyes and look at him, and when I did, he showed me an impossibly large, wooden dildo. I moaned as he inserted it and held it just an inch inside me. The muscles of my rim and sphincter undulated over it, again trying to pull it inside. I was open to it and the knowledge that I was—Richard's exclamation that he'd been in almost up to his wrist—coursed through my body like electricity.

And then it was inside me, pressing deeper, pausing at my prostate, rubbing me there, sending charges of electricity through me. Withdrawing when I felt I was about to explode and holding its thicker bulb just inside my hole as my rim pulsed around it, slowly calming down, my panting and twitching subsiding. Then invading again, the thick, smooth bulb rubbing the prostate again.

"You may release now," Teng said in a low voice, and I did so, with a cry of passion. The polished wood dildo went deeper inside me and Teng moved it in and out, fucking me with it. I had gone soft and spongy inside, not just taking the thick wooden phallus but undulating the muscles of my channel walls over it as it moved deeper inside me and Teng twisted it this way and that to the sounds of my deep moans.

"Good, you are open to it now, joining with it as one, Lingam and Kundalini working together to achieve cosmic energy. The perfect balance of Yin and Yang, only missing the full essence of the Yang," he whispered. "I will be your Yang now. Later, your partner."

I *was* gloriously open to it, feeling no pain, experiencing only pleasure. I almost cried at the loss when Teng pulled it out of me, but I rejoiced when I realized he'd only done so to come up on the table himself and push his knees under my buttocks while pushing the pillow that had been under the small of my back off to the side of the table.

He too held for the longest moment with only his bulb inside me and then I cried out at the long slide of him into the depths of my passage, my central core now soft, yielding, wanting.

"The complete balance of Yin and Yang," he whispered.

204

He was gigantic inside me, and throbbing, as the wooden dildo was unable to do. I sobbed and went even softer, more vulnerable, for him inside, my muscles gripping his staff and undulating over it. Truly as one with him. It wasn't just him. My pelvis was in motion, moving with him, leveraging off my feet on the surface of the table and thrusting up as he thrust down, taking him deep and deeper. Matching my rhythm to his. There was no question that he was in to the hilt. He fucked me and stroked my cock with a hand until I was hard again. Then he left me, and I felt Richard coming up onto the table and sliding inside me.

"Yin and Yang. Lingam becoming one with Kundalini," Teng murmured, and Richard and I did, indeed become one—as much one coordinated act of nature as I had achieved with Teng, moving together as one, pelvises in one coordinated action, sighing together, groaning and moaning together, crying out in ecstasy together, as, after what seemed an eternity of the prolonged arousal state Teng had called Karezza, we came not more than five seconds apart.

He lay on top of me, still throbbing inside me, his lips pressed into the hollow of my neck. Teng released my wrists, and I wrapped my arms around Richard's back. We cooled in a prolonged state of ecstasy, and I felt him stirring inside me again, and I began moving my pelvis, willing the muscles of my channel walls to grip him again and ripple over his staff as it hardened again, and started to move inside me, to probe me deep, once more.

* * * *

I straddled Richard on the bed in my apartment, him on his back, his hands gripping my waist, as, facing him, the palms of my hands pressed into his pectorals, I rode his cock—his Lingam, in Teng's terms—in circular and rocking motions, taking him deep in what Teng called my Kundalini. We were doing the Yin and Yang thing in spades. Also the Karezza thing, me holding still whenever I felt either one of us was going to blow and then resuming the ride when we had calmed—not when we had cooled down, but when we'd backed off a bit so that the next high and "close to exploding" was higher than the previous one had been.

I was completely open to him, and his cock was hard as a rock, engorged to his limit, and throbbing inside my soft inner core.

He took my cock in one of his hands and stroked it in rhythm to my rise and fall on his staff. "This time. All the way this time," he growled through gritted teeth.

"Talk me in," I begged. "Let me know when. Let's try to come together."

We did, the first time we'd achieved a mutual ejaculation.

We soaped each other in the shower and fondled each other until, rinsing off under the cascading water, he bundled our cocks together and stroked us off to a second mutual explosion. We'd had three session with Teng. He'd said we could achieve mutual comings by being entirely open to each other and, he said, "embracing the natural energies of our bodies and becoming one with the other."

In my book, what had been needed was for Richard to understand that he had to seduce me each time—prepare me and not stick it in until I was open enough to take it without pain, without closing down to him. If he wanted to buy Teng's tantric mumbo jumbo and be able to tell himself that it was all me being trained to it, that was OK with me.

I left him in the shower and padded out to the kitchen to make our breakfast. He came in with just a towel around his waist. I think it was the same inadequate towel he'd worn a couple of weeks ago, the day he made the appointment for us with Teng, because it slipped down his legs again as he leaned into the kitchen bar while I brought our breakfast to the table in the bow window overlooking the Baltimore Inner Harbor.

I was naked and he was watching my every movement. My movements were informed by pamphlets on tantric sex that Teng had given me. "Dance for him; put him in the mood," Teng had said. It was working. We'd fucked and frotted, but he was half hard again.

We ate our breakfasts quickly. I reached over and laid a hand on his forearm.

"Do you really want to go into the office this early?" I asked.

"Do you want to go for a third mutual?" he asked hopefully.

"Of course," I answered, "but you forget. Clarissa and the girls are coming home tomorrow."

"Ah, yes," he said, a hint of regret in his voice. "I have to do some straightening up today. I'm not planning to go to the office at all."

"Too bad," I said, showing him a bit of a pout.

"Just a minute," he said. He went back to the kitchen island and retrieved his cell phone. He leaned into the bar as the connection went through, and I went over, knelt in front of him, and took his cock in my mouth. He valiantly suppressed a groan as Clarissa picked up. "I thought I'd call you just before leaving for the office," he said. He listened to her briefly and then said, "Well, that sounds too good for them to pass up. Another week then? I'll miss you, but we'd agreed that the summer was for the girls."

When he rang off, he held my head briefly into his crotch as he gave way to deep moans, and then pushed me gently away. "Clarissa's parents want to take the girls for a beach week. They won't be coming home for another week. I don't have to straighten the house up today."

I rode him with him sitting there in his chair and me straddling his lap, rising and falling on his cock using the leverage of my bare feet on the floor on either side of his chair. I held his mouth to my nipples, in turn, and moaned deeply for him. He was lost to me now. I'd known before that he could be because of all the effort he'd put into melding with me. And now we melded. We did Yin and Yang perfectly. I made melting love to his Lingam, trapping it deep in my Kundalini with the newly trained muscles of my channel walls. We mastered Karezza.

We could set a record for consecutive mutual shoot offs with another week of practice.

I was enjoying the ride, but I already was planning my day for after Richard left. Teng was holding an afternoon session open for a one-on-one tantric lesson. There was no way I wanted to miss that.

Making of a Porn Star

"Here we are again with our favorite American sub porn star, Brady Boyd. Say hello to your fans out there, Brady." The voice behind the camera at the foot of the bed was a low, sensuous one, speaking in English, with an accent—slightly English English but something else as well. I, of course, knew that Costas was Cypriot and that we were in the studio in his house in the hills overlooking Limassol on the southern coast of the island.

"Hello fans," I said, giving a bit of a wave and a smile. I was sitting against the headboard of the bed to the right of a big, black hunk of a man, similarly propped against the headboard. I was in gym shorts and a tank top; he was just in gym shorts. He had a beefy arm around my shoulders and his left hand on my thigh, just above my knee, the fingers underneath the hem of my gym shorts. I had my legs bent and spread, with my feet flat on the surface of the bed. Costas had posed us there before starting to film. There were two other cameramen, out of range, on either side of the bed. As Costas asked the question, and as he had instructed me to do, I moved my leg to lay on top of the other guy's thigh, and he ran his hand further up my thigh under the material of my gym shorts.

It wasn't an accident that his hand puffed the material of my shorts out so that the camera could see all the way up to my balls.

"You are our star for this film, Brady, and you are quite experienced now, but you haven't been doing this for long, have you?"

"No, just a few months," I answered. "But this is my fifth shoot."

"And you aren't yet nineteen, are you?"

"I'll be nineteen next month," I answered. I was older but I passed as younger, and those subscribing to Costas's subscription Web site apparently liked to think of me as younger.

"Where are you from and what do you do?"

"Other than porn films?" I asked, and gave a little laugh. I was told to do that—to act the innocent.

"Yes, are you a student?"

"Yes, I just started college. And I'm from a farm in Colorado. Just left home for the first time." I'd actually started graduate school before this came along, and I was from further north, where they still were producing sunny Scandinavia blonds. My gig here, though, was freshness, submissive vulnerability.

"Well, we have a real treat for you and the viewers today, Brady. You've told me before, but tell the viewers what you like in a man."

"I like bulls. Big black bulls," I answered, looking into the camera Costas was holding and giving a shy smile.

"Contrasts," he'd said. "Give them sweet and savory."

"I like to be dominated and manhandled," I added. And it was true—I did.

"And we just happen to have that for you today," Costas said. "This is Sami, who will be fucking our porn star, Brady, today. My, you are a big one, aren't you, Sami? Where do you come from?"

"I'm French. But I'm from Algeria." The voice was a bass, the French accent noticeable. He'd been told to speak slowly and distinctly—and not much. But he wasn't here to talk.

"He's a big brute, isn't he, Brady? You think you can handle him?"

"I'm hoping he'll handle me," I said and gave a weak little smile. We'd practiced this line before, as well as the expression I'd put with it. "But, yes, he's big."

"How old are you and what do you do, Sami?"

"I'm twenty-four and I fuck little white boys." Costas laughed. This too had been a devised line to parallel the one I'd given earlier.

"Are you a student too? And have you done porn before?"

"I work in construction," Sami answered. "And, no, this is my first time doing a movie."

"But you like topping young men like our star, Brady, here?"

"Just what I like, yes. I'll break him if you let me." On cue he gave a mean, thuggish look and then changed it to a grin. He moved his big, beefy hand from my thigh to my belly, running his pinky in under the waistband of my gym shorts as he'd been instructed to do. This, of course, wasn't his first film. He was a star top in his own right, but mostly in regional films in France until Costas had gone on a recruiting drive in the States and stopped in Paris on his way back to Cyprus. Costas's studio was international.

"That should be interesting," Costas said, which was an understatement. It was the whole hook of this film—the contrasting sizes, the submissiveness of me and the dominance of the big black bull.

"The differences between you are striking," Costas said, as if this had just occurred to him. "You are small of stature, Brady, and Sami here is so big. Does that frighten you?"

"A little bit, yes," I answered. "But it arouses me too." Sami moved his hand to my basket and pulled me closer into him. I laid my head against his bicep and moved a hand to his basket. I gave a little look of surprise and concern when I felt how big he was—just as I'd been coached to do.

"Let's give our viewers a sense of the differences. How tall are you and how much do you weigh, Brady?"

"I'm five foot six and weigh 142 pounds," I answered.

"That's 170 in centimeters and sixty-four kilos. And you, Sami?"

"I'm 198 centimeters tall and 104 kilos."

"For our American viewers, that six foot six, a whole foot of difference, and nearly ninety pounds of difference too. And the more vital measurement?"

"You mean dick size?" I asked, and then answered, "Let's just say I'm normal sized."

Sami gave a grin. "twenty-one," he answered proudly.

"That's over eight inches. Very impressive. You think you can handle that, Brady?"

"I can try," I said, showing him a cringe.

"I'm not sure we have a condom to cover that, Sami."

"I don't use condoms," Sami growled. Barebacking was a hallmark of Limassol Films, and Costas liked to work it into the introductions that it was going to be barebacking, to enhance the audience's arousal. He also liked to reflect that it hadn't been planned to be barebacking. Sometimes he had the actors get into the film and either "forget" to use a condom or be too much in heat to take the time to use one, or, for some other reason, bring one out but toss it aside without using it. That gave the viewer an extra little jolt.

"Brady?"

"That's fine with me." And it was, we were tested and medicated to make it as safe as possible, and I did prefer the raw effect of flesh directly on flesh, the release of cum inside me, and the cum serving as extra lubricant when the brute kept on stroking.

"You're so much bigger than he is, Sami. You are going to show him mercy, aren't you?" Costas said, milking the anticipation for all it was worth.

"No, I'm going to fuck the shit out of him—leaving him sobbing like a baby."

"So, do you want to back out of this movie, Brady?" Costas asked.

"No, it's what I want," I answered. "If he can break, me, I want him to."

"Show it to us—show us what's going to stretch you to the limit, shred you, if he can. Pull it out, Brady."

I pulled Sami's gym shorts down and he lifted his buttocks to aid in that. He took over and pulled the shorts completely off, leaving him fully naked on the bed—and magnificent both in form and erection.

"Don't be shy, Brady. Hold it up for us."

I didn't have to hold it up. It was proudly jutting up from his trimmed, kinky pubes. I moved my hand up and down it, though, and I could feel Sami shudder. His hand of the arm he had around my shoulder closed tightly on my bicep. "It's black, jet-black, darker than the rest of him," I said, in amazement. I wasn't really all that amazed, though. He'd fucked me already—when we'd first been introduced, later on the terrace of the Limassol house by the pool just because we wanted to fuck, and earlier today in rehearsals for the filming. And it wasn't really jet-black. It had a bluish tint to it.

"Yes, really black. Just the way you like it," Costas said.

"Yes, just the way I like it," I agreed.

"Then perhaps it's time to stop talking and to do something useful with it," Costas said.

That was Sami's cue. He pulled the tank top over my head and brought us closer together by pressing on my bicep with his hand. I turned my face to his, and we went into a kiss. His left hand pushed the front of my gym shorts down, and he fisted my cock. I was already stroking his with my hand.

He pushed me down, into his lap, and I took his cock in my mouth, nearly deep-throating it. Gagging on it. Just like I was supposed to.

* * * *

I didn't seek out appearing in porn films. That was the farthest intention from my mind until after I already was in them. I was entering graduate school, or at least appearing for my first graduate degree semester at the anthropology department of the University of Arizona in Tucson. I wanted to be an archeologist and had shown up in Tucson on a hope and a prayer. I'd barely been able to scrape together the money for undergraduate studies, and here I was, at twenty-one, an orphan with no means of support and bills appearing for tuition and room and board. I'd applied for scholarships but none had come through.

I was in a last-ditch effort to gather some experience in archaeology before the university discovered I wasn't going to pay any bills—that I couldn't. That's what led me to be on a study project right off the bat at the Mesa Verde National Park, in Four Corners, where Utah, Colorado, New Mexico, and Arizona met, where a group from the university was included in excavating an eight hundred-year-old Pueblo Indian cliff dwelling that had recently been discovered. We were to be there for a month. Other groups, of course, would be there longer and at different times. It wasn't going to be a dig that would be completed in a year or even five years. But for that month, I'd have a tent over my head near the dig and meals provided. It would take the university that long, I thought, to discover that I couldn't pay for the classes that would build on this excavation experience. I was holding out hope that a scholarship would come in before then or that one of the senior archaeologists would decide that I was such a brilliant student and worker that they would take me under their wing and pay my way.

That's essentially what happened, although not nearly in the way I imagined or hoped it would.

I'll also establish that I wasn't a complete innocent sexually by the time and I knew I probably was gay—probably, because I hadn't done all that much about finding out for sure. I had tunnel vision concerning becoming an archaeologist. Just a smaller-and-younger-looking Nebraska farm boy, born late in life to a couple who didn't make it to the end of my undergraduate days, with a blond, oh-my-gosh look, a small, but toned body, and a dream about what I would be doing with my future.

I had done some fooling around, but nothing too heavy—a bit of fondling during wrestling practices with other guys my age—I had been a high school varsity wrestler in the 140-pound weight class and a gymnast as well and had been good but not good enough for a collegiate scholarship. There also had been some hand jobs and a few blow jobs with a coach who got skittish and convinced me that we should forget

214

it ever happened. I'd done enough to know I liked that better than the alternative, but I'd never gone any farther than dreaming of bottoming for another guy.

So, although I was taken advantage of and maneuvered and coaxed into films, I can't say that I said no anywhere along the line and, if I regretted it, which I don't, really, I couldn't really blame anyone but myself.

There were several groups working the Mesa Verde cliff house excavation when I was there. The professor heading up the university's group decided that we'd get better exposure if he assigned us individually or in pairs to other established teams. I was assigned to a European one. More specifically, the team was from the island of Cyprus in the Mediterranean, an island that had a rich history in settlement that went all the way back to the Neolithic period. I had read about the excavation that was going on there in Cyprus, and I knew I'd give my right testicle to do work there.

That's essentially what I did.

The archaeologist in charge was named Costas Nikolides. He had gotten his doctorate in England and his was a name I had heard before. He was an imposing man, with a booming but velvety baritone voice and charming mix of Greek and English accent. He had a commanding presence and the physique of a Zeus—a thick, but muscular body that brought "powerful" to mind rather than "fat." He wasn't tall but he was a handsome man, always giving the impression that he was moving with purpose and determination. He had the dark, olive-toned skin of the Mediterranean man and black hair, which lightly covered his body in tight, curly swirls. He liked to work bare-chested, wearing low-riding khaki cargo shorts, a bush hat, and construction boots with thick, white socks.

Although his team at Mesa Verde was a hodge-podge of Europeans and Americans of all ages and both sexes, all of whom were in awe of him and treated him almost as a god, he had two right-hand men he'd brought with him from Cyprus. They both were young. One was a Greek Cypriot named Xantos Michaledis, who was maybe in his late twenties and was gaunt and sinewy. He was handsome in a foxy or hawkish sort of way, but he was quiet, hanging on every wish and order of Nikolides. He was the ultimate gofer and "would die for" Costas appendage. I was told that his family went back to the time when Genoa ruled the island and that he was of Jewish Italian descent, long having, by necessity, dropped the Jewish for Greek Orthodox.

The other assistant was a big, black man, central African by descent, Benji Ougala, and I never quite figured out how he had hooked up with Costas, although it evidently was connected to his talent as a photographer. He always—except sometimes when he was fucking someone—had a video camera or still camera in his hands, recording whatever Nikolides pointed to. He was big, strong, and muscular. Like Nikolides and Michaledis, he worked on the dig in just shorts, bush hat and construction boots. His body was nearly overdeveloped muscular, hairless, and gleamed ebony in the sun. He probably was closer to forty than thirty and he was always smiling—not necessarily a friendly smile; more of an "I could eat you alive and I just might" smile. I stayed out of his way as much as possible for as long as possible—but then, once he's fucked me I couldn't get enough of him.

The style of dress of Costas and his assistants caught on with the team, and it wasn't long until all of the men were down to shorts and a head covering of some sort and the women were only adding halter tops or bras. I didn't have the fancy cargo shorts and construction boots, but Costas didn't seem to mind my skimpy cut-off jeans shorts and sandals and remarked a couple of times that I was turning berry brown and had a nice, lean body.

I desperately wanted to go work for Costas Nikolides on Neolithic excavations in Cyprus from the very first days I was with him. He was thoroughly professional and brilliant in his deductions and discussions of what we were working on. He was mesmerizing and charismatic. My focus changed from studying at the University of Arizona to following him to the ends of the earth. I made myself as indispensable and promising, as an archaeologist, as I could, nearly throwing myself at him in worship. And he noticed. At the beginning of the last week I was to be with the dig, he said he had a proposition for me and would I come have dinner with him at the park's lodge, the Far View Lodge, that evening. He wasn't tenting with the others near the dig site. He was staying at the park's hilltop hotel.

There was no question whether or not I would attend him at the hotel that evening. It was what I was hoping a praying for.

"You can drive up to the lodge with my assistants and me," he said. "I'll have Xantos drive you back afterward."

* * * *

"You are a very impressive young man."

We were sitting on the Spruce Tree terrace, Costas Nikolides and I, after having dinner in the Far View Lodge's Metate Room Restaurant. The lodge in the Mesa Verde Park was a balance of rustic and sophisticated. The views over the semiarid red rocks cliff area were breathtaking. Twilight had fallen while we were eating dinner by a window wall and watching the deer and other wild animals coming to the stream in the meadow below to drink. Costas had been quite solicitous of me, sitting close to me and touching me when he spoke to establish a connection that Mediterranean folks like to have when they were conversing—or that's the explanation he gave me.

We had moved on to the terrace with a bottle of wine and two glasses. It was our second bottle, and, being nervous and wanting to make a good impression without thinking that drunk didn't produce a very good impression, I had a buzz on. I'd drunk most of both the first and second bottles of wine. Costas had urged the wine on me, and I couldn't tell him no politely. I also felt the sexuality of the handsome, charismatic Greek Cypriot, and a small thrill went through my body at those moments that he touched me with his fingers on my forearm.

"I'm happy that you like my work," I said. "I've tried hard to learn the basics of site excavation."

"You do that well, yes—you are quite competent with the basics of the work—but you are impressive for more than that. You are a beautiful young man."

"Sometimes I feel like I'm not as strong—as well developed as, say Xantos or Benji, to be able to do the heavy work."

"It's your youthful look and supple body that makes you impressive in that way," Costas said. "You can go into tight places that Benji can't and you are more careful, better at working with artifact fragments, than Xantos is. But there are other aspects about you too that impress me and have prompted me to make a proposition to you."

(God, I was being dense, I now realize.)

"A proposition?"

"Yes, if you can delay your studies here in the United States, I would like for you to come back to Cyprus with me—to work for me on the excavation we are doing at the Lemba Neolithic site on Cyprus. I've watched you when I've told the team of this work, and I can see that it interests you."

"Yes, it does," I answered.

"I can see you look at me too," Costas said in a lower voice, "and if I'm not mistaken, I think I interest you too."

I didn't respond to that, but looked away, down into the meadow, at the shadows of the deer moving around the stream. I couldn't deny it. He did interest me.

"Sexually," Costas whispered.

I couldn't deny that either.

"Are you, Jeff? Are you interested in me sexually?" My name was Jeff then. The stage name, Brady Boyd, was picked up later. "I ask," he continued, "because I'm interested in you sexually. I go with men, and I am interested in covering you. Do you go with men too? Could you be interested in lying under me?"

I still didn't respond, but surely he could see me trembling.

"Jeff?"

"Yes," I said in a low voice, struggling to get it out.

"Yes, you go with men? And, yes, you would be interested in me bedding you?"

"Yes, I'm interested—and flattered—but I'm afraid. I have little experience with men. You say bedded. You want to fuck me? I've never gone that far . . . I don't have experience in—"

I heard him give a low laugh. "I have enough experience for both of us. By bedded I don't mean that I want you just once. I want you in my bed to enjoy over and over again, in many different positions. I am a highly sexed man. I could pleasure you beyond your wildest dreams. Your freshness is a large part of your charm. I would develop you. Train you. I would like you to sign contracts to come to Cyprus with me, but I would want it to be contingent on you serving me fully—for you to be in my bed, writhing under me. I would work your beautiful little body hard. Make no mistake about that. Can you do that?"

Did he know just how destitute I was? How much on the edge I was living? How I couldn't afford to continue my studies here even if I wanted to without a scholarship—or a mentor? And did he know how persuasive he was in his raw sexuality? I was hard just from what he said to me.

Yes, I'd thought of giving myself in exchange for being supported through my studies. I knew there were professors and administrators in Tucson who had signaled the possibility of such an arrangement. And I had come to the place of considering them. How was this different from what Costas Nikolides was proposing? If he paid me over and above all the rest, I could come back to Arizona for my studies and I'd have important archaeology work on my resume. I'd always figured I would be in some man's bed some day. This was an opportunity.

"You have contracts to sign, you say?" I asked.

"Yes, here in this briefcase. Have another glass of wine while you sign them."

After handing me the papers and a pen, he placed a hand, with long sensuous fingers, on my thigh and squeezed. I could barely do more than scan the top few papers as his hand moved to my basket. I was trembling almost uncontrollably as I signed here, there, and there again. I only now was realizing that I very much wanted him to make love to me—that I'd ached for him sexually almost since the first moment I'd seen him.

It didn't help that he put his lips to my ear and whispered, "I can't wait to be inside you. I am very big, you will find. I will take you with a passion such as you have never felt before. I will work you to a glorious exhaustion."

* * * *

Finding Xantos and Benji, bare-chested and in their low-rise cargo shorts and with video cameras in their hands, in Costas's room when we got there was a shock, but, his hands already on me intimately to add to the effect of the drink in stripping my inhibitions away, Costas was quite straightforward.

"You said it would be your first time having a man inside you. It's a special occasion—for both of us. I work in film, in recording history. This will be just for us; you'll be glad—we'll be glad—to have this recorded for us to enjoy later." He was whispering, Xantos and Benji already were recording, and Costas already had our shirts off and our trousers and briefs pushed down off our pelvises and his hand frotting our engorging cocks. He was moving us both toward the bed, which dominated the room.

And he completely dominated me, not giving me the time and space to object to two men filming us fucking—or, rather, Costas fucking me, dominating me completely. Having his way with me.

It was only later, when I was fully enthralled to him and dependent on what he gave me, that I learned how much of it was lies. His comment on working in films—which was the most truthful thing he said to me as he was taking me totally—could have alerted me if I hadn't been half looped and aroused to the heights by him. The film wasn't just for the two of us. That had been an idiotic assertion on the face of it. Xantos and Benji were in the room too, recording it when they weren't participating in it. It was my debut on Costas's subscription Internet site.

He was more pornographer than archaeologist, and among the contract papers I'd signed on the terrace of the Far View Lodge, while he was distracting me with his sensuality, was a release on the viewing and distribution rights for my maiden porn film. The film in which I lost my anal-sex virginity became a best-seller. Costas later told me that my response to the popping of my male cherry was one of the most realistic scenes he had in his collection and continued to sell month after month. I knew how real and excruciating painful and, ultimately, passionate it was. I was there.

That maiden film would be followed by films in which I symbolically would lose my virginity again and again before Costas moved me to the big black bull taking category. The fantasy of it became more important to buyers than the reality of it.

My first time started off on familiar ground, standing against Costas and receiving his kisses and the touch of his sensuous fingers, and moved slowly into escalating intensity so that when the height of being taken—and not so gently— came, I was as well prepared as I could be and it wasn't abrupt. He told me to pay no attention to the cameras and soon was working my body to the point that the cameras were the least of my concern—nor were Xantos and Benji when Costas gave way and let them ravish me as well.

I had sucked a man before, so it wasn't new ground when Costas sat at the foot of the bed and pressed me down on my knees between his legs and presented a thick, hard cock to slide along the roof of my mouth and to my throat, where he would withdraw when I gagged, but soon was pressing again until I was able to take him deep. When he pulled me up onto the bed, our bodies stretched against each other in reverse and he started doing the same to me that I was doing to him, this both engaging at once was new, but not a great leap from what I'd done before.

When he was tonguing my entrance and whispering to me what he was preparing me for, these were new, not unpleasant sensations. At this point the camera, held by Xantos intruded, coming close to my face to capture my facial expressions in response to Costas's attentions, while Benji recorded the action lower on my body. I know I was being expressive and vocal, and Costas encouraged me not to hold back.

I certainly didn't hold back when Costas turned me on my stomach, coaxed me up on my knees, covered me close from above and behind, and slowly, painfully, relentlessly entered, entered, entered me. Unsure, not liking the pain of the entry, I struggled against the invasion—enough to get across my apprehension; not enough to make him consider stopping. He said he liked having to fight for it a bit. When he was inside me, though, which entailed a good bit crying out and grunting, groaning, and begging for mercy from me, I went docile and submissive for him. I already was undone, I had known that I would be undone at some point, and the man who grabbed my virginity from me was a magnificent stud. Costas later told me that he liked my complete surrender to him as much as my initial struggle.

Once saddled and me cowed, he held there, waiting for me to open to him, which, miraculously, I did, slowly and with much panting, groaning, and whimpering, all of which was caught in close-up on tape, with Costas whispering encourage murmurs of "Good, yes, open to me. Take the cock. You are so sweet, and so tight. I'm going to be so good to you."

Initially, he worked me slowly, solicitous to my ability—fuck my willingness at that point—to receive him, cooing encouragement to me and assurances that the pain would recede into pleasure as he inched inside me, his hard, throbbing cock relentlessly moving deeper, stretching me, coaxing me to open to him, which I did as I trembled and nearly sobbed from the possession of him. And I believed him about the pleasure overtaking the pain and I could feel that that was becoming so. But he suddenly changed, raising to his feet and crouching over me, covering me close from above and behind, grasping my wrists, and beginning to mine my channel with rapid, possessive deep strokes. Breathing heavily in my ear, muttering obscenities of what he was going to do to my body, how totally he was going to master me, how relentlessly he was going to pound me. That he was going to break, conquer, and reduce me to his sex slave.

222

And then he proceeded to do all of that.

I surrendered all to him, my mind no longer on the cameras and Xantos and Benji moving around the bed, vying for the best angles and careful to stay out of each other's field of camera vision.

Costas turned me over on my back, slapped my legs open, grabbing them under my knee and spreading them, kneeling between my thighs, sliding inside me again, and pounding me deep. I flung my arms wide, arched my back, and moaned my submission, with Benji coming in close to get a total surrender shot.

Costas came deep inside me. He hadn't worn a condom. None of them did. None of the men who subsequently covered me on film would. Barebacking was a hallmark of Costas's films, with the signature shot being the cock coming out to the surface enough to catch the ejaculation and then sinking inside again, the deep stroking continuing as long as the top could do it. That first time, he took it on faith that I'd never been anally fucked before. After that it was a stringent medical checkup of all men involved in the films.

The moment of ejaculation and the sinking of the cock back inside me, sliding through the cum, was, I'll have to admit, a moment of high arousal for me—all three times that night. When Costas did it, when Xantos did it, and, most assuredly, when the horse-hung cock of the black bull, Benji, did it. Each successive time was made easier by the extra lubrication of each additional man.

After he had come, Costas pulled out of me and went off the bed at the foot, pulling me down to him with fists grabbing my ankles. He pulled me all the way down to the floor on my knees, with my back against the foot of the bed and my head arched back onto the mattress. I stretched my arms out along the edge of the bottom of the mattress, suggestive of a crucifixion position, Costas whispering for me to do so as a symbol of my sacrifice and surrender and because he said the camera would love it. He stood over me, facing me, grabbed the hair on the back of my head, and made me take his cock in my mouth again to clean it and to let it probe the back of my throat.

Meanwhile, Xantos went down behind Costas and between his legs, took my cock in his mouth, and invaded my entrance with the fingers of one hand, while filming what he was doing with the other. What he was doing extended to pushing his knees under my buttocks, hooking my legs on his hips, getting his long, thin cock inside me, and stroking to an ejaculation while I was servicing Costas's cock with my throat. Xantos was easier to take than Costas. The apprehension that there would be no pleasure to overtake the pain was gone, and, though he was longer than Costas, he wasn't nearly as thick.

He lacked Costas's stamina. He came quickly and withdrew quickly to return to filming the scene from a distance.

Benji was the last, the most taxing, the thickest and longest, and the most virile and longest lasting, as I lay, docilely, and moaning slightly in surrender under him on the bed, as he went into a pushup stance and fucked me in the missionary position on the bed, with Costas and Xantos capturing everything on camera. With Benji, the pleasure far outstripped the pain—the exotic sensation of being taken by a man of color, with a beautiful, muscular body, and of now being able to sheath a man as thick and long as he was heightened the arousal. Added to that, I now was well open and lubricated. I sighed and nearly was purring at his ejaculation, my arms outstretched in supplication, my chest arched up to his mouth devouring my nipples, Xantos's camera trained on a close-up of my face, showing an expression of ultimate surrender and satisfaction.

Days later, when we reached the rambling stucco and glass house in the hills overlooking Limassol, Cyprus, and I learned that I now was under signed contract to star in porn films on an equal basis with excavating at the Lemba archaeological site and that my initiation film wasn't really something just for Costas and me to share, I learned that my first film had broken all records of download sales on Costas's Web site.

At the Limassol house, I joined a large group of other men who were featured in Costas's films in three separate studios in the house and who were kept busy around the clock working on or in the productions, or both. There were three directors, but Costas kept my films for himself, and he starred with me in several films.

I was making good money above the free room and board—and the experience I was gathering and the credit for my résumé from working on the Lemba dig would give me free sailing through graduate school at the University of Arizona and on to a professional position in archaeology.

Someday. I couldn't play the young innocent on film forever and those who remained stars as they aged were mostly tops. I was a submissive. And I'd found that I loved having a man—or two or three—fucking me. And I loved watching myself being fucked on film.

I didn't know when I'd move on from this.

* * * *

I heard Costas whisper that they were coming in for close shot of me deep-throating the Algerian's thick, black cock. I knew just what beleaguered look I was to give at that moment. I could even make my eyes water.

"Ever the virgin," I heard Costas whisper approvingly in the background. "Incredible. Provides the illusion of popping his male cherry each time." As long as I could play this role . . .

When Sami was on his back on the bed, his broad, strong hands gripping my waist, as I straddled his pelvis, the bulb of his big, bluish-black cock nestled in my hole, I cried out, on cue, in pained ecstasy as he pulled me down on the impossibly thick cock. Xantos and Benji moved around the bed, catching close-ups and long shots, ever mindful to keep each other out of the camera lens and their shadows unseen as well. In the background, Costas whispered directions in a voice that would be edited out of the final film. He was excited and I caught glimpses of him stroking his shaft as he watched. He would fuck me either on or off camera after the scene with Sami was concluded. And as long as I could keep him interested in doing that . . .

I cried out and flopped around, pressing my fists ineffectually into Sami's meaty pecs as he slammed me up and down on his cock. He was filling and working me hard inside and I was in ninth heaven, but my responses for the camera had to show that I was being taxed to and beyond the limit.

On instruction from Costas, I swooned and went limp, as Sami continued slamming me up and down on the shaft. I arched my back, letting him hold me in position with his hands gripping my waist. I let my head arch back too and my arms to go limp at my side. There would be some who would interpret that I had been fucked unconscious and was continuing to be fucked—the virgin taken beyond the realm of endurance. At length, Sami pulled me up enough to show his bulb emerging from the hole and shooting off. I groaned a low, exhausted groan, and he slammed me down on the cock again, showing his cum oozing out of the hole around his shaft. A few more slides, and Sami let me fall back between his legs onto my back. He came with me, covering me in a missionary, and continued shafting me.

To the extent that being broken by a fuck could be shown on film, this was it.

The camera came in close to my face to show a beatific smile and my eyes rolling up into my head. The camera panned out as I flung my arms out wide from the sides of my body, taking on a cruciform stance of total surrender, as, his knees pushed under my buttocks and his hands grasping my waist again, Sami continued pulling my inert body on and off his cock.

The crucifixion surrender stance was my signature position. The buyers on Costas's Web site loved it and snatched up every new film showing it.

I was a porn star.

I am a porn star.

Ed, Frank, and Mark

I took his cum on my cheek, wiped it off with a Kleenex from my jeans pocket, and stood up from the park bench, ready to move on after he paid me. Instead he motioned me to sit on the bench beside him and, after passing me the two tens he'd had folded in the palm of one of his hands, stuffed his cock back inside his trousers fly and zipped himself up. He put an arm around my shoulders along the back of the park bench, used that hand to turn my face toward his for a kiss, and stroked my bicep with his fingers while we kissed.

"Can we just talk for a few minutes?" he asked.

"Sure," I answered, thinking this might lead to an opportunity for a couple of more bills from someone I wouldn't have to do a buildup with.

We were sitting within the shelter of a large pine tree with sweeping branches and looking out on one of the large open spaces in the center of Patterson Park in southeast Baltimore, not too far from the inner harbor, which then, in the early seventies was under robust redevelopment into a showcase city center. Redevelopment hadn't reached this far out on Eastern Avenue yet, though.

The park wasn't exactly deserted this hour before twilight, but there were many private places, like this bench, where men could meet for a tryst and not have a great risk of being seen or interrupted. This was a well-known place in

Baltimore—the gay bar district was close by—for just exactly what I was doing here with a guy who called himself Tom and who I had met right here, less than twenty minutes ago, and had walked by a couple of times until we were both comfortable that the other one knew what we were here for and were interested. He'd wanted to talk before I gave him a blow job too. Often it was a quick suck and no talking. But this guy wanted to talk. He obviously wanted company as badly as he wanted sex.

He wasn't really named Tom, of course, nor was the name I gave him, Dane, my real name—although it was close enough—but we both knew how it was with names. About as far as he'd gotten in revealing who he was was that he was a businessman in Baltimore for a couple of days on business. He was wearing a suit, which gave evidence to that. I just told him I was taking a year off before resuming school. I was dressed like a student would be.

We sized each other up. I could tell that he was attracted to my blond, curly hair and blue eyes and to my body, which was muscular, but toned just right for my size—not threatening but certainly not bringing "weakling" to mind. For his part, he was probably in his early forties but was trim and good looking enough. Not a standout, but definitely not a throw away. And he was dressed for success. Even was wearing a tie out here in the park, though it was pulled down from the knot. His suit coat was draped over the back of the bench beside him. His shirt cuffs were rolled up on his forearms, which showed a matting of curly black hair. I think he might have just come from meetings.

"Just out of high school?" He'd asked when we were sitting on the bench, sizing each other up.

"Yes," I'd replied, "but I took a year longer at that than usual. I have trouble applying myself, they told me." I didn't tell them that I'd gotten set back a semester and moved to another school just because of that business with some guys on the football team.

"I want to go to college," I said, "but I'd like some time off first. I'm kicking around the East Coast."

"Where have you come from?" he asked me.

"Pennsylvania. West from here." I didn't tell him it was from a small farming community near Pittsburgh. I'd learned fast not to tell the guys I ran across everything about me. I'd also learned to make them come up with any suggestions. Which, of course, Tom had eventually. He obviously had wanted his cock polished. He seemed proud of it, and he had a good reason to be so.

"If you're just drifting around, how are you covering your expenses?" he asked. "You doing odd jobs here and there? Is that enough to get you by?"

"I worked for a landscaping company while I was in school," I answered. I let that cover what I could do to earn money here and there while I traveled. I didn't mention that I had money stashed in a locker at Penn Station up on North Charles Street, enough to see me by for several months of travel on the cheap. That's because I had, indeed, worked for a landscaper while going to school.

"But is it enough to see you by?" he asked.

"It's never enough, of course," I answered. He was angling for service, I could tell. That was what I'd been hoping for when he said he wanted to talk. I figured he had the money and was good for it.

That's when he worked his way into telling me what I could do for him to earn some money. After all the roundabout talk, when it came down to it, he was very direct.

"I have this problem," he said. "It's called an ache in the balls. I'll give you twenty dollars to suck me off."

My response to that led me to kneeling between his spread thighs, unzipping and fishing his tool out, and giving him a twenty-dollar blow job while he leaned back in the bench, arms stretched along the bench back in both directions, and moaned his pleasure. I knew how to give a man pleasure with a blow job. I had developed the skill with the guys from the football team.

"Such a soft mouth," he said, his voice dreamy, his eyes closed. "Yes, there, like that. Again, please. Ahhh, shit. Fuck. Oh, Christ. Is that a bead you've got in your tongue? It's driving me crazy."

Yes, it was a bead I had pierced in my tongue.

229

He'd come quickly and hadn't make demands for me to deep-throat him. Very polite about it, he was. He moaned as I licked it off, and he remained, leaning back, eyes closed, and dong hanging out of his fly, as I made to rise and leave.

"No, please, not yet," he'd said, opening his eyes and motioning me to sit on the bench next to him. That's when he'd said, "Can we just talk for a few minutes?"

I'd thought that would be it; he hadn't mentioned going any further. But I began to wonder about that when he wanted me to sit and make out a bit with him and "just talk" after I'd sucked him off. I did a bit of a look around on where we could go if he wanted to fuck me. He was nice looking and built well enough and his dick was nice, but not frightening, so I was willing to do it if he offered at least fifty. I could see that, in back of us, there was an ideal spot—hidden under the sweeping pine tree branches, the ground under there covered with pine needles.

That isn't quite what he wanted, though. He was nuzzling the side of my neck and had his left hand on my thigh, when he whispered in my ear, "I'll give you another ten if you let me jack you off."

He did it right there, right then. He pulled my face into his for another round of kissing, while he unzipped me, freed my cock, and stroked me to an ejaculation. It was kind of nice, and he wasn't at all dominating or threatening. He might have been perfect if I wanted it soft, but I was sort of partial to getting it rough.

"What are you doing for the rest of the evening?" he asked, after he was done and he'd pulled a package of Chesterfields out of his shirt pocket, offered me one, and then lit us both up with a flashy silver lighter. "Do you have plans? I don't have any meetings tonight and am foot loose. There's a club here—the Apollo Club—up, just off Eastern Avenue, in the Canton district I'd like to try out. I'd rather not go alone. We could stop in someplace for dinner, my treat, and then take in the club."

"That sounds good," I said.

"And then . . . maybe . . . I'm staying at the Belvedere on North Charles. Do you know that hotel?"

"No, I'm not from Baltimore. I'm just passing through."

"But you might be willing to go to a hotel room with me?"

"Yeah, sure, if—"

"Maybe for, say . . . a hundred dollars."

"OK." I would have gone to the hotel room with him for less. I would have gone just to be able to sleep in a hotel room, even if there was a guy on top of me doing pushups on my body. This guy seemed a little soft to be doing pushups on my ass, though.

And that's where, I guess, my Goldilocks story from the early 1970s started. Well, a bit after that. The deal with Tom didn't go much further. But it *was* Tom who took me to the Apollo Club.

The Apollo Club was in a row of townhouses a block off Eastern Avenue that had been converted into various commercial enterprises. The club was in the upper stories of one of these row houses and there was a separate entrance to the basement with a sign, Nate's Gym, over it. I was later to learn that these were connected businesses. The Apollo Club was a gay bar and music venue and the gym was for the club's members—one membership card covered both, and there was an internal staircase between the floors as well as the separate outside entrances.

The main club room took up most of the first floor of the building. There was a bar at the side, a group of tables at the street side of the room, a raised stage for the bands at the back wall, and dancing and swaying space in between. The dancers took a position near the tables and the swayers lined up in a semicircle in front of the stage.

The band that night was one called the Drive Shaft, which was an OK name for a band playing gay clubs up and down the East Coast. They played loud rock and they were the personification of rockers—long hair, garishly colored tight pants, high-top boots, no shirts, and headbands. I think they were picked to be in the band as much for being hunks as for their music ability. I was taken with both. They definitely were studs and the music was about the same level of competence as the band I had done some singing for back in Ivywood, Pennsylvania. It wasn't so much that it was great, as that it was familiar and made me a bit homesick.

Tom was sitting back in his chair, butt on the front edge, at one of the tables. Most of the clientele was younger than he was and I'm not sure that the Apollo Club was what he was expecting. I was up with the swayers, right in front of the lead singer, gyrating to the music and lip-synching his songs whenever he was doing one I knew. I caught his eye and he caught mine, and we swayed and sang together, cutting the rest of the room out.

Next thing I knew there was a late forties, balding guy in a cheap suit, a shirt open down to his navel, a hairy chest, a thick gold chain around his neck, and a collection of chunky rings on his fingers putting a hand on my shoulder. I looked around, but he was looking up on the stage. I did too and saw the singer giving him a nod.

The man leaned in to me and yelled in my ear over the noise, "You a player, son? For men?"

"Yeah, sure," I yelled back. Why not? We were in a gay bar. I really shouldn't have been in here because I wasn't old enough to drink. Of course I'd had a couple of beers already. But I was gay and I fucked for money, so that part wasn't anything to hide.

"Want to meet the band?" he asked.

"Yeah, that would be great."

"They're off in another ten. Come on back to the lounge, where they unwind. I'm Ed, their manager."

I looked over at the tables to see what Tom was doing. Tom wasn't sitting at the table. I don't know if he just went to the john, or was at the bar refreshing our drinks, or had had enough of the club and had left. And I would never know, because I was following Ed through a beaded-curtain-covered doorway at the side of the stage and back to a dressing room with couches for lounging—and, as I found, for fucking.

There were five guys in the band, and, as far as I know, I sucked and was fucked by all five of them over the next couple of hours. Thanks to a stash provided by Ed, I was high after the first fifteen minutes or so, so I couldn't be sure.

Before that fifteen minutes were up, though, I had the lead singer's dick inside my ass and the drummer's dick in my throat—at the same time. They had lines of cocaine set and I was offered that, but declined. I didn't decline the reefers, which must have had something stronger than pot involved, the poppers, and the bottles of assorted liquor they passed around.

The lead singer held me in a standing clutch as soon as they entered the room, and we kissed as we felt up each other and he got my jeans and bikini briefs off. Then he had me on all fours with my mouth on the drummer's cock, while he mounted and fucked me doggie style. He was replaced by the bass player, and after that it got fuzzy. Ed, the manager, was floating around managing, or at least functioning as a gofer.

I woke up in the morning, hung over, in a cheap hotel room. A neon sign running alongside the uncurtained window on the outside was flickering in red. I could see a lit R, followed by an unlit I, and then a lit L and E. Presumably the sign continued above and below the window. I was lying on top of the sheets, naked, on my back, my legs spread and bent. A hard pillow was stuffed under my tailbone. Ed, the manager, also naked, was sitting on the side of the bed, leaning over the nightstand, and taking a line hit of cocaine.

From the soreness and spasms gripping my channel I knew I'd been fucked royally—often and recently.

He rose from the bed and padded into the adjoining bathroom. From the back, he looked a bit pear shaped—but not too bad. His ass was fat. I heard him pissing in the toilet and the toilet flushing and then he was walking back to the bed. He had a beer belly, but again not bad for his age. He looked maybe five months pregnant. His chest was hairy and his pecs on the verge of going flabby. He was still wearing the gold chain. He had wisps of brownish hair combed over a bald spot on top of his head, but not enough to fool anyone. If he'd had the hair on his head that he had on his chest and his bush he'd be OK. He was stroking himself and I couldn't see what he had to stroke, which wasn't a good sign for him, but it meant I wouldn't be taxed—or hadn't already been taxed, I guess. From my position on the bed, I'd have to assume he'd already fucked me—along with some country's army. The last I knew it had been dark and I was in the club. Now it was light and I was in his bed.

He dropped his hand as he approached the bed. He'd managed to stroke himself to an erection. He couldn't have been more than four inches, but they say if it's enough to reach the prostate . . .

And it was enough. He came onto the bed, grabbed my ankles and wishboned my legs, crouched over me, thrust up inside me, and began to pump me. Yes, he must have been inside me at least once in the night. It felt squishy inside my channel from an earlier deposit or two—recently—and I'd remembered being douched late the night before. The band had thought that was amusing. I grabbed his biceps, such as they were, with my hands, moved with him, and made the noises of pain-pleasure I knew were expected of me. We both managed to come. He came quickly but held inside me and worked my cock until I'd come for him.

It was pretty much like that for the next five nights. He paid me fifty a day plus meals, minor drugs, and a few hours of sleep time in this luxury hotel.

When we'd "done it" the first morning and he was sitting on the side of the bed, smoking, and I was propped up against the headboard, also smoking—his smokes—he said, "Last night you indicated you had some experience working with a band."

"Yeah, back where I came from I was in a band," I answered.

"If you'll be in my bed every night, we can take you on to help carry, set up, and tear down the instruments. Free food and booze. Coke and pot if you want it—if you let the band members do you too—and fifty a night. Interested?"

"Sure, what's not to like?" I said. The translation for that was that it would be a string of days I didn't have to dip into the stash I had in the locker at the train station.

"Oh, and you'll get a club card too. There's a gym in the basement. You'll have plenty of time to work out there if you want. And your bod is so nice that I'll bet you work out a lot."

With that, he took my cigarette from me, stubbed both mine and his out on the surface of the nightstand, climbed on top of me, and fucked me again. He must have been extra horny that night, because there were nights he couldn't get it up at all. Even when he did me twice, though, he couldn't manage more than ten or fifteen minutes at a crack. He became my "too soft" Baltimore experience—not as soft as Tom, but not as nice either. By the second day I was regretting that I hadn't gone to the hotel room with the businessman named Tom.

I, however, did like to work out in the gym. I didn't think much at the time about him giving me a club card that included the gym, but that turned out to be the best thing that Ed, the band manager, did for me.

* × * *

The first time I saw Frank he was fucking a guy on a bench press at Nate's Gym. It was the sort of place where that went on in the open and no one was shocked—more like everyone stood around watching and chanting "Fuck 'em, fuck 'em. Give it to 'em good." And Frank was certainly fucking the guy hard. The guy was on his belly on the bench, which rose in incline under the bar hung in the stand at the end of the bench. His feet were pressed into the floor on either side of the bench and he had his tail raised enough to give Frank a good thrust angle. His arms were raised over his head, his fists gripping the bar. He was screaming bloody murder about Frank killing him, and, indeed, from what I could see of Frank's weapon, pulling out of the guy's ass, thrusting home, and then withdrawing to the bulb, and thrusting to the quick again, he could kill a man with it. He was hung like a bull, thick and long. His low-slung balls make a slapping noise on the guy's inner thighs as Frank plowed him.

Even though the guy was complaining about the fuck, he held himself in place for it, so he must have had at least mixed feelings about it.

Frank was covering the guy from above, crouched over him, trapping the guy's fists to the bars by his own fists. He wore brown leather driving gloves on his hands, the kind that left the fingers exposed. Frank's sinewy-muscled legs were bent and pressing the other guy's legs to the sides of the bench, and his feet, in gym shoes without socks and planted just to the outside of the other guy's bare feet, were being used to leverage the rapid stroking of Frank's cock. The bottom wore only a jock strap. Frank also was only in a jock strap, but his pouch was tucked up under his balls. Frank's butt was tight, buns of steel. The cheeks were contracting and expanding in synch with his vicious thrusts.

Man was that guy getting fucked. I shivered from imagining it happening to me. I wanted to pull my eyes away from it, but I was mesmerized. The bottom was making a lot of noise, the signals on how well he was taking it and how much he wanted it mixed enough that no one was moving to extricate him.

Frank looked to be in his early fifties. I asked and was told that he didn't say much but that he apparently was a cop and pretty high up in the rankings. He had been a Marine, I could tell—or had wanted to be one. The Semper Fi symbol tattoo on his bicep wasn't the only clue to that. He had a buzz cut of graying stubble; the demeanor of command and purpose; a mean, piercing stare; and he was a man of steel— muscular but not muscle bound. Hard as steel, veins popping out all over his smooth body other than the trimmed salt-and-pepper bush, sinewy and gaunt. Each muscle was perfectly defined, hard, and no bigger than it needed to be to get the job done.

I was also told that he came and went as he liked, did as he wanted, and picked out whoever he wanted and fucked them to a puddle of whimpering Jell-O. He certainly did that that night to a young, twenty-something guy, who was more pretty than handsome and with a bit more meat on him than necessary.

Frank was fucking the guy when I came to the gym and still fucking him when I left. I left, that first afternoon I tried out the gym after Ed had hired me and between gofer jobs he gave me in the early afternoon and having to help set the band up in the evening, thinking I wouldn't be back, that Frank was too scary. But I couldn't help thinking about him all evening, and, of course I was back in the gym the next afternoon.

Frank was there too, working out hard. I am almost ashamed to admit that I flirted with him. I worked equipment near him and gave more ogling attention to him than anyone else working out. He noticed, and gave me some hard looks. He was zeroing in on another young guy, though—a different guy from the one he'd fucked the afternoon before. He did come over to spot me a time or two and stayed around long enough to feel me up, get my hand on his crotch, and growl in my ear, "You get a ticket to cum. Gonna spike you into next week."

I gave him a shot of the bead in my tongue, teasing him, and he gave me a harder look, knowing what I was telling him I could do with that.

Fool that I was, I didn't perceive the danger of him happening until the next week, and I figured the band would be on its way somewhere else by then.

When I went to the shower, I didn't see him still on the gym floor—or the guy he was working out with either. I discovered they were in the sauna. I opened the door to go in, only to see that Frank had the guy bent over on a shelf and was doggie fucking the other guy. He was grasping the guy's hips and pulling all of the way out of him before slamming all the way in him—again and again. The guy was jerking and wailing with each thrust. I fled back to the shower and then out of the gym.

I had reason to put Frank into the back of my mind that evening because it was Saturday and the club was crowded during the performance sets. I helped set up the band and then stood in the wings while they were practicing an hour before the doors of the club would open and they'd start performing. When the lead singer started into his songs, there I was, in the wings, singing a harmony backup line in a low voice. I didn't realize that Ed, the manager, was standing beside me until he put a hand on my arm and said, "That ain't half bad, Dane. (I hadn't told him my real name either and, as he paid me under the table—or, in my case, under the sheets—I didn't see the

237

need for him to know that much about me.) You didn't tell me you could sing like that."

"I told you I knew bands—that I'd been in a band," I said. "I was the lead singer."

"Let's get you out there behind Snake and see what you can do," he said.

Snake didn't mind and we sounded real good together, and suddenly I wasn't just a groupie helping to fetch and carry for the band. I was singing backup in the band as well. Later, in the lounge, Snake gave me a lot more respect than he had before when he fucked me. But he did fuck me. Ed was the same old Ed that night, although he'd drunk enough that he couldn't get it up at all. Instead, he lay there beside me, close, jacking me off. By thinking back on having watched Frank plow two guys, I managed an ejaculation in Ed's fist.

I avoided the gym the next day, but I was drawn to it on Monday afternoon. And I knew as soon as I entered that today it was going to be me. I hyperventilated, but I didn't flee. It was like a moth to the flame. I knew I was going to be burned to a crisp but I wanted it so bad.

Frank came to me, just in gym shorts and sneakers without socks as soon as I entered the gym in shorts and a T-shirt. His body was magnificent, especially for his age. Hard as steel, both threatening and enticing. Rock hard pecks, with veins running along the surface and nipples bulging out. He came to me and pulled my T-shirt over my head, exposing my torso.

"I'll be spotting you today, and I'll want to see the effect of the individual exercises on your muscles." It seemed like a logical reason and he did seem to pay attention to the definition of my chest and arm muscles, moving his half-gloved hands over them as I exercised on the chest press and lat pulldown machine. The feel of the leather of the gloves on my flesh made my skin tingle and my cock pay attention. I could tell he was hard too. I knew this would end with him fucking me. I knew he knew he'd fuck me. But I knew he wanted something else too.

"You still got that bead in your tongue?" he asked.

"Yes," I answered, showing it to him.

"Good. We'll make use of that later."

I was trembling when he slid my gym shorts off, leaving me only in a jock strap when we moved to the leg press. Once again he said he wanted to be able to feel my muscles—my legs and glutes—while I was working them. Once again there was logic to it. But we both knew he was undressing me, preparing me for him to cover and fuck me right here on the gym floor with all the other guys watching and cheering for him to drill me a bigger one. Already they were beginning to gather, to lick their chops, to move their hands to their own crotches.

I was on the incline bench press, lifting a bar bell, when he grasped my waist between his hands and started to turn me on my belly, in the same position I'd seen him fuck the guy a couple of days before. I balked, though, which surprised him and he let loose of my waist and I rolled off the bench and away from him.

"OK," I said in a strangled voice, "but not here. Not in front of the others." I scrambled up and headed back to the locker room area and the showers. Frank caught up with me at the door of the sauna. He pulled me inside; slammed me down on one of the shelves, taking the breath out of me; and hooked my legs over his shoulders as his face buried itself between my thighs and he worked my cock and balls and ate my ass out. Moaning, I just lay there for him, not offering any resistance, holding his head between my hands. The men who were in the sauna moved away from us, but they stayed in the sauna, all of them watching us closely. More men, ones who had been on the floor when Frank had made his move and who knew I was going to be fucked, crowded into the sauna to watch.

He was huge, entering me. There would have been nothing he could have done to prepare me fully for mounting. He didn't half try. He obviously enjoyed being the battering ram at the gates. He invaded me without mercy, reveling in my cries, ignoring my beating on his chest, waiting for me to surrender and to go limp, a whimpering, conquered captive. He was only half way inside me when I reached that stage. When I did and relaxed and went limp, I discovered that I opened for him more easily, and he slid in the rest of the way more easily and began to pump me.

He didn't finish me there, though. To make his point and to wipe away all thought that I had any say in this, he'd been pumping me for ten minutes or so, when he rose from me, pulled my limp body off the sauna shelf, and slung me over his shoulder. He handled me like I was weightless, and I was too cowed to resist him in any way. He walked through the audience in the sauna, which parted for him to pass and followed him back to the gym floor. He put me down on my belly on the incline bench press, lifted my hands to grasp the bar bell overhead, bent my legs so that the balls of my feet pressed into the floor on either side of the bench, and mounted and thrust inside me from above. It was the same position I'd seen him fuck the guy in that first day. It was the position I'd tried to resist to avoid the audience earlier. The audience gathered just as before. He was making his point of who was in control. They began to chant for my destruction, and he proceeded to do just that.

He fucked me on the bench for a good twenty minutes. Near the end I was open enough to take him without much pain, and the pleasure of it rolled over and over me.

Then he fucked me again in the shower, against the tile wall, me plastered to his chest, my knees hooked on this hips, and him showing his phenomenal strength by holding me prisoner and sliding my back up and down on the slick tiles with the strength of his up-thrusting cock.

"Time to make use of that bead," he said, as he forced me down on my knees in front of him. "Clean it, and make love to it with that bead," he growled. I did, and he managed another afterglow ejaculation down my throat. He left me in a puddle on the shower stall floor, moaning under the cascading water. The watchers at the entrance to the stall followed in his wake when he left. No one helped me up, dried me off, or gave me assistance as I painfully dressed in the locker room to leave.

I was back in the gym the next, Tuesday, afternoon. I was determined to deny him, to get a little of my own back. He had been too hard for me, too much. I wanted to tell him so. I wanted him to want me again and for me to say that no one should be treated the way I was—that he wasn't that good, even though, truth be known, he *was* that good. I entertained the possibility of letting him fuck me again if he promised not to be as brutal as he'd been. It wasn't long before I'd moved to moaning for him to fuck me again. This despite having already categorized him as "too hard."

But, although he saw that I was in the gym, he ignored me and was working on spiking another guy who, as far as I knew, was in there for the first time. The fucker ignored me. I was just a one-time piece of tail for him. He was hard, unyielding, cold steel.

I had been warned beforehand by the guy at the check-in desk that it was all the conquest and conquering for Frank. One time and that was it. I hadn't absorbed that. I had thought it couldn't possibly be true for me, but it was.

Deflated, I went upstairs to the club to start setting up for the Gear Shaft's sets that night only to find their gear was gone.

"I let them go early," Mark the club manager said. "I have a more popular band coming in earlier than expected. They didn't tell you? You're not with the band permanently?"

No, quite clearly I wasn't with the band permanently.

* * * *

"They didn't tell you they were pulling out?"

I looked at him—seeing him for the first time. He'd been there, of course, moving around, overseeing everything, but I hadn't scoped on him before. I wondered why not. The man was a hunk and a half. Late twenties or early thirties and really built. Now that I thought about it, I'd seen him in the gym, working out, and he'd been bloody beautiful. Blond, curly hair and blue eyes. A lot like me, I guess, but more powerfully built. I'd first thought he was a bouncer here until someone told me he was the manager. Someone else said that, no, he owned the place. I hadn't given any thought to him beyond this. Until now.

"No. I haven't been paid either," I answered. It didn't occur to me that this Mark guy would think that we were talking about more than a couple of hundred dollars. His response was immediate and sympathetic, though. And he put a hand on my forearm that almost made me hyperventilate. The man was beyond sexy.

The question remained whether he was . . . but, then, if he owned a gay club and gym chances were good that he was gay.

"That's tough to swallow, I know," he said. "Say, I've heard you sing with Gear Shift and I've seen how you work with getting the amps set up and working. As you know we have a house band here. You could work with them until you decide what you want to do."

"Thanks, that's generous of you, but—"

He interrupted me, though, and came in close, and gave me a look like I'd seen several times before. "I know what you did for the band and for the manager. I can offer you a place to stay too—for certain services rendered. My digs are up on the third floor of this building. What say you come up there for dinner with me and we'll discuss the possibilities?"

He took his time preparing me, lying on top of me between my spread thighs lengthwise on his sofa, with my shoulders propped up on the sofa arm. We kissed, with lots of tongue, while we felt each other up. He sucked me until I moaned and I sucked him big and throbbing. He wasn't as big and threatening as Frank was, but he was way beyond Ed. A great cock, really, built to stretch and dig but not to threaten to split or come up into the back of my throat—a real pleasure tool, and he knew how to use it. By the time he did use it, stretching me internally to deep moaning and taking me to heaven, I was begging for it. And he gave it—on the sofa, in his bed, in the shower, in his bed again. He was insatiable and so was I. We fit together perfectly. And he varied it. He could be the lover, but he could give it to me rough too when I begged for it—and he loved the bead in my tongue.

Like in the Goldilocks story, Ed had been too soft; Frank had been too hard; Mark was just right.

He was just right through the rest of the summer and well into the fall as I worked with the house band on stage and he worked on me in his bed. And he was just right when I was

242

"discovered" and offered a band of my own. And he was just right when he came to New York with me and became my manager and opened another club—and then one in Chicago and Houston and San Francisco. My band played in them all, and he fucked me in them all.

He is still just right forty years later when we are both retired and enjoying the high life in Jamaica. I still have the locker at Penn Station in Baltimore and we still call Baltimore our home. I never got farther than that on my own on my precollege journey. For that matter, I never got to college. But I've traveled the world with Mark since we met. I still keep that original amount of money I brought with me from Ivywood, Pennsylvania. It looks like a pitiful amount now, but I mark my life a success because I've never had to dip into it.

Well, no, I mark my life a success because I met the "just right" man—Mark.

Under the Skin

"You must be Mr. Markham. I'm afraid you're almost too late," the elderly lady said at the cottage door in the sparsely populated outskirts of Lelystad, itself on the outskirts of Amsterdam. "And there will be no chance of getting material for your article, I'm sorry to say. Perhaps you might as well have the taxi wait."

"I'm sorry, should I not bother to come in?" I answered her. "I've come a long way, and I'm actually an old friend of Alfred's. I've not only come to interview him. I am concerned about how he's doing."

"Oh, I didn't realize you were personal friends. I didn't mean you shouldn't come in and visit. I'm sorry to leave that impression," the woman said, backing up from the door so as not to appear to be blocking my entry. "He won't be able to speak with you and may not know you were even here, but you've come all this way. From New York City, isn't it? Please do come in. We can always call a taxi to take you back to Schiphol Airport when you're ready."

I turned and waved the taxi off and entered the home, which was comfortably furnished.

"Perhaps you would like to visit the facilities before visiting with Alfred. I'll make some tea." The woman seemed anxious now to make me welcome.

"Yes, please," I said, and she showed me where a guest bath was. I watched her waddle toward the back of the house, where the kitchen must be. Her English was very good, which was a relief. I didn't speak Dutch, and I was afraid of what I might find here. It had taken me some time to track them down and more time to convince the paper that there was a story here. That had been on false pretenses, as the story didn't mean nearly as much to me as seeing Alfred again. I'd read in the press that the movie actor was seriously ailing, and it had been far too long since we'd touched base. I should have known he'd have a house here in the Netherlands—even here in Lelystad—but I hadn't given it much thought.

I'd left it almost too late. I'd heard of the stroke the week before I left New York. I had been intending to see him since I'd seen the South African film he'd been in. I had been pleased that he'd finally made his peace and gone back there. It then had taken time to form up a story idea on Alfred Sobhuza. It wasn't that I couldn't afford the travel; it was that I was so busy at the *Times* that I couldn't get the time off for a private trip.

When I came out of the guest bath, the woman was standing nearby. She had a tray with a small teapot on it and just one cup. Looking at the solitary cup brought home to me for the first time just how one-sided this visit would be.

"Just so you know. He's not alone in the room," she said as she paused in our walk down the hall.

"I know that Jan Martans is here too," I answered. I could see that a slight look of concern slipped off her face and she turned to continue leading me down the corridor.

"I'll take you in to them," she said. "Be aware that the doctors can give us no idea how much Mr. Sobhuza will understand and how much Mr. Martans will retain. You did say on the phone that you know Mr. Martans too, didn't you?"

"Yes. We've met. We didn't know each other as well as Alfred and I knew each other, though." I almost laughed at that. Alfred and I had known every square inch of each other. We'd known how it felt for Alfred to be inside me, pumping me hard as I writhed under him and moaned for him. No one had possessed me as Alfred had.

She led me down a corridor and into a cheery room, with windows on two sides that brought in the afternoon sun.

It had rained all the way from the airport to here, but the clouds had cleared after I'd entered the house and all was bright now. The windows facing the door I entered overlooked a garden. There were several windows in the roof giving the effect of bringing the garden inside. The tops of the colorful flowers showed above the window sill, glistening in the sun from the raindrops still adhering to their petals, and an apple tree in blossom could be seen in the yard beyond.

A man in his mid fifties—I knew he had been born in 1963—was sitting in a straight chair with his profile to one of the windows. Although the view to the garden was dazzling, he was looking into the room, at the bed, placed against the wall to the left of where I stood. He was looking intently at the bed, but his eyes were blank. They gave me the impression that he could see but that he couldn't fully comprehend.

This would be Jan Martans. I'd met him once—here, actually, in Lelystad, but in another house in the early 1990s. He'd been much younger looking then, and beautiful—blond and willowy and full of humor and vitality, even though, at the time, what we had to speak about was sadness. I guess he was much as I was; we probably would have been nearly identical in our early twenties. At least Alfred had said so. Jan was a fine looking man even now, but the impression he gave was one of being vacant—here in body, but not in mind. I wasn't surprised. I understood that he had Alzheimer's and hadn't been "here" for a number of years. Alfred had become his caregiver, increasingly pulling away from the movie world to be able to devote time to Martans.

Now Alfred needed a caregiver of his own—if only for a few more days.

The man in the bed also was still handsome, but he had withered since I last saw him. I'd always thought of him as a mountain of a man—powerful, ebony black, with an overpowering voice and presence. He had done very well in movies, but his forte had been his stage work, his Othello second to none, his voice of such resonant richness that his voiceovers were recognized by all and were highly sought after by movie producers and makers of television commercials.

Well, there would be no more voiceovers. I could see that by looking at him lying in the bed, under the covers—a withered old man at sixty. This should have been the height of his vitality and presence in the world, but a series of strokes had laid him low, the last of which, just a few short weeks ago, had put him into a virtual coma that was now drawing to an end.

I'd almost come too late. Undoubtedly too late for either of them. I hoped it wasn't too late for me. I had much to tell Alfred about how he had influenced my life.

"You can draw that chair up from over there if you wish to stay for a few moments," the woman said. She was being kind, giving me a chance to say I couldn't stay. There was nothing really to stay for—two shells of once-vital men who now were in worlds that trapped them from connection outside of their shells—and, worse, kept them from each other.

"Thank you," I answered. "I would like to sit with them for a while, if you don't mind. I have quite a bit to tell Alfred." I had instinctively taken my pen and notebook out, but now I slipped them back into the satchel I had hanging over my shoulder. The woman gave me an approving look. I could tell that she had harbored an apprehension that I was here to exploit the two men who were in her care in some unknown way. I could tell by the way she looked at them and now moved around the room tucking in this and that around them that she did care for them both.

"I'll just place your tea over here on this table and give you time alone with them. I'll be in the kitchen if you need me. Take as long as you need. It may not seem so, but I think they'll know, in their own ways, that you are here and visiting with them." After giving a searching look at both of the invalids to see if there was any more way she could give them comfort, she gave me a little smile and left the room.

I pulled the chair over to the side of the bed and sat down. Alfred's eyes were open, looking up at the ceiling, not, I'm sure, seeing anything—although I told myself, because I needed to believe it, that there was a slight hint of recognition there of my presence. Jan's eyes remained focused, to the extent that he could focus, on Alfred from over near the window.

I could see a framed photograph on the nightstand by the bed. I knew the photo well, although I hadn't seen it for nearly thirty years. Alfred and Jan, as young men, smiling hopefully into the camera. I knew it had been taken in Cape Town, South Africa, sometime in the early 1980s.

"Alfred, it's me, Luke Markham. Remember me? Remember that miserable Off-Broadway play we were in, *Brothers All*, back in 1988? So much has happened since then— since a few years later when we last saw each other. I want to tell you what I've been doing since then. Remember how you said I'd never make it as an actor—that I cared too much and that I was too intense, too naïve? Well I wanted to tell you that . . ."

* * * *

About all we had going for us in the 1988 production of *Brothers All*, according to the director, were the tension chemistry between Alfred Sobhuza and me—which Aly was too repressed to realize was sexual more than it was racial— and Alfred's anger. When Alfred put anger and indignation in his role, he was a lion on stage. Once the anger was gone, merely a week into the Off-Broadway run of the play, all of the pizzazz sank out of the production and we closed to empty halls. I didn't have the courage to tell her that the dissipation of the anger was probably my fault. I thought I wanted to be an actor and you don't piss off directors if you want to land parts. Alfred was the only real actor on stage in that production, though.

And, unknown to the rest of us—at least initially— Alfred wasn't really acting.

The play was doomed from the start. It had, I'm sure, been selected to galvanize and showcase Alfred's powerful black body, voice, and charismatic acting, and it did that, at least. It was one of those self-righteous, preachy, civil rights plays that were popular in the sixties, but it was being staged in the late eighties. The subject was Apartheid and how inhuman

Apartheid was and how degrading it was to the noble black African races. But the play was staged in 1988 and by 1991, Apartheid was officially over—it already was on its way out in 1988. It didn't need the anger and exposure of unacknowledged injustice that would have worked in the sixties. It just needed an exit strategy that wasn't as damaging as Apartheid was.

The play also was wordy, a dialogue between just two players, Alfred Sobhuza, playing the black activist on trial for insurrection in Apartheid South Africa, and me, Luke Markham, playing his foil, a white prosecutor, whose arrogance, prejudice, and ignorance are eventually stripped from him and beaten to a pulp in nearly two hours of largely, at the time, unnecessary indignation raged by Alfred's character.

I was wrong for the role on so many levels, only having gotten the part because I had slept with the manager of the theater, who gave us a cut rate in booking. I was much too young for the part. Alfred, at thirty-four had to play something closer to twenty, which he did admirably. But I, at twenty had to play something more like thirty-four, and that just didn't work. I was small of stature, blond, and somewhat lean and androgynous of features. No manner of stage makeup could convincingly make me older or even halfway believable as a foil to the charismatic black man who was Alfred Sobhuza. Beyond that, although I believe I was a halfway decent actor, I was no way on par with Alfred. I couldn't hold my own with him on stage even after he had lost his anger.

Alfred knew I wasn't up to it and spent half his time suggesting other professions I might try. He seemed stuck on my becoming a writer after he'd seen a portfolio of the short stories I'd written. The other half of his time with me he spent in legitimately being disdainful of my motivation and politics. What impressed me, though, and that made it so easy for me to lay under him and open my legs for him was that he didn't give up on helping me realize my fulfilling path in life. He seemed genuinely to care for me when it had been so hard for him to find people of my color who cared about him in any way, indeed who were willing to consider him as human at all.

"You're a 'stay in your comfort zone' activist, especially on the subject of Apartheid," he'd say. "You know nothing about the effects of racial inequality. Your views are simplistic and pie in the sky. You want to be angry about it and an activist on it just because it's popular to do. You'd never bleed for it."

Although I thought at the time that he was being hypocritical, because I was as critical of Apartheid as he was being—indeed I was mimicking his expressed anger at the institution—I also slowly came to realize that my being raised in the American South, in Danville, Virginia, hadn't kept me from being imbued with the racial prejudices that I mouthed opposition to.

It required Alfred to fuck those prejudices out of me, a process that led to the demise of our stage production.

The first three nights of the run had gone well enough, with the house being a bit more than half full and a good review—at least of Alfred's performance—promising to put more bums on seats. Neither of us could act on a full stomach, so we were going to various restaurants around the theater after the performance in search for a satisfactory balance of food quality, quantity, and inexpense. As we sat in a booth, menus in hand, waiting for service, we fell into going over the lines of one of our troublesome scenes.

"It isn't whether you are black or white but who you are under the skin that makes you a man." Alfred was bellowing out one of his lines.

Only then did we realize that not only were the other patrons in the restaurant nervously eyeballing us, but that we had landed in one of those still-existent establishments where, even in 1988 and in New York City, favor was not shown on a black man sitting with a white man and sharing a meal. Especially appalling to the type comfortable in this restaurant was that, through our stage play lines, the black man was making mincemeat of the white man's prejudicial statements. No one had taken our order. We'd been so engrossed in going over our lines that we'd been there for a half hour and no one had taken our order—and everyone had been angrily staring at us—at Alfred.

Alfred saw it before I did. He slammed down his menu, rose majestically from the booth, and made an exit from the restaurant that, if done on stage, would have gotten him a standing ovation. That is, from some other crowd than those who were in this restaurant. A waiter picked that moment to smirk, saunter over to the booth, and demonstrate an interest in taking my dinner order. He was full of sympathy for me for what I had to endure from what he called "that darkie."

The meaning of life—or at least in terms of how race entered into the meaning of life—all came together for me in that moment. Suddenly I understood. I'd been blind and just playing at it before then. They had just been lines from a play, but having them play out in a real-life scenario brought them into raw reality for me.

Embarrassed and ashamed and now angry myself, I dropped my menu, shoved the waiter aside as I rose from the booth, and left the restaurant in search of Alfred. I found him in a nearby alley, bouncing off the walls, seething with anger.

The chemistry that the director kept saying she saw between us in the play—the chemistry that was sexual, not intellectual—reared its head at that moment and I threw myself on him, hugging him tightly, trying to stop him from hurting himself by bouncing off the brick walls in the ally.

And I told him what I wanted from him—what I had known I wanted from him since the first day of rehearsals. It wasn't because I was sorry for him for how he was treated for his color. It was purely sexual—that I wanted him inside me, the two of us merging as one. That color didn't matter to me. I wanted him to master me; I wanted to be his sexual slave.

He took me to his room in a fleabag hotel, not far from the theater, and he fucked my lights out. He took me hard and rough, pinning my relatively small body to the bed with his magnificently muscular one, taking the breath from me, and keeping me on the edge of not finding my next one. He was the most massively hung man I'd ever taken inside me, and he pounded me mercilessly, mustering up all of the anger he had with the world, and punishing me with it in a no-captives-taken ravishment in which pain, pleasure, and ecstasy rolled over me in almost equal proportions until we had both exploded. I lay

251

there, under him, entirely open and vulnerable, sobbing, panting, and moaning, while, still half hard—and even then thicker and longer than any man I'd taken before—he throbbed inside me.

"Sorry," I heard him mutter as he rolled off me and to the side. "I lost my head. I've been wanting to fuck you—but not like that. I let my anger get the best of me. Not at you, not really. But . . . I'm sorry. I've hurt you."

There was no reason for him to apologize for fucking me, just the intensity of it. I'd begged him, back there in the ally, to take me someplace and fuck me. I'd begged for it.

"I understand," I said, and strangely enough I did. I didn't understand all of it, though. But I understood enough, just from that "gestalt" shock in the restaurant, to know that I hadn't understood any of it, not really, up to now. And that I wanted to understand it now. "You haven't hurt me," I said—although, physically, he had—"You've completed me. For the first time. It was like the ultimate first time. I am completely open to you, though. You can make me or destroy me now. The next time—"

"The next time? You don't want this again. You'll want to leave. I hope you won't—" He was moving away from me, getting ready to sit up on the side the bed and maybe even leave me—maybe to cover his magnificent, naked body, glistening in its ebony glory. That's not what I wanted.

"No, I don't want to leave. And I don't want you to leave either. Hold me. Please. Don't make this be the end of it. But I'm completely open to you now, vulnerable. If you care—and I completely understand if you don't—but if you care, don't just fuck me. Make love to me. If this is just sex to you, though, do whatever you want. I'll take whatever you have to give. I'll be grateful for whatever you do. You're body is magnificent. I die to have you inside me."

He turned back to me, stretching his body along mine, and took me in his arms. I turned my face to him and we kissed, a long, lingering kiss. I moaned as I felt the bulb of his cock come to rest at my entrance again. I lay there, groaning, as he teased my hole, probing it with the bulb as the muscles of my channel walls rippled in anticipation. Then he palmed the small of my back with a strong hand and I gasped as he pulled me into him, drew my passage, already reamed to his thickness, onto his cock in a long glide, and then started taking me in long, languid slides, fucking me deep, and, with a jerk and a little cry of his own, releasing his seed far up inside me.

Although it was not the hard, vigorous fucking I subsequently wanted and got from him, it was just as possessing, moving deep inside me when I was my most vulnerable to him and merging with me respectfully and with love. And it was the coupling that told me that, despite all that had been done to him, he was capable of caring. I can't say how often that sustained me in all the evil in the world that I observed and reported on in the following years. Through those years I'd wanted to tell him how great the gift was that he gave me with this insight and I almost left that to too late.

We just lay there afterward for a while, each gauging the breath of the other, trying to bring our breathing into synch with each other—not fully realizing that was what we were trying to do. As I cooled down, I looked around the room, trying to pick out in the dinginess of the temporary hotel room signs of him—clues to who he was—who he was other than the most forceful, virile, satiating lover I'd ever had. My first black lover—because of him and the desires he nurtured in me, not my last.

About the only thing I saw that was his was the framed photograph on the nightstand. It was of two young men, obviously in love, embracing and smiling at the camera. One, the smaller one—one who for a moment I fancied was me—was white. A willowy blond of androgynous features. The other was a younger Alfred.

"The photograph, the men in that picture . . ." I murmured.

Then he told me. And then I understood. Then I understood more than I'd ever understood before—not just about Alfred, but also about Apartheid, about why he was in this play, about why he had so much anger to galvanize for the play.

"That's Jan Martans," he said. "We found each other in Cape Town. His family found out about us. They sent Jan to Amsterdam. They sent me to prison."

There was much more, of course, but that was the essential core of it all. Alfred spoke for over an hour, telling me how it was—Apartheid. How it really was. And how it was to love someone of a different race under Apartheid. What the loss and consequences were of being discovered.

And after an hour, I understood so much more than I ever had before. And I understood that I couldn't leave it like this.

"Fuck me. Take me again. Take me like you took Jan. Make love to me like I am Jan," I whispered. "Let me be Jan for you for tonight."

And he did. He rolled over on top of me, coaxed my legs open to him, shoved a pillow under the small of my back to turn my pelvis up to him. And he entered, entered, entered, me as I groaned and worked hard to open to the invading shaft moving deep up inside me, reaching deeper, feeling thicker, than he had when he was fucking me in anger—even than he had when he was fucking me to show he cared. I palmed his buttocks, holding him inside me. We kissed. And he fucked me and fucked me and fucked me.

He made love to me every night through the short run of *Brothers All* and for the week after that until we both had moved on. He fucked me in the dark, and when he was most tender, moving the deepest and thickest inside me, I would hear him murmur the name Jan. I wasn't jealous; I knew what we had was temporary and a substitute. But I understood, and for that time, to the extent I could be, I was Jan for him.

The play fell apart after that. Alfred had lost the edge of his anger that had fed what little vital there was about the play. The director couldn't figure out what the problem was. But I knew, and I'm sure Alfred knew too. We closed during the second week.

Alfred went on to better parts in better plays. Taking his suggestion, I enrolled at NYU in journalism, endured the lean years of catching part-time work here and there during the day and attending college in the evening, and eventually landed a job at the *New York Times*.

My first celebrated feature was for a series in 1995 on the effect of Apartheid on individual lives. The crowning piece was the result of having gone to Amsterdam while Alfred Sobhuza was on stage as Othello to thunderous applause in London, finding Jan Martans in Lelystad, and taking him to London to meet up with Alfred in his dressing room. I'm not sure they even noticed when I slipped out of the room.

After that, life became very busy for me and I moved on to being an international correspondent, keeping a touch on my bent to activism and idealism, and immersing myself in life to the extent of letting my contact with Alfred slip out of my hands—until I read of his illness and going into seclusion. It took me weeks to find out that he was in Lelystad. When I knew that, I knew who he was with. I didn't know, however, just how ill they both were.

* * * *

I talked so long with Alfred, all about how my life had changed by having encountered him and then as it spun out from his suggestion that journalism might be more appropriate for me in life than acting, that I didn't realize that it was dark until the overhead light in the bedroom switched on. I had had no idea how major had been the impact of the black giant on my life, based just on a few short weeks of a failed play and of moving under him on his bed in that fleabag hotel. He'd opened a greater understanding and a whole different world to me.

During the years I had roamed the world as a correspondent, I had lain under men of different colors and religions. None quite measured up to what Alfred had given me, but several were satiating and quite satisfying in what they had to share with me, and I would not have lain with some of these men if Alfred hadn't taught me the important lesson that all men are the same under the skin. All men could penetrate and possess me and could move with me to our mutual satisfaction—if only for that coupling and if I was willing to

255

give as much as I took. The men I would not have given a second look at without the "under the skin" wisdom Alfred had imparted to me invariably turned out to be the most satisfying lovers—black men, in particular.

I felt blinded by the light at first, unaware of how it had come on. I looked over at Jan. He'd been quiet the whole time, but even in the dark his eyes had been directed to the bed where Alfred lay in his coma. There was a little smile on Jan's face.

Then I turned and looked at the door from the corridor. The elderly woman was standing there, her hand on the light switch.

"I'm sorry," I said to her. "I lost track of the time."

"I heard you talking, but I couldn't hear what you were saying," she said. "I'm sure they enjoyed your visit."

"I'm just sorry that I came too late for the three of us to talk of old times."

"They were quiet. Usually on an afternoon like this, they will stir and I will have to come in and do something for them. Mr. Sobhuza has seizures now and then, even though he's in a coma. And they set Mr. Martans off. He can't take having Mr. Sobhuza jerking and possibly in pain. It's almost like they were listening to you—like they were thinking on all of the things you had to talk over with them. It's been good having you here today. They've both been calm. I wouldn't have interrupted you, but it's time they were put to bed. If you'd just step out of the room, I'll take care of that—and I have a bit for you to eat in the other room before you leave for the airport."

"Can I . . . do you need help putting them to bed?"

"Well, I don't know . . . I don't think—" the elderly woman said. She seemed a bit disconcerted, and it suddenly occurred to me why.

"If it's about knowing them . . . knowing what they were to each other. I know about that. They sleep in the same bed, don't they . . . still?"

"Yes sir, they do. And, yes, if you wouldn't mind that, I could use the help." She seemed relieved to know that I was aware that the men were a couple.

When we'd gotten Jan over to the bed and put him under the covers, he emitted an audible sigh, turned on his side toward Alfred, and put an arm over him. I almost could have thought that I heard a sigh from Alfred too.

When we'd left the room, the woman said, "I don't know how much longer Mr. Sobhuza will hang on. The doctors are amazed that he's lived this long."

I didn't tell her, but I knew why. Alfred was the strongest-willed man I'd ever known. My opinion was that he was waiting so that he and Jan could go together.

I hadn't taken any notes. I'd have to come up with some article that would justify the expense the *Times* had gone to to bring me here, but it wasn't going to be about Alfred and Jan specifically. They had earned their privacy. I would protect their dignity. Maybe I could get something worthwhile—maybe something about all men being the same under the skin—that I could write from what I'd let pour out of me in talking with Alfred and Jan this afternoon. Maybe I could step up to taking my own stand publicly on the interracial gay lovers issue.

I'd write this story—Alfred and Jan's story—but to protect them, I decided I'd write it as a short story. And to a bit of an extent, it would be my story too.

~

About the Author

Habu is one of the pen names of a former supersonic spy jet pilot, intelligence agent, male model, movie actor, and diplomat. A wild youth in Southeast Asia was spent enjoying whatever sexual opportunities came his way, and much of his gay male writing is about recalling incidents from those days and inventing ones he'd perhaps have liked to experience. He now leads a very quiet and ordinary happily married family life.

An American, he is a published mainstream novelist and short story writer under another name and in another dimension of his life. He has written or cowritten (with Sabb) approaching 1,000 published short stories and over 100 published erotica e-books, primarily of gay fiction but also memoir, straight fiction and ménage fiction. His hand and creative writing can be seen in stories and books by habu, sr71plt, Dirk Hessian, Shabbu, and Stephen Kessel—among unrevealed others that might surprise readers. The fictionalized GM memoir *Flying High, Diving Deep* is loosely based on his life experiences. He can be found at the adults only gay male site www.BarbarianSpy.com, which he shares with Sabb and Dirk Hessian.

Our authors always like to receive feedback, and appreciate it when readers post reviews at distributors and other sites.

BarbarianSpy

FOR LITERARY HEAT

BarbarianSpyBooks

Not all books listed below may currently be on release.
* indicates the book is available in paperback and e-book.
BOOKS BY CHRIS CROSS
Multisexual Adult Romance
Pulaski Square
Chocolate in Vanilla (MF)2
Christmas with Chris (MMF) (MM) (MF)
BOOKS BY ALEX LOCKHEED
Transgender Romance
Meeting Jenna
Transgender Other
Being Sarah
BOOKS BY DIRK HESSIAN
Xtreme Historical Erotica
Dirk's Ancient Times Collection (Print only Bundle)*
The King's Men
Shores of Tripoli*
Prophecy of Noto
Pretender's Fate
General Historical Erotic Romance
Dirk's America's Founding Collection (Print only Bundle)*
Soldier,Spy
Ridden West
Deliver a Virgin
Clouds and Rain
Confederate Gold
Puttin on the Ritz
To the Hessian Hills
Fire Down the Valley*
Constantinople*
The Beautiful Way*
Blue and Gray
Colonel's Treasure
Beginning of Time
Labyrinth
BOOKS BY HABU
Gay Erotica

Memoir Faction
Flying High, Diving Deep*
Xtreme Erotica
Fist of Gold
Liaisons
Chain Gang Banged (Short Story)
Tramp Steaming*
Escape to Girne
Silas' Choice*
Last Call
Choke Hold
Apyko: The Greek Pimp
Visits of the Schlange
Second Coming: Emile La Cour Unleashed*
Vortex: Sacrificed by Curiosity*
Dark Angel Sounding *(in e-book & included in Sounding:Ultimate Control paperback)**
Sounding: Ultimate Control *(Print Only)**
Sounding Five *(in e-book & included in Sounding:Ultimate Control paperback)**
Romance
Gift from the Sea
Shore Leave
The Aviators
Poison Pen
Need to be Needed
Key Westing (short)
Finding a New Sam
Bangkok Summer Seduction
The Photograph
Inevitable Case
Turn to Love
Rain Check
Built for Pleasure (Sci Fi)
Danny's Choice*
Pull of the Groove
Sugar n Spice Christmas
Friday Nights with Lenny (Christmas Romance)
Snowy, Snowy Nights (Christmas Romance)
Tank n Bull
Sail to the Sun
War Letters
Ravens Roost
Caribbean Cruise Top to Bottom
Arena Stage
Trading Partners (Valentine's Day)

Four Coins
Lower Than the Heart (Valentine's Day)
Brambleton
Fincing Amnad
Platres Conclave
Other Novels/Novellas
Also Want to Thank
Ranger Guided
Key Westing
Syrian Ram
Temptation's Clutches*
Descent into Chaos
Escape to Girne
Journey Through Abilene
Harmony and Dissonance
Stallion Station
Racing With the Devil (espionage suspense)
Prepared in Cape Verdi
Gilded Cage
House on Park*
Anything for Ambition
Dance of the Ravishers
Hard Knocks U*
My Neighbor's Spa*
Man's Man: Tales of a High Priced Gay Hooker*
Trip Money
The Indian Doctor
Sailorboy
Home to Fire Island
Murder Mysteries
Retribution (Hardesty)
Snitches (Hardesty
Gotta Keep Trying (Hardesty)
All Fools Day Foolery (Mike Kavanagh)
Inevitable Case (Mike Kavanagh)
Vanishing Laura
Death on a Ping Pong Table
Clint Folsom Mysteries Compendium Volume 1*
Death to Blonds - Stolen Judgment (Clint Folsom Mystery)*
Clint Folsom Mysteries Compendium Volume 2*
Gay Erotica Anthologies
Earth Cry*
Shunga
Habu's Christmas Balls
Eight in D*
DevilMENt

Silas' Choices*
Stallion Station (A Novella in Parts)
Eleven to the Dogs*
Fifty Seventy*
Spy Tails 001*
Spy Tails 002*
Doubled*
Doubled Again*
Tails in the Tropics*
Tails in the Med*
Tails in the West*
Rough Riders*
Grab Bag 1*
Grab Bag 2*
Grab Bag 3*
Grab Bag 4*
Grab Bag 5*
Grab Bag 6*
Grab Bag 7*
Grab Bag 8*
Grab Bag 9*
Grab Bag 10*
Grab Bag 11*
Grab Bag 12*
Beyond the Beaded Curtain*
The Sporting Life*
Fetish Galore!*
Literary Gay Erotica
Cairo Surrender*
The Handyman*
Homeward Bound
Journey to Mirage*
Bisexual/Menage/Multisexual Erotica
And Eat it Too
Two Men, One Woman*
Every Which Way
Summer of Denial
Death on a Ping Pong Table
Cruising Gigolo
13 Ways for Halloween
Luther*
The Indian Prince*
BOOKS BY SABB
Spanish Lovers
Driver Reliever
Hiring in Hollywood

The Legend of Holleystone Grange
Surprise Encounters*
She is He
Wrong Man
Loyal to his King
Barbarian Tales - Book One - Traveler's Tales*
Barbarian Tales - Book Two - Journeys Begin*
Barbarian Tales - Book Three - The Inheritance*
Barbarian Tales - Book Four - Road to Persepolis*
BOOKS BY SHABBU
A Season in Galicia*
Blind Dates*
Velvet Interrogation
Finding Jason
Dirty Pool
Operation Black Jade
Cigars!*
Angel in the Barn
Gayly Complicated*
Despoiling David
The Tree of Idleness*
I Met a Man
Rough Road to Happiness
BOOKS BY STEPHEN KESSEL
Gay Romance
The Forever Man
Two Chances
BOOKS BY KIM BLACK
Lesbian Romance
Transfixed on Tammie (F/T lesbian)
~